SOMEONE ELSE'S SOUL

MERADETH HOUSTON

OWL HOLLOW PRESS

Owl Hollow Press, LLC, Springville, UT 84663

Someone Else's Soul
Second Edition

Library of Congress Cataloging-in-Publication Data
Someone Else's Soul / M. Houston — Second edition.

Summary:
There are 14 strangers who share her face, and someone is determined to erase them all.

Cover Design by Pocket Hollow Designs

ISBN: 978-1-958109-04-5 (paperback)
ISBN: 978-1-958109-05-2 (e-book)

CHAPTER
ONE

THERE WAS a close correlation between the amount of body spray a man used and his perceived attractiveness to the opposite sex. Tonight was no exception. My mark was surrounded by a giant cloud of fumes, which was apparently doing its job, because he hadn't had a moment alone since he arrived.

Though that might have more to do with the Rolex on his wrist and the shoes that cost more than the contents of my entire closet. The women here were hunting, and my mark, Eduardo—Eddy—was a prime catch.

A woman in a stunningly miniscule mauve dress with a major eating disorder giggled and batted her lashes at him while he ordered another round for his table at the bar. His gaze raked over her, but his smile was polite, dismissive. She could tell, her weight shifting back and away, but she still tried another tack—asking him something about his friends.

When he didn't bother to answer, she rolled her eyes and flounced off, her dress not even attempting to hide any of her willowy frame.

Part of me wanted to go tell her she was better off. He was shorter than her, and part of a family that communicated through violence. Didn't she see the scar on his jaw? The burn on his inner arm? The way he favored his left arm? All reminders of an insurrection he put down last year. This man was bred for violence, and he would continue his family's tradition.

Unless someone took them all down. Which was exactly what I planned to do.

"I swear, if someone doesn't up the budget for accessories, I'm never doing one of these jobs again," I grumbled into my earpiece. Stuck in the shadows off to one side, I surveyed the dance floor in the slivers of frozen time the strobe light offered.

Five men carried guns, and at least one woman, though I wasn't sure how she hid it beneath her tight skirt. Three Ecstasy deals had happened since I arrived, far less covert than they thought. Expensive jewelry painted the wearers with a catalogue of their daddy's jobs—banker, CEO, founder, along with a few that stood out, their straighter posture marking them as minor royalty.

The music pounded through the floor—some new DJ from New York to wow the crowds. While I appreciated the talent deployed in his mixing, I didn't enjoy it, and thankfully my earpiece kept the sound to a dull roar. I needed to hear conversations, not shout above them.

I set my soda water with a curl of lime rind on a nearby table and ignored the surly looks from the couple standing there. They were already too high to remember the drink, my face, or anything else.

Across the room, a gaggle of models surrounded the reason Eddy was here in the first place: a B-list celebrity with a figure that reminded me of a ripe fruit. During my recon over the past week, I'd heard him laughing with his buddies about what he'd like to do with "dat fine ass."

Now Eddy was keeping an eye on her from across the darkened room. From the way he twisted his watch around his wrist, he was nervous about approaching her. Not that she'd noticed him at all, despite his slicked back dark hair, carefully selected too-tight shirt, and the unending cloud of cologne.

Between the snippets of light, I took careful stock of him while moving forward. He resembled his father—one of the top cartel owners in Miami. His mother had stopped him before he headed out for the night, and I could see where a bit of her distinct shade of lipstick was rubbed onto his cheek. He'd had four drinks but was still steady on his feet.

He couldn't stop looking over at the woman, which warmed me a little, because it ensured that I'd be able to do exactly what I needed to do.

Sliding up to the bar, I finagled my timing so that another man slammed into me, pushing me into Eddy's arm.

"Ouch! Oh, shit, I'm so sorry!" I hadn't hurt him, but it's easy to feign concern. The right tilt to my head, slant to my eyes, and he'd never know.

"Are you okay?" he asked, polite, a light hand on my arm. I felt the dampness of his palms and barely held back a flinch of disgust.

"I'm fine. Sorry. I hope I didn't spill anything." I knew he didn't have his order yet, but made sure anyhow, polite if a little unsure on my feet. I may have been the only sober one in here, but no one else needed to know that.

"No, no, you're fine." He patted my arm distractedly and went back to inspecting the bar, waiting for his drinks with a foot on the low railing, his posture held just so, in case the woman glanced our way.

"She gave me something for you, you know." I leaned in a little closer, pitching my voice to as low a whisper as the pounding bass allowed. I let in just the right amount of laughter, hinting at my inebriated state.

His body angled away, clearly hoping I'd stop talking to him. Good. I didn't want to alert a friend or guard to my presence and be ushered away before delivering my package. "What are you talking about?" He had just a hint of an accent that belied his Columbian roots.

"Her." I didn't dare point but nodded in the celebrity's direction. She was busy laughing with her posse, her blonde head a beacon in the dimly lit club, as if her fame lit her all on its own.

"You haven't been with them." But he frowned at me all the same.

"I'm her assistant. Obviously, I'm meant to be in the background." I shrugged, keeping my tone just right, my posture relaxed, my honesty written all over my carefully controlled body language.

"Hmm." He shrugged, but his fingers tapped on the bar.

"She's seen you, and she's interested," I divulged. "Told me to give you this. It'll tell you how to find her." I materialized a tiny flash drive, hardly bigger than a nickel, its surface gold and studded with CZs that caught the light. I offered it, a little impish grin tugging at my features. "I promise you'll like it."

"Why doesn't she just give it to me herself?" he asked suspiciously, crossing his arms and staring down at me with dark eyes that reflected the dancing lights.

Holding back a sigh of exasperation, I shrugged like it were blatantly obvious. "You know she's constantly being watched by the paparazzi. Just look over there." I motioned toward the thick, red velvet curtains that led to the front door, where a man stood in the shadows. He was my backup, but no one needed to know that. "He's one of them. Neither of you want any extra attention if you want to get to know each other."

Eddy sized up the man by the door but seemed to listen to my reasoning. He looked me over once more, taking in my petite form, long hair artfully mastered by the woman in charge of wigs, and my little black dress that screamed *clear-*

ance rack at Nordstrom's. Finally, he took the drive. I mentally did a little happy dance-slash-sigh of relief.

"What's on it?"

"Just some photos she thought you might enjoy." I winked at him. "Have fun!" And with that, I backed away, sliding into the shadows so I could edge around the corner of the bar and outside. What was *actually* on the drive was a little different—the tools to track and hack into all his father's security measures, which would hopefully be enough evidence to bring him, and his operation, down. Thanks to Eddy's libido, I had no doubt he'd be plugging in the drive as soon as he got home.

"Nicely done, Diana. Now let's get the hell out of here before I go deaf," my backup whispered in my earpiece.

"I'll meet you around back." I blended into the shadows along the far wall, heading toward the exit I scoped earlier. I watched every face, ensuring no one paid me any attention.

That was when I saw them. Eddy's father's rivals—a pair of brothers—stationed back by the long line to the bathrooms, staring Eddy down.

"Well, shit, we've got trouble." I wedged myself in by a table full of people who were laughing a little too loud to be sober and grounded.

"Who is it?" an agent from our get-away car chimed in.

"The Gomez brothers. They're definitely aware of Eduardo." I edged closer to the duo, swearing again when I realized they were carrying, and from the way they stood and their angry hushed conversation, they were about to take their revenge for what Eddy did to their father the year before. Probably with collateral lives.

"We need to get Eddy out of here, now!" I snapped.

The others chattered about the best move while I took a good long look at the brothers. They hadn't changed much since the photos taken at the insurrection led by their father. They'd managed to escape with their mother before Eddy could track them down. I didn't know a lot about them, but from their cheap jeans, the ill-fitting jackets, and hair too long to be stylish, they stood out. They'd been on the run, and their shoes showed it.

I wobbled out from the shadows—only half pretending, my heels were killing me—and made my way toward them. Too bad they blocked the bathrooms where maybe I could get my wig off and my natural dark brown hair might have made me look a little different. Hopefully they hadn't seen me with Eddy minutes ago.

They both looked past me as I came closer, not even noticing when I came to a stop, nearly pressing myself up against them.

"Hey boys, why don't you buy me a drink?" I spoke a little too loudly.

The older brother looked down at me, a frown marring his otherwise good-looking features. At least he didn't smell as though he'd bathed in sandalwood.

"Sounds like you've had too many already."

His brother elbowed him. "Don't mind him. I think I want a drink, too." His smile was genuine and he leaned a little closer, interested.

I shifted my weight so that my heavily padded boobs were at a better angle. Kudos to the costume team—they did their best, and maybe in the dark I could pass for someone with real assets.

"We need to be thinking clearly. No drinks." The older brother made to push me out of the way, but the younger snagged me and nestled me against his side.

I ran my hands down my dress and laughed a little. This was the kind of improvising I hated—no plan, no escape route, and the potential for a very dangerous situation to erupt in a crowded place. The guy's gun, tucked into his pants, dug into my ribs.

The song faded into something with a slower beat and the

frenzied dancers on the floor shifted their rhythm. A quick survey of the room left me wishing I hadn't seen what they were doing—I was sure a few couples out there were actually having sex. But there was no sign of Eddy. I couldn't speak into my earpiece and prayed one of my damn coworkers would fill me in before I got stuck with the Gomez brothers all night.

Then, on the other side of the club, I noticed Eddy slipping out of the room with his bodyguard. I didn't know who'd tipped him off, or whether he was just eager to see what was on the drive, but I breathed a little sigh of relief.

In a flash of inspiration, I clutched my stomach, then my mouth, doubling forward in a classic "I'm gonna puke" look, and turned to race for the bathroom line.

The brothers groaned and chuckled behind me, but their footsteps didn't follow as I hurried alongside the line of women. The hallway was close and dark, and it didn't take long before I was out of sight from the main floor and able to drop my act. I didn't slow my feet, and the green Exit sign up ahead kept me moving.

I really wanted out of my heels, out of this dress, and out of the close confines of the club. My head pounded from the music, and my brain kept randomly collecting information on the club and people within it (it had been a solid three years since anyone swept this hallway, and the couple making out were both high on cocaine). I needed to get away before my brain overloaded.

The back door pushed open to the alleyway, where I expected my team to be waiting for me. It smelled of vomit and cigarettes, and the light at the corner—maybe twenty yards to my left—flickered in its halo of moths.

Instead of my team, I stepped out to see Eddy smoking with his buddy, the door to their Escalade open behind them. Cigarette smoke curled up in the dark, humid night. They didn't turn to look at the sound of the door opening, instead laughing and continuing a bullshit discussion on how best to land a woman in their bed (they didn't seem to find it ironic that neither of them *had* a woman).

Grateful for the dark and for my black dress, I slid my heels off and silently wedged into a crevice of the alley where they couldn't see me.

"Where the hell are you?" I demanded in barely a whisper. Of course they weren't close by, or letting me in on what was up—the last people anyone could ever trust were spies for hire.

"We had to move or else they'd be onto us," my backup replied. From how out of breath he sounded, they must have had to haul it down to the far end of the block, which faded in the opposite direction.

I was silently trying to estimate exactly how long it would be until Eddy and Company left when the back door to the club opened. The Gomez brothers emerged, one by one, each with a pistol drawn and trained on Eddy.

Fuck. Seriously, fuck. I was only armed with my knife and my heels, and these two would start a full-scale drug war when they killed Eddy. We'd never get the virus onto his father's systems.

My hiding spot kept me from the brothers' line of sight, not that they were taking their eyes off Eddy. The latter finally clued into what was going on, and I heard his bodyguard whip out his weapon and the panicked footsteps of Eddy's friend running away.

Tucked into my little corner, I tried to reason through the best plan. Disarming them all was impossible, especially without shoes or a gun. Distraction wasn't likely to work again. Eddy was too stupid to play along with any ruse I could muster up. No, there was no way I could get out of this without getting everyone shot.

I knocked my head back, trying to come up with a path out, when my phone dinged. It was so loud it echoed. It was *his* tone, too. The one I'd changed the settings on, because I was always eager for his messages. It wasn't on silent like every other possible call, so I wouldn't miss it.

Tonight, it distracted everyone. The Gomez brothers both turned their weapons toward me. My heart leapt, and a little whimper escaped as I edged forward.

Both brothers looked confused to see me, and I put on a sheepish face. "The line to the bathroom was too long."

Eddy's bodyguard seemed to realize this was his chance, and the ping of a shot took the older brother in the shoulder. He fell with a grunt, followed by a crunch as he hit his head against a pile of bricks. He lay unmoving, and after a moment, his chest rose and fell. Eyes wide with panic, the younger brother shot back and I heard the slump of a larger body—the guard hitting the ground.

Immediate problem taken care of, the younger Gomez looked between his brother and Eddy, as if deciding what to do.

I solved the problem with a loose brick from the ground. When his gaze flicked to Eddy, I sprang toward him and swung. It was a solid blow at the back of his head, and his body tipped forward. A third dull thud as his body hit the pavement. Now to make sure Eddy wouldn't be the fourth...

The cartel owner stood there, cigarette smoking in the streetlight, watching with a slack jaw.

"Get the fuck out of here!" I screamed at him.

That seemed to wake him up. He looked at the unconscious brothers, then at me, and shook his head. Like it didn't add up.

"The paparazzi are vicious," I explained, dropping the brick to the ground. Not that it explained anything, much less how I knew how to hit someone over the head, but it was enough for Eddy.

Two seconds later, he was nothing more than the screech of tires at the end of the street.

"I need medical aid, now," I shouted into my earpiece. I bent over the bleeding brother and used his crappy jacket to apply pressure to his wound. Hopefully my damn backup would get here soon.

Not all was lost—Eddy would still look at the drive. The Gomez brothers were alive. And I'd gotten my heels off.

Best of all, I had a new email to read as soon as I washed the blood off my hands.

CHAPTER
TWO

IT TOOK hours until I was back on our private plane, flying to headquarters, finally out of my dress, showered and clean, when I managed to get another look at my phone.

I caught serious flak for letting the thing ring in the middle of a mission. Perhaps the intrigue was making me take risks. Perhaps I just wanted a connection badly enough that I didn't care.

Settling into the leather seat and tucking my legs under me, I tuned out the world. Sure, my brain might have been merrily cataloguing which colleague was having an affair, which one was musing about finding another job, and which one switched their shampoo two days ago, but I just wanted a moment to relish my message, to enjoy the jump in my heart rate and swirl of butterflies in my belly. To let my brain whirl away at the possibility of who was on the other end.

The first mysterious email had hit my inbox about a month before.

"Do you usually read Schrödinger on the train? I always thought his views on pet care were rather morbid."

It made me laugh.

The email though—no name, just initials and a generic

@gmail account. Tracing it back to where it'd been sent from didn't take much work. Whomever it was must have wanted to be found. But that turned into dead end after dead end—all coffee houses in various parts of the city with no record of who the person behind the emails could be. No purchases on a card that I could link to a name.

My amused response was more because I was curious to know who this person was, especially if they managed to work out my email based off the only clue I could find in my outward appearance from the day in question: the Oxford scarf I grabbed for no particular reason other than I felt nostalgic that frigid morning in March.

This was someone else who played the Game with the world around them—piecing together every little bit of data to get the clearest picture. If that was the case, I was sure to win.

The notes went from every other day to multiples a day. To be safe, I varied my route home. Guarded any bit of personal information. Played the Game to ensure no one would show up on my stoop. The topics we covered varied from life on Mars to the potential for the lower class to revolt in a return to the revolutions of centuries past. And it was fun. The truest fun I'd had in years.

Thus far, I'd only worked out three points about the sender: he was male (from the way he spoke about his father and brother), lived in the city but wasn't born there (from the lack of knowledge of where to get a decent cup of coffee), and occasionally took the train (from how he spotted me).

That was about to change. After confessing the emails to Celine, she urged me to try to meet him face-to-face. Celine was my best friend, ever since she and I had hit it off in our freshman high school English class where we were the only two who had enjoyed reading Shakespeare.

"You can't keep doing this forever. He's obviously interested, and what's not to be interested in?" Her British accent and the sharp jut of her hip made me smile. I trusted her—probably more than anyone else. And maybe more than that, I wanted her to be right.

The new message sat at the top of my queue and I opened it with a decisive tap. The message was simple: "I think it's time we meet in person, don't you?"

My response was a single word.

Two minutes later: "Tomorrow night," followed by details on where to meet.

Smothering a grin, I rested my head against the back of the seat.

————

My boss idled by, running his hands through his hair. I really ought to do him a favor and anonymously drop some decent shampoo in his office, if only because I worried his dandruff would fly onto my desk.

The day felt like it had stretched over at least a week as I filed paperwork at headquarters, taking care of reports on what happened during the past week and the very near miss of an all-out drug war the night before. I checked my messages at least twenty times an hour but didn't receive a single message—something that both left me on edge and heightened my expectations for tonight.

"You leave for Belgrade in two days. Is your report filed?" My boss had paused to watch me drop lipstick, keys, and a jumpdrive into my black leather bag.

The report had been in his inbox for two hours, but I smiled and nodded. "Of course! I just have a meeting to run to. Your new cufflinks look great, by the way. Gift from your wife?" I tilted my head. They were a gift from his mistress, which I could tell from the perfume that lingered around him.

He didn't blink, just nodded and walked off. Point to me.

My phone buzzed. A text from Celine, stating that she was

already settled at the café—my safety net for the evening. No one meets strangers from the Internet without someone nearby with the police on speed dial. She was the only human on the planet, after my parents' deaths, that I would even consider asking to be my backup.

It was a struggle to keep from skipping down the stairs and out the nondescript front of the building. All I wanted to do was run, but the two snipers on the roof might view that as odd, and I didn't need to explain myself to anyone, least of all my boss.

The café was no more than a block away, which made it easier to get to. My office building was in the main hub of the city, leaving me certain that the locale choice was not because he knew anything more about me. I made a quick sweep of the area, peeking in the window before I entered through another set of doors. Celine didn't look up from where she sipped tea and typed furiously on her phone.

Plenty of people filled the seats scattered around. One more test. Which one was him?

The tall and lanky man in the corner was too old—he'd never have understood the reference we'd laughed about regarding the Power Rangers. The other man with the laptop on the couch wore a wedding ring and twisted at it like he wished to throw it across the room—not him either.

The last unaccompanied option sat with his back to the door. Dark hair spilled over the collar of his leather jacket. Long legs stretched to make the tall chair he sat on look tiny. And then I spotted it. My clue. A hint of the Oxford colors nearly hidden in his jacket.

A tingle of nerves ran up my arms and down my back— delicious in its own way, though I hesitated before taking another step forward. I couldn't wait to meet this person, and yet, and yet... A million possibilities ran through my mind, not the least of which was me ending up dismembered in his trunk.

Celine glanced at me, her expression perfectly blank, but the challenge still rang in her eyes. She'd never let me live it down if I didn't at least go over.

Fine. I could play this Game.

My feet seemed to have a mind of their own, walking too fast across the room. I was nearly out of breath as I stepped up to the empty seat across from the man.

Not the best entrance, nor the best set-up for my next move. But when he looked up, I realized I didn't quite care.

"Tea, right? Earl grey with honey." He pushed the mug across the table, along with a pot of hot water and a tea bag.

"Thank you. How very thoughtful."

"Just a lucky guess," he said with a little smile that made me very grateful I'd settled onto my seat.

Luck had nothing to do with it. He'd been reading me—every last clue in every message—learning everything he could about me. For the first time in forever, I realized that maybe I would lose the Game. And perhaps I'd be completely okay with that.

THE SEAT LEFT my feet dangling a good foot and a half from the floor and made me feel like I was six again, sitting at my parents' table.

My blush crept to my hairline and I kept my eyes on my tea, watching the current form eddies in my mug, until the blush dissolved.

Then, and only then, did I allow myself to look up. With the tea steeping, and steam wafting toward my face, my eyes met his.

Dark brown irises. A tiny scar under his left eyebrow. Straight nose and lips that were just a touch fuller than I expected. Had he been biting them in apprehension of meeting me? They looked chapped. I made him nervous. Good.

Somehow that made me want to smile and I ducked back to my tea, removed the bag with a practiced hand, and added honey.

"How did you know?" I asked, waving at my drink.

"Oxford. So, tea, of course. Earl grey because it's evening, and that would be your standard type when out where the tea collection may be dodgy. Honey, because you're still

American, but health conscious that you wouldn't go for something artificial." He grinned, his straight white teeth catching the light.

I remembered reading once, when I was a kid, a book titled *Jacob, I Have Loved*. In it was one of those lines of truth, distilled to perfection, about how watching someone's hands was the best way to know intimate details about them. I thought of that often. However, I found that watching someone's teeth was far more informative. His said money for braces. Wealth for the veneers. Healthy, and therefore he took care of them. Not stained, so he wasn't a heavy coffee or red wine drinker. Add to that the clean-shaven face, and I tacked meticulous to the list—although I knew that already.

I stirred my tea before taking an idle sip. I could feel Celine's eyes on my back, wondering why we were sitting in silence. By now she should understand how I got to know someone, by watching, counting, observing. And something, some small voice that wasn't backed by reason but by hope, told me this man did the same. A little part of me wished I could dance, just so I could express how joyous that thought made me.

Oh, this was going to be fun.

"I imagine you have a name that might make for a good start to this evening," I said, giving him just the right tilt of my head to convey coyness. A few loose strands of my dark hair played along, tickling across my cheek.

The man chuckled, a comfortable sound, and he leaned back in his chair. The scarf wrapped loosely around his neck told me that he was in the sciences and had done graduate work at Oxford. Okay. That paired nicely with his Schrödinger joke.

"It's David. And yours?"

"Diana."

He extended a hand across the table and I shook it. It was warm but dry, so he wasn't as nervous as me. His nails were clipped close and clean, but not manicured, so he wasn't obsessed with his appearance. His grip was strong but lasted a beat too long, clueing me into his own slight awkwardness.

"Thanks for the invitation to meet in person. I had been about to ask you about meeting, but it was a pleasure to have you beat me to it," I said, mixing formality with a hint of my own truth. It had been lovely not having to ask myself. That had been what happened the last date I went on, and within fifteen minutes I found myself regretting it.

David grinned. "I should have asked sooner."

I sipped my too-hot tea and shrugged. "I should have, too."

His chuckle was a good sound—the kind that spiked my heartrate a little.

"Physics or bioengineering?" I asked, settling my hands back around my mug.

"That was too easy. I knew I shouldn't have worn the scarf." He sighed, and from the little glance to the older gentleman in the corner, I realized I hadn't been the only one with a safety.

He caught me lingering on the man with his back to us. They were both tall, similar hair, though the other man's had gone to gray at the temples.

"My father." David spoke before I could ask.

"That was kind of him."

David shrugged. "He knew the weight of this meeting."

At that, I lifted an eyebrow. "Weight?" For the first time, a tinge of "oh crap" twisted my gut. And here I'd come to think that this was just a simple date; something casual between two people who enjoyed each other's conversation.

Celine would have laughed at that description for very obvious reasons. Yes, I had hoped there might be more. Of the handful of men I'd dated throughout college and grad school, none were able to handle me—the way my brain worked, the fact that secrets didn't work when I could read every little thing about them in their body language, or even the way they hung their coat. I couldn't turn my inner analysis off, even when I wanted to. I'd hoped this might be different. I wanted a connection, someone who understood the way I ticked. I wanted someone I could trust with my true self.

And now?

Suppressing a sigh, I gathered my bag from the back of the chair, ready to hop from my chair and leave.

"What? You're going?" David managed to look thoroughly perplexed. An act? He was capable of it.

"I don't want to deal with whatever agenda you've got for this meeting. I only wanted to meet you." It was more than I needed to say as I slid from the height of my chair. My feet hit the floor a little harder than I'd intended and the weight of my frustration seemed to help gravity as it tugged my heart toward my toes.

"Diana." The way he said my name, the rough urgency of it, forced me to pause, if only for an instant.

My eyes met his as I wrestled my bag over my shoulder.

"Please. Hear me out."

"Thank you for the tea, David. Please do me the courtesy of not contacting me again. I'd really rather not have to ensure you never find me." Just as I worked so hard to ensure my appearance and tone made people trust and like me, ice now crystallized in my voice, and I could almost see his tea freeze on the table between us.

David sighed and ran a hand through his hair. Damn it, why did he have to have good hair?

Off to the side, I could see Celine watching us, her phone forgotten in her hands. She knew better than to make herself known, but I could almost smell the gunpowder-like scent of her anxiety.

"What do you know of your sister?" David asked, his hand reaching to lay flat on the table next to me. I flinched back.

"I don't have a sister." Panic brought the room into much sharper focus around me, my brain doing overtime with the mad swirl of information to be gathered—from the affair the two were planning on the couch, to the man who'd lost his job today nursing an Irish coffee at the bar, to the need for someone to replace the receipt tape at the register.

I took a deep breath, forcing the air all the way to the bottom of my lungs. I held it there for a long count before letting it out through my nose. A trick I'd learned in high school. Before I learned how to control that part of my mind, to dim it down to just the information I wanted. Otherwise it went haywire and I could be easily overwhelmed, throwing the switch like a power breaker leading to a blackout. I should have known this was all too good to be true. That this person was after something, trying to sell some lie, or worse.

If David noticed my brush with overload, he didn't mention it. Instead, he rocked to the side and pulled an envelope from under his leg. It was bent, just a little, from its hiding place.

"Look at these and tell me you don't have a sister. A twin."

I pressed my lips together and made for the door. *A twin.* What the hell was he playing at?

I didn't take the envelope, and with a weary look, he set it on the table between us. "This is important. Please. Just take these and look at them."

I shook my head. In my line of work, I knew full well what an innocent piece of paper could carry, and I would accept nothing from this stranger. Already I regretted my sip of tea. What if he'd done something to that?

Something about my reluctance made David pick up the envelope and crack the seal on the back. With expert hands, he pulled out a short stack of photos. Their glossy surfaces caught the light from the overhead lamp and the colors wavered for a moment. It had been ages since I'd seen actual prints—they brought a rush of longing for my mother and the meticulous care she took of our family photos.

Then I caught a good look at the first image. I froze, my bag numb between my fingers.

The photo was of me. Or what I might have looked like if I'd had shorter hair. She stood in a soccer field, surrounded by people, shouting onto the green expanse of the field dotted with tiny players. At her feet, a small child, less than a year old, played on a blanket. She clearly had no idea someone had snapped the shutter for the shot.

There were ways to detect a falsified photo. I mentally checked through the list, looking for every telltale detail that might suggest someone had manufactured the image.

My gut—that was the most frightening aspect. It screamed that this was real, that it hadn't been faked, the implications of which were overwhelming. But there was no logical way this could be true. The memory of my mother swirled into something more, a dark void that reminded me I was alone in this world, the only surviving member of my family, my safety net nonexistent. Whatever mysteries this presented were mine alone. No one could help me.

Celine buzzed my phone, but I waved indiscriminately in her direction and settled back into my chair—truthfully, I needed to sit, or I might give away how much this affected me.

"Show me the rest." I didn't bother looking at David as he slowly flipped through the rest of the prints.

Each were analyzed to see if they were real. None stood out as fake, but I'd have to run them to a specialist to be sure. And even then, it was possible someone was just that good.

And yet. There was something about them, the odd angles someone—David?—had taken them from, the genuine way the woman spoke with her children, their cute little house, the way they touched so easily, the dirty car she drove, that screamed reality.

"What are you playing at?" I asked as David settled the pile of photos on the table, tapping the stack so it settled neatly.

"You've never seen her before?" David asked, his lips pressed into a fine line.

"Only every day when I look in the mirror," I replied.

"Did you know you had a twin?"

I didn't bother to respond. That answer was obvious and he knew it. I was an only child, and my mother was very blunt about her desire for more children. If I'd had a twin I would have known about it. I grew up wishing I had siblings, hoping for someone who had to be my friend, despite all my quirks.

A low rush of air blew out of his mouth as he stared at me. "Tell me... how did you start working for Global Incentives?"

My head jerked back, my heart all but stopping in my chest. I immediately hated that I let on that he'd guessed right, but there was no helping it. "How did you know that?"

Even Celine didn't know. I scanned the café, looking more closely this time for some kind of device, anything that might demonstrate I was being watched. They were easy to hide, wireless mostly, but I'd worked with them enough that I could generally pick up the odd pin, hair clip, or something that might hide a mike or camera. Nothing stood out, but that didn't mean I couldn't have been overlooking it.

"Have you ever heard of English United?" David fiddled with the small container of sugars on the table, switching several out so that the packets of the same color were aligned.

"They're our counterpart, overseas. I've worked with them on several jobs." I was admitting too much. If this man were actually investigating me, what I'd just admitted to could cost me my job.

But right then, I didn't care. I had to know about the woman in those photos. Or at least what this man would tell me about her—if anything that came from his lips could be true.

"I used to work for them. Until about a week ago, actually," he admitted. His accent, faint until now, clipped his consonants and gave me more information about him: raised in London, England, in an affluent household. Schooled in Germany and the US grad school at Oxford. All in the way he said those short sentences.

"And?" I prodded. Why did I have to know? What could possibly come from this? And yet, there was something about the woman's expression. She looked… happy. In a way I couldn't begin to comprehend. It was odd to see that expression on a stranger's face. Odd enough, I felt compelled to know more.

As I watched him, David glanced away, and a string seemed to pull him taut. He did a scan of the room just as I had, but he didn't relax, even though I knew there was no one in here who was a threat. Still, a deep curl of unease settled in my gut.

"That's more than I can tell you here. Really, we should go somewhere more private."

"You'll tell me more. Here." It wasn't a question. He couldn't give me that big a hint and then let it drop. No way was I ever trusting him enough to have any contact with him in the future.

"I will. Tomorrow. And next time, you might want to leave your friend at home." He nodded in Celine's direction.

"Same to you." Still, I grimaced. Okay, so he managed to work it out. It *was* rather obvious. But I hated the thought that whoever this was now knew Celine's face.

David's father didn't shift as the two of us looked over to him.

"You'll want to meet him. He has… information about this mess." David's brows drew low over his eyes, and I knew then that he was upset with his father for some unknowable slight. It added to his unease and thickened the tension he'd already brought to the table.

"I need something more. Tonight," I insisted. "You can't possibly drop that kind of bomb and then expect me to wait." I didn't let my voice betray the whirlwind of emotions within me, though my palms grew sweaty and my back tensed. I could play it cool and calm, though I did need to know more. He didn't need to know I intended to ensure he never saw me again.

David set the container of sugars aside, his moves deliberate, his eyes still hooded when he looked up at me across the tiny table. "I want to, Diana, and I know you want to know more. But I can't right now. Take the photos. They're safe. I swear it." His glance flicked to the dark glass mirroring back the interior of the coffee shop. I couldn't see a thing beyond them, but something about his look raised the hair on the back of my neck.

I watched him as he spoke, careful to gauge his pupils. They didn't dilate. So either he was as good a liar as me, or the photos were okay. He had touched them himself, so without any more options, I took the stack and settled them into a plastic bag left over from my lunch. I risked another look at the empty street beyond the doors. There was still nothing I could see out there, despite the way David now angled himself away from the window.

"Where will we meet tomorrow?" I asked. Another lie, but one that felt imperative to my safety.

He shook his head. "You'll work it out." With that, he stood, the full extent of his six-five height towering over me as I sat in my chair, unsure I'd be able to move quite yet.

"I promise I'll explain more." He extended his hand. I watched him for a moment before taking it.

His hands were much warmer this time. He ducked his head, hiding his face from the security camera. What in the hell was he playing at? Was he trying to scare me? Certainly he'd tell me if there was something dangerous about the photos. Right?

I watched, my eyes glued to his back, as he walked out of the café and onto the darkened street, ducking quickly out of view. I turned to scope out his father, but the older man had already left—right under my nose.

Celine waited a minute before coming over as I sat there, desperately attempting to get my mind in order. My internal overload switch seemed altogether too close to being thrown as information rattled through me at lightning speed. I couldn't tell if anyone around me was paying too much attention to us, but something about David's sudden switch in demeanor, coupled with his weird news, unnerved me.

She settled in across from me, taking David's place, her eyes boring into mine.

"Okay, spill. You look like you've seen a ghost."

I managed a tiny smile. In some ways, I had. A ghost of another me, in a life so vastly different from my own I couldn't comprehend it.

But I couldn't tell Celine that, as much as I wanted to. It wasn't as if she weren't smart enough—the woman was an amazing lawyer, having made partner at a prestigious firm at only thirty-five. But this had to be filed under the same heading as work: if I didn't tell her the details, she could be safe.

If I spilled, then whatever Pandora's box those photos might open, it meant she would be involved. Right now, I needed to know more about what that entailed before risking her safety.

Back to the aspect of the Game I was best at: keeping secrets.

"He's nice," I offered lamely. "It was strange, though. A bit like… like meeting someone you've known forever because they're awfully similar to yourself."

Celine quirked an eyebrow and leaned in across the table.

"At one point, I thought you might kill him. The look on your face, Di… I've never seen you look that way."

I laughed, praying it sounded as natural as it needed to. "A stupid misunderstanding about his marital status. He *is* single." Not that he said it, but I knew. And he was straight. I could study and parse out how I'd come to that conclusion, but it wouldn't change matters.

"So, will you see him again?" she asked expectantly.

I took a deep breath, the photos seeming to scream at me from my bag. "Yes. I will definitely see him again." It was the only thing I could say to let us drop the conversation. I needed to nurse my disappointment on my own, because whatever David was up to I wanted no part in it.

I WALKED CELINE HOME, turning the conversation to the "undeniable prat" she had for a boss, and gave her some fun ideas of how the man could get what he had coming to him. It involved a bit of Nair and a means of helping his biggest client become Celine's. We were laughing and falling over ourselves by the time we reached her flat. I did a quick inspection of the apartment, without her knowing, to ensure no one lurked inside or in the shadows out back.

Satisfied with her immediate safety, I took a circuitous route to my place. It had become my standard way home in the last few days to ensure David didn't find me, but tonight it felt superfluous. If David already knew what he did about me, my physical address was the least of my concerns.

Which meant that he was kind enough not to randomly show up at my home. Which meant... what? That he didn't want to bother me at home?

A small kindness and respect for my privacy. I wasn't quite sure what I felt about that.

Inside, I kicked off my heels and sank into my couch. I designed this room with the intent of making my guests as comfortable as possible, the furniture unassuming and light but comfortable all the same. I stuck to neutral beige and cream, though accenting with a few turquoise pieces—a bowl, a flash of color in the paintings on the wall, and several small baskets. The color reminded me of a Mexican beach I'd been to as a kid with my parents, where the ocean had been the most unbelievable teal color in the way that only childhood memories can conjure.

Massaging my feet from the stiletto assault I'd put them through, I refocused on the photos. Just what did they mean?

I cleared the magazines and books on Rome and Kyoto off my coffee table, then grabbed paper towels from my kitchen and layered them into a covering. It was silly to still be worried, but something about the photos and situation put me on edge. I spread out the photos, each one face up, and studied them carefully.

Staring down into the glossy pieces of paper, my mind couldn't help the flare of panic at the sight of her—*my face*—going about such a normal life.

What the hell did it all mean?

Grabbing a magnifying glass, I spent the rest of the night poring over every image.

With each photo I picked up, I hoped I'd somehow find a clue to what made these false, an infinitesimal nuance that made this situation a fake. But nothing came to light. Each image seemed to solidify the nagging ache behind my breastbone.

The one in the car got to me the most. David—or whoever took the photo—caught her, me, whomever, singing in the car. Her children's hands were raised in the back seat, caught in mid-dance. The light settled over her, giving her a look that stole my breath. How could she be *that* happy?

Each of the images testified to that, calling to some part of me that I'd denied for so long. My forgotten biological imperative in this world. Hitting thirty-five a month ago meant my chances were dwindling, and fast. My mom's photo, a black-and-white snapshot of her and I from after my graduate school graduation, sat in the corner. I'd already been five by the time she'd been my age. The thought weighed on me, along with the familiar pang of wishing I could ask my mother these questions, discuss their implications, understand what it all meant through her practical lens.

Here was this other woman with two kids in tow and happy. It was so real. I touched her face in one of the photos, longing to ask her: *What made you this way? How are you content with the life you're leading?*

Even more, I wanted to know how she turned it all off. How she ignored the risks, the world falling into oblivion around her. How could she not want to change that, as I did, every day? Every mission I took with Global went toward that end: to make the world safe for this woman and her children. For a moment I wondered if Global knew about this woman bearing my face. If they did, would they worry about her fate if my cover was ever blown?

Instinctively filing it away to ask David about it in some veiled manner, I stopped myself.

When, over the last month, had that become a habit? When had I become excited, wanting to share every detail with him?

The thought made me shove the photo back onto the table with a twist of my lips. Damn it. And damn David for dropping this in my lap.

Why couldn't he have just been normal? Or at least my kind of normal—the kind who I could actually have a solid conversation with? Someone I knew wasn't trying to play me?

Ignoring the bubbling annoyance in my chest, I took three photos from the pile and slid them into a clean baggie from my kitchen and settled them in my purse. I left the rest of the photos sealed in an envelope and placed them in my safe, content that they'd wait until after I verified the validity of the three.

No sleep, though I wasn't a stranger to that. Still, in the morning, after washing my face with icy water to lessen the puffiness, I layered on a bit of extra makeup under my eyes. The finished product still looked exhausted in the mirror. I pushed my hair away from my eyes and pinched the bridge of my nose.

Maybe it was all just some strange coincidence, and he was paranoid. Clearly, he was not right in the head. It was a simpler explanation than the hypotheses my tired brain spun out. There was no hope for ever trusting someone like that.

I left an hour early, but instead of heading to my office, caught the train to the fringes of the city, where strip malls took over and one of my sources worked. Ron used to work freelance for Global, but after a leak of classified info, he was sidelined. I knew beyond a doubt that the leak wasn't his fault and trusted him, but my boss, who wasn't quite smart enough to realize that *he* was the one who inadvertently leaked the info, felt differently.

The little store was next to a panaderia and a cake-decorating place, filling the morning air with the scent of baking goodness. That was the only hang-up about this location. I never escaped without purchasing something I shouldn't eat.

A bell over the door announced my arrival to the small camera shop, and I stepped into the hushed interior and scanned the shelves of equipment. Most of the merchandise was digital, though Ron had a penchant for film and still stocked the chemicals and equipment to use the old medium.

He was also one of the pioneers in the development of Photoshop, and could fake any image, if paid well. I was fairly certain that was the only way his business kept afloat these days.

Inspecting the rows of lenses behind the counter, I waited patiently for him to make his appearance. The tiny camera by the register would scan me and alert Ron to my presence, as well as whether or not I posed a threat. That was something I learned the hard way the first time I came here carrying my standard issue firearm. It took Ron two more of my visits before he coded his alarm system to override my "danger signal," as he called it.

"Diana." Ron appeared behind the counter, far more graceful than his large frame should have allowed. If I could have written the Wikipedia entry on what a true nerd should look like, Ron's picture would fit the bill. Tall, overweight, with unruly curly hair, and an honest-to-goodness pocket protector. Add to that broken glasses taped together at the bridge. It took a monumental force of effort not to laugh.

"Morning, Ron. How's the girlfriend?" I smiled and put all my energy into ensuring I came across as the caring, friendly woman Ron occasionally opened up to. Several months before, he'd asked me to look at his online dating profile and provide feedback. I helped him make it as good as it could be, and in the ensuing months, he'd managed to find a lady friend. From what I could tell, the two made quite the pair.

Ron blushed deep red and ducked his head. "She's wonderful."

I peppered him with a few more questions, and learned she was going to an RPG conference with him in a few months. It warmed my heart.

"So, what brings you in?" Ron asked, all but throwing up a white flag to get me to stop with the personal questions.

"I need you to take a look at something." I pulled the photos from my bag, making sure my hands didn't shake.

He slid them across the glass countertop, then frowned as he picked them up and scanned the top image. He wouldn't ask any additional questions, which was part of why I brought them here. He wouldn't care what the photos were of, just what he could do with them.

"If these are fake, they're well done. May I?" he asked solicitously before opening the bag.

I motioned him to go ahead, and folded my arms across my chest as I watched him work. He flicked on a bright light on the far end of the counter and used a slide-viewer to inspect the images.

I stared, unseeing, at the prices of the lenses behind the counter, my mind flipping through the myriad of potential situations that might remotely explain the photos.

1. They are fake.
2. It is an elaborate scheme by David.
3. Work is testing me in some way.
4. Someone is going to blackmail me.
5. The woman in the photos found me and is concerned.
6. Celine put together a massive prank.
7. They are real.

Each of the ideas didn't fit, and I kept attempting different scenarios to make something snap together. Yet, I kept circling back to the last possibility.

"May I keep these? I'll have to do a hi-res scan and look at them on my computer. I can contact you in a couple of hours."

I nodded and pulled out the hundred dollar bills, fanning them onto the tabletop.

Ron gathered everything up, turned, and disappeared into his back room. The door slid shut behind him.

I walked outside and stood in the sunshine, warming up after the chill from Ron's blasting air conditioner. Then I walked into the panaderia and grabbed a carb overload, munching as I went to work.

———

I'd expected there to be a message from David this morning. But nothing appeared. My heart grumbled at this news like a damn traitor.

My boss wandered by, and I smiled sweetly. Without a word—he was still sore about my wife comment from yesterday—he slid the Belgrade paperwork onto my desk and left.

I was due to leave in a day. Which, at this point, felt like an impossibility. There were far too many loose ends here to leave behind, all of which felt far more pressing than some stupid diplomat who needed to be reminded he was not a pawn of the mafia.

Bringing up my encrypted browser, my fingers hovered over the keyboard for a good while as I fought to figure out what to search for. While running a facial recognition search might turn up some results, our technology was slow and clunky, and would more than likely set off alarms some-where. Searching for my own face might get me in trouble for wasting time and resources.

No, I needed something else. The license plate on the car the woman drove had been mostly cut off, but revealed she lived in California. Of course, that was the most populous state. But I had two of the digits on the plate, and started running a search based on the numbers, the make, and the color of the car.

A half hour later, I had a short list of five potential people, scattered throughout the state.

Each with a name and address.

After that, it wasn't hard.

One of the women lived in Palm Springs, and from the green hills behind the soccer fields, I dropped her from the list.

The next was over sixty. Dropped.

A quick scan of social media left one single with too many drunk shots, and the other potential was Asian. That left the last one. I typed in her name and sat back as the screen populated with what information it could gather.

Married.

Two kids.

Address in Sacramento, California.

College at UC Davis.

Another car registered to who I assumed was her husband. Same last name.

Worked at a start-up and was a part owner.

Husband was an engineer.

No health concerns for any of them.

Her photos, more of them now, still carried my face.

I settled back in my seat, my fingers back to the bridge of my nose. What did this mean? Maybe I just had a doppelganger. She could simply look remarkably like me. But was that really feasible?

Her birthday was exactly nine months from mine. Parents listed as living in a nearby small town in central California.

She'd done exceptionally well in school, but something happened and she never entered grad school. The discrepancy made me frown and click through several of the school documents that were dredged up during my search of company records.

She'd been accepted. Of course she had been—her scores were even better than mine were at that time. But according to a small note on one of the pages, she received a rejection letter by accident, and no one ever thought to fix it.

Which would have been odd, but not horrible, if it hadn't happened at each of the six places she'd applied.

CHAPTER
FIVE

I GOT CAUGHT up in planning my next assignment for the rest of the day. My boss didn't even bother asking me why I'd been using the company access to motor vehicle databases —not that he would. Years of being exceptionally "squeaky-clean" at work (actually, just very good at covering my tracks) had killed any suspicions. As it should have. I'd played him just for times like this when I needed information for myself. Or Celine, when she'd been dating that douche and needed incriminating evidence to ensure he lost his job after she caught him cheating on her.

Usually, I stayed late at work, busy with whatever project came next. But tonight, I needed to see what Ron had uncovered, so I gathered my things and hustled out with the bubbling secretaries, acting as if I planned on joining them at the bar.

I split as soon as we got around the corner from our building, feigning forgotten plans. The secretaries were good about things like that, a sea of faces I carefully memorized and kept track of, though there were days when I wondered why I bothered. None of them would want to be friends with me, with an agent, with someone who wanted to talk about difficult things. It was incredibly snotty of me, but I knew full well who I was. Some things just were what they were. That meant I would probably be single forever, drinking wine with Celine and her husband—whenever she met him—and being a perfectly amazing aunt to her two-point-three children.

Damn, I hated David right then. More so for the momentary glimmer of hope that he'd given me that maybe I wouldn't be alone forever.

The train was full of commuters for the ride out to Ron's shop. I entertained myself with assigning each of them their day-jobs (computer scientist, professor, fifth grade teacher), then challenged myself with trying to decipher their hobbies (one was a writer, another rode horseback, another cooked—poorly). The Game passed the time, at least.

I walked to Ron's shop, and as soon as the door came into view, I knew something was off. The Open sign in the window hung crooked. Ron, with all his little quirks, would have never allowed that.

The plate windows into the shop were dark, and I swallowed hard against the flare of panic that started to crawl up my throat. It was one thing to face a situation like this on the job, but quite another to find it in the business of someone I knew well, someone I'd visited just that morning.

Careful to avoid touching anything with my hands, I edged inside. Maybe Ron just got sloppy—maybe he and his girlfriend knocked into the sign while having wild sex.

Ron would never do that. Not in a million years.

Shaking the random thought from my mind, I took a couple of steps inside. Everything appeared to be in order, except for the camera Ron used to alert him to people arriving. It was gone.

Shit.

"Ron?" I called.

Taking great care to avoid any possible source of evidence, I walked around the counter and toward the door to the back room. My heart felt like it had lodged itself somewhere in the back of my mouth, which wasn't helped when I realized the door wasn't latched.

Definitely not a good sign.

Taking note of the door's precise angle so I could reproduce it later, I stepped into Ron's lair. Really, that's what it was. He had a thing for sixteenth-century knights and the walls were painted to resemble stone, with several large sword replicas hung about. They juxtaposed well with the array of computers that dominated every other space.

So cliché, really.

No sign of Ron, but one of his computers was still on. This set my nerves even more on edge, and I pulled out the knife I kept just under the hem of my skirt.

After a quick survey of the small space and tiny bathroom, I felt a little better that I wasn't about to fall to the same fate as Ron. But the same inspection didn't reveal my photos, either.

I took a long look at his screen, seeing my face peering back. He'd already scanned the images and was apparently studying them when something, or someone, interrupted him.

A sticky note pad and pen rested on the otherwise pristine desktop. Ron's loopy, almost feminine writing noted the three file names for the images. Underneath them, he'd written and underlined twice, "Not fake."

Now, to find my photos and get out of there. I could call the cops from somewhere far away.

Pulling on gloves from my purse, I did a hasty search of the documents I could find. Most were tucked neatly into a filing cabinet. The scanner was empty. The trash too. There was nothing.

It took me a moment, standing still and peering around the room, for it to sink in.

The photos I brought were completely gone.

Then I heard it. A faint trickle of droplets. The room was nearly silent, and from some remote part of my brain, I wondered how I'd missed the sound before. Tracing it to the back door of the shop, the drips grew louder.

Ron sat in the alley behind the building, in a second desk chair that must've come from his office. Someone had strapped him down and slit his throat no more than ten minutes ago. The blood pooled in his lap and dripped onto the pavement.

"Holy, holy shit," I gasped.

Gulping back the bile that blazed up my throat, I retreated a step and let the back door swing closed.

Without knowing how or why my brain reasoned it out, I knew Ron had been killed because of those photos.

My fault. My fault. My fault.

I'd killed two men while on the job. One in Cambodia, when he'd discovered my true identity and tried to drown me; the other while sneaking out of a safe house in Dubai, when I found myself staring down the barrel of a gun. I still remembered the final look in their eyes, and they continued to haunt my sleep. Both were situations of kill or be killed, and while I logically knew it was my life or theirs, it never made it any easier to handle.

This was completely different. Nothing should have happened to Ron. My foolishness led to this. I had to get away before anyone traced this back to me.

I did nothing to stop the tremble in my hands as I gathered my things and took a great deal of extra care to avoid any evidence that I'd been there. I deleted the files off the computer and ensured they weren't stored anywhere on a backup drive or other random memory. A dedicated hacker could still find them, but I hoped the police wouldn't dig too far into that.

I peeled off one glove. Then the other. Stuffed them into my purse. And edged my way out of the shop, careful to keep my head angled away from any potential cameras, which I had forgotten to do on the way in.

Running was out of the question, but walking felt far too slow, too obvious, as I made my way back to the platform. I ignored everyone around me and waited off to one side, wishing the image of Ron's surprised face would leave me, that I could ignore the guilt over what his girlfriend would feel when she found out. But I knew better. Ron was a friend, and because of me, he was dead.

CHAPTER
SIX

NOT EVEN MY little Game could distract me while I rode home. My mind circled back, again and again, to the expression of pure terror that popped Ron's dead eyes wide, followed by the second grin below his chin.

I did that to him—all but held the knife. My knees wanted to give out at just the thought of it, of his poor girlfriend, his family.

All because of some damn photos of my doppelganger.

And David—what did he have to do with it? Was he the one to do it? He was the only one who also knew of the photos' existence. It was going to cost him everything, just as soon as I got my hands on him.

My mind whirled and buzzed through a million different scenarios, each with their flaws and loopholes. Nothing quite made sense, and all the while, my breath felt short and painful, my chest tight over the loss of Ron.

I headed home, tempting myself with a bottle of wine and a hot bath, needing time to think once I felt safe behind my own doors. The actions wouldn't keep the analytical part of my brain from working, but I wanted to work out the perfect payback for what had happened to Ron. I was a big proponent of revenge being carefully planned out.

The footsteps behind me were stealthy, but not hidden.

"Not terribly worried about someone following you?"

I wheeled around, keys in hand, ready to use them as a weapon if needed. I'd almost made it home to my carefully constructed safe house, but David, of course, had to ruin it. Somehow it felt like I'd summoned him with the extensive imaginings I'd been entertaining of how to kill him.

"Who the hell are you?" I spat as I glared at David, standing a step below me on my front stoop. He still towered over me.

This close, his scent hit me. Not too strong, but clean, comfortable, a part of his Game. Any woman would think, "Safe, considerate, handsome."

Not me.

David considered his answer for a long moment, his dark eyes scanning my face, hair, and bag. I knew he was logging every faint detail. A part of me wanted to push him down the steps, but I wouldn't be that petty.

Not when the neighbors could see, at least.

"What happened?" David's voice dropped low and his hands clenched at his sides. Every bit of him said he was concerned for me. An act, of course. One that would rival any one I could manage.

"Nothing." I shut the frustrated and grieving part of my brain behind a steel door, clearing my head—the mental equivalent of shoving everything in the closet before guests arrive. I managed a polite smile for David and crossed my arms, and then drew myself up to my full height, eyes level with his clavicle. A quick consideration of the situation left me few options. Technically he had the upper hand here, while I was unarmed and unprepared. His height and strength would work against me. For now, I needed to get away, get a plan, and then strike back.

"Nothing's wrong," I repeated. "I assumed you knew where I lived and didn't feel like bothering to circle the block."

"Are you going to go in?" David asked, leaning forward this time to make our conversation appear a little more intimate.

"Not with you." Before he could respond, I turned and jammed my key into the lock, and with practiced ease, got myself inside. I slammed the door shut, then caught the handle just before it closed.

David's fingers had arced around the edge of the door, his plain but well-kept nails white as he held it and braced for pain.

For some stupid reason, I couldn't bring myself to do it. I wanted to hurt him, and pushing him down the stairs still seemed like a pleasurable option. But I didn't particularly like the thought of slamming his hand in the door. It was just a horrible way to lose a few fingers that I'd have to clean up.

And maybe the woman inside me who had so loved his emails just didn't want to think he could have anything to do with all of this, even if I did find it entirely too coincidental that the photos he'd given me had been what Ron had been investigating when he'd been murdered. My gut still squawked his innocence, but I knew better than to trust it.

I held the door almost shut, pressure trapping his fingers between door and jamb. I waited, one beat, then two.

"Why not?" David asked.

My grin was quick, more teeth than lips. But I said nothing.

David sighed and pulled his hand back, allowing me to shut the door and throw each and every bolt home. I had five.

The security system my work had installed engaged and I breathed a tiny sigh. Even though I knew it wasn't foolproof, it was better than nothing.

I set my bag in its spot by the door and kicked off my

heels. My feet felt miserable, like I'd spent the day balancing on broken glass. Wearing them, however, was part of the Game. No one at work would ever know my feet hurt, and there was no denying that walking in with heels leveraged a little extra bit of power when I needed it most. So, I kept wearing them, and knew I'd have to find a podiatrist at some future date.

An old family portrait from when I'd been eight hung by my entry—I looked like a terribly awkward child and I placed it there to put my guests ease. Today, I touched my dad's face, his geeky glasses slightly askew. He'd always been so protective of me when it came to the guys I dated, and I wished I could get his help dealing with the ridiculous situation I was in now.

It took exactly one minute before my phone dinged.

David's email notice.

Even though I expected it, it still irked me. Why bother? I'd made myself clear. I needed to call into work and have someone do a sweep of the neighborhood, in case David wasn't the only one lurking outside. Hopefully they wouldn't be lazy about it and be done before I got out of my bath.

I fished my phone out and stared at the screen for a moment. I was keen on not bothering to read it, but since I was learning all kinds of new things about him, I was afraid to find out just how crazy he might be.

The message was simple: "What did you learn today?"

I closed the message and sent a quick note to the security director at work, instructing him of a suspicious character outside, and asking that someone to come collect him and await additional instructions. David was too smart to be caught by such simple means, but I felt safer having done it.

Then, I went back to David's message and replied, "I have made it clear that I don't want to have anything more to do with you. Please stop harassing me." Documentation would be key if anyone ever linked me to his demise.

The response took no more than a few seconds. "Or you'll have your bosses haul me in as well?"

Did he hack my phone? Or did he just assume my actions? Both were possible.

Both were terrifying.

I flicked on every light on the way to my kitchen. Shock left me freezing, and I needed hot tea. I dropped my phone on the counter with every intention of not responding further.

I set the tea kettle on the stove and counted down from ten, allowing myself to breathe out as I did, forcing my mind back on track. The shock of seeing Ron had derailed me, but something bigger was going on, and I needed to be sure I handled it right.

By the time the teapot sang, I felt a little more like myself. I peeled an orange and ate that, too, knowing the sugar would help.

While my tea steeped, my phone dinged again. I wanted to turn it off, but I had to wait for work to reach out.

His message this time shot a spear of ice down my back. "You shouldn't have shown anyone the photos. Now they know you know. They saw me at the café last night."

Swallowing, I took my tea and drained the cup in a single swig. The honey I'd poured in had gathered at the bottom and made the dregs overly sweet.

Then, I picked up the phone and dialed his number. When he picked up, I kept my tone cool, not about to take no for an answer. I owed Ron that much. "Who knows, exactly?"

"Those who are behind the experiments. If you let me in, I can explain more."

I actually laughed. "Not a chance." My curiosity only went so far as ensuring my own safety. If he thought I'd let him inside my house, even with the promise of learning what hell I'd landed myself in, he was delusional.

"When you need more answers, you know where to reach me," David said after a longer pause.

I didn't reply. Instead, I made another mug of tea and went upstairs to my room. I locked the steel reinforced door and checked the windows. Only one of them would open, from the inside only, if I needed to escape—I wasn't about to be cornered—but at least I felt safe there.

If only I could stop my mind from replaying Ron's image.

Then there were the photos. The woman with my face. The fact that Ron was killed because of them seemed too likely. David had been clear that the photos were dangerous. But, I really did not want to think it was David who would have done that to Ron. I didn't have enough information to guess who else could be responsible beside David, and that irked me. Tomorrow, I'd figure out what was going on. I'd use my work resources and get to the bottom of it all.

And if David was at all linked to what happened to Ron, he was going to regret ever emailing me.

CHAPTER
SEVEN

I DIDN'T GET TRULY WORRIED until I woke the next morning after a very fitful "sleep" and realized no one from work had called to say they had the tail in custody.

That was the moment I realized I was in over my head.

Despite the early hour and the fact I was still in my pajamas, I called in to the security office. Perhaps my message hadn't gone through correctly. As unlikely as that was—our teams relied on the system with their lives; it was meant to always work—I wanted to believe something had simply gone wrong.

No one picked up. I left a terse message.

Next came my boss. Yesterday he'd been wearing a tie his mistress gave him, so I called his private line.

No answer.

Called his home. His wife, sleepy and with the sound of a small child crying in the background, hadn't heard from him. From the tone of her voice, I guessed she hadn't had a proper amount of sleep in at least a month. Her shitty husband was sleeping around. I really needed to replace his shampoo with Nair. What a weasel.

These small facts didn't distract me from what else I had

to do. My travel bag sat ready, as it always did, inside my closet. I'd added several items yesterday morning in anticipation of my work trip. Now, I was grateful.

The vest I strapped on before dressing was from our R&D department—light and barely noticeable. It still didn't make me feel safe. The rest of my outfit was designed to blend in. Jeans. Shoes I could run in. Nothing too clingy or constricting.

Before I left my room, I texted Celine. It was nothing but a string of numbers. Anyone checking my or her phone wouldn't recognize them, but she would. It was the house number and zip code for the place we'd lived in together back before getting our own addresses. It meant something was going down and she had to get out of Dodge until further notice.

Two minutes later, I got a message back. Another code. This one told me to be safe.

Celine may not have known what I did for work, but she knew to trust me.

Armed with both a Taser and a gun, my bag strapped to my back, I left my room.

The house felt eerily still, like it held its breath, waiting for something to happen.

Or maybe that was just me.

Then, a sound. In the kitchen.

The adrenaline took over. I'd trained for this. Knew what to do. Took pleasure in letting my mind pull taut over the points of action.

Gun out, I slipped down the stairs. Silent, I edged around the corner, headed for the door. I'd go around the back, get my car parked there.

"Going somewhere?"

I almost shot him. My finger tightened on the trigger, and it was a hair from releasing when I stopped myself.

The old man from the coffee shop. David said it was his father. Sitting on my couch, reading the paper, legs crossed and face hidden behind the expanded pages, his voice was similar enough.

One deep breath. Two. I lowered my gun a fraction.

"You can put the gun down, Diana. We're not here to harm you." David emerged from my kitchen, my favorite mug steaming in his hands.

"Then what the hell are you doing in my house?" The urge to shoot David was nearly overwhelming. Was he here to do the same to me as he had done to Ron? Even without any logical indicators that he had been involved, I didn't feel any better about the situation.

"We're here to get you out of here. Safely." David's father folded the paper and set it neatly on my table.

"By breaking into my house?" There were more than a few things I wanted to add to that, but I took the opportunity of them exchanging a glance to edge my way toward the front door.

"I wouldn't do that," David's father warned. "You grew a tail in the night." He pushed a hand through his graying hair, the morning light catching on the silver strands.

Keeping my gun handy, I went to the window, peeking out to see that several people, not bothering to be inconspicuous, lounged on the bus bench, against the brick wall of the house across the street, and in a car a few houses up. Dark suits and glasses. It was like some terrible movie set.

"And how am I supposed to believe you're not with them?"

"Maybe because we're not dragging you out the door already?" David said with a wry grin at his father.

"That's hardly evidence. There are plenty of other ways you could be colluding."

David's father laughed. "David, I was sure I'd never meet someone else who would actually use the word 'collude' aloud."

I rolled my eyes but not before I noticed a faint pink tint in David's cheeks.

"Why don't we go in the kitchen? Have a cup of tea. Talk for a few minutes. And then we can get out of here," David suggested.

They outnumbered me. I might have been able to take the old man, but against both, I gauged my odds to be about thirty percent. It was better to play this calm. There'd be a chance to make a run for it shortly.

I knew this house. Knew how to ensure I got away. All I needed was a chance.

———

Several coffee cups from the place down the street sat on my counter. Two dirty plates sat in my sink.

"You came prepared." I stowed my gun in the holster under my arm, looking around for other traces of what they'd been up to. The slightly ajar cupboard door told me where they'd searched. My purse on the table, not where I left it, made it clear they'd gone through that as well.

Bastards. Not that I left anything important anywhere accessible, but it still gave me a grimy, icky feeling.

"We had to be sure," David commented in a low voice, catching my murderous glance.

"Of what, exactly?"

"That you weren't the one who killed the man at the photo shop." David's father sat down on one of the seats at my breakfast bar, steepling his fingers under his chin.

My jaw dropped an inch. "You really think I'd do that to Ron?" I shook my head, the thought making me want to tase them both and then toss them down the front stairs.

David shook his head. "I didn't think so, but after all we've seen…" He trailed off, shrugging. "We had to be sure."

A list of five very different questions ordered themselves

in my mind. Torture would have gotten me the answers, but instead I walked to the sink, rinsed out my teapot, and set it on the stove.

Once my tea was prepared, I turned back to the men, both now seated across the stove and countertop from me.

"I did *not* kill Ron," I said flatly. "I thought you did." It was a leading statement, one I hoped would build up to more information.

"It wasn't us," David's father answered calmly, his dark eyes never leaving my face. "We don't know for sure who did it, but we have a good idea. It's the same organization that has men staked outside your house. We arrived shortly before they did."

"And what organization is that?" I took a sip of tea, grateful I could hold the cup without it spilling.

"The one that's responsible for what you saw in the photos. They've gone to great lengths to ensure you don't learn about her and are now going to assess what they should do with you."

Despite my best efforts, my mug rattled against the saucer as I set it down. "Excuse me?"

The two men made the exact same expression—lips in a flat line, brows drawn together. It was like they were the same person, separated by several decades.

It was the older version who finally spoke. "There's so much to explain, Diana, and very little time to get to the details. What is most important to know right now is that these men are serious. Deadly. And they are distinctly displeased that we've interfered with their experiment."

The word "experiment" rattled around in my mind for a few extra heartbeats. The possible ramifications of what that meant were miles long.

David spoke next. "Did Ron tell you anything before yesterday's events?"

I shook my head, thinking about what I learned the day

before—or rather, what I didn't. "All I could find out was that the photos weren't fakes." As much as I might wish they were.

Ron's frozen expression, and all the blood, slipped through my mind again. "He shouldn't have died." The edge to my voice was one I only used when I interrogated someone.

To their credit, they both flinched.

"I'm sorry. I didn't think that just the photos…" David sighed. "I didn't think that something so small, something that couldn't be directly traced back, would lead to anything. He must have done some digging and started to work it out." The last part of David's comment seemed to be directed to his father, who nodded as if this made perfect sense.

"Well, maybe you should have considered that and at least mentioned there was the possibility of real danger." My voice rose and I glared at the men, my horrified anger surfacing.

"Would you have listened?" David's eyes glinted, meeting mine.

I swallowed. Damn it. "I would have taken it under advisement."

Both men made an identical laugh that sent a shiver up my spine.

"We had nothing to do with Ron's murder, but we truly are sorry about what happened," David's father said. He sounded sincere. "It's not something we anticipated, but I do think it gives you an idea of what's going on here. How serious all of this is."

"Serious" felt like an understatement. Complex, deadly, and at this point, a complete mystery—that was more like it.

As I watched the two men over the rim of my mug, my whole being hummed with distrust. They got me into this mess to begin with. Who was to say they weren't attempting to drag me into it deeper?

"So, all I know is that there's someone with my face living

in Sacramento with a couple of kids. And she was somehow screwed out of getting into a grad program several times."

David raised a brow. "You found out more, then."

I shrugged. "Standard things." He knew where I worked and how simple the information would be to look up. "Should you be worried about her as well?"

"At this point, we hope not. She doesn't know what's going on, and that will help keep her safe. For a little while, at least."

"Safe from what? I keep waiting for some kind of explanation."

David drew a deep breath and both men exchanged a long look. "There's a lot to tell—"

"And a lot of it may be hard to digest," his father interrupted.

"We aren't attempting to keep secrets, we're just trying to find a way to explain it so that you aren't..." David met my eyes again.

"So I'm not what? I think I've demonstrated that I can handle myself." I gripped the edge of my marble countertop, my knuckles blanching white. Nothing pissed me off more than two men thinking they knew better than I did what I needed, or didn't need, to know.

David was about to speak when the bell for the front door rang.

"SURELY THEY'RE NOT GOING to just ring the doorbell," I scoffed. Logically, I knew that was a relatively safe way to get someone to open up. On the other hand, there were enough people outside that bypassing the door would be easy.

"They'll want to appear… peaceful. At first." David's father's eyes narrowed.

"Ready?" David asked.

From their expressions, we would be leaving soon. Which left open the one possibility I'd been waiting for.

The two nodded at each other before turning to assess me. I crossed my arms over my chest.

David, in an eerily calm voice, stated, "We've got a car. We have to leave. Now." This was the kind of voice I'd assume was behind all of the emails we'd sent to one another. The kind of calm that I used when I tried to get a suspect to be compliant.

Nodding once, I retrieved my travel bag from where I'd set it near the door, sparing a quick glance at the old family photo, and snagged my purse from the table where the boys had rifled through it.

Another ring of the bell.

"They'll be entering in about twenty seconds," David muttered under his breath.

Just long enough for us to get to the back door. David slid out a gun, its silencer extending the barrel to comical lengths. But as soon as we edged through the back door off the kitchen, the one that led down my back steps to the alley and my parking garage, a dark form appeared around the side of the house.

Two muffled puffs of air, and he fell.

"It's just a tranq," David whispered.

That did not make me feel any better.

David's father took out a second pursuer as we crouched low behind the wall that guarded my back stairs, then ran toward the garage at the end of the block. The intruders still hadn't shot at us. My heart rate calmed. The real threat was David and his dad. They had to be daft if they thought I was about to trust their sorry story.

Fifty yards. Twenty. I could see the edge of my bumper through the open slats of the structure.

No way in hell was I getting into a car with either of these men. I did not care that they hadn't just killed me outright, that they acted like they were trying to help me—whatever nonsense they were dragging me into, I wanted no part in it. I had work to do, and just because I looked like some woman in Sacramento, I was not going to haul off with them. Work would handle the weird people hanging around my house, and I'd be on a plane later to get away from all this insanity.

Remaining behind a step or two, I scanned the buildings around us. I kept my gun out—the non-tranq kind—and made a show of covering our backs.

My keys were already in hand. David and his father didn't look back as I slowed my steps.

One quick beep and my car unlocked. In a move I'd practiced a hundred times, I opened the door and pushed the button to start the engine a split second later. Less than five seconds and I was behind the wheel.

The doors locked with a clunk.

David's face loomed in my window. I didn't look.

My foot slammed on the gas, and I whipped back out of my spot.

David's father jumped out of the way. I almost clipped him.

I slammed through my gears, and with squealing tires, screamed out of the garage.

David and his father ran after me, a lone tranq bullet pinging off the bullet-proof glass of the back window.

"See ya later, boys."

They disappeared from my rear-view mirror as I raced around the corner. Hopefully all the shit they'd dumped on me would be taken care of by the time I got back.

At the next stoplight, I closed my eyes and took a deep breath. First things first.

I grabbed my phone and made one more call in to work—the emergency line, the one reserved only for the direst of situations. I'd only ever used it once, when I was trapped in a terrorist cell in Alabama. It went straight to the director.

Today, it rang fifteen times before clicking off.

"Shit." I threw my phone against the passenger seat, where it bounced against the leather.

What this all meant settled poorly in my stomach. Nothing should have interfered with someone picking up that call. What if another agent actually needed aid?

Another red light and I stretched out across my seat to grab the phone from where it had slid.

If, indeed, someone had infiltrated our program, I needed to be untraceable. Prying off the back of the phone, I grabbed the extra memory card and the SIM card before dropping the phone out my window as I passed over the river.

That should take care of the worst of it. Unless they'd bugged my car.

I took extra precautions on my way to work. Extra turns and every lesson I'd been taught on how to ensure I wasn't followed. Today, I didn't know if it was superfluous, but I'd much rather err on the side of caution.

By the time I pulled onto the familiar street, my grip on the steering wheel was white and painful. I got my reserved spot in the garage across the street, stowed my purse in my bag, and strapped it onto my back.

Whatever was going down, I sure as hell wasn't going in unprepared.

That included the gun tucked under my arm.

And the thud of my heartbeat in my ears.

This whole insanity made me wish I'd never responded to David's initial email. What possessed me to play this stupid Game?

Boredom.

The answer, so plain and simple, didn't make me feel any better.

I kept my eyes open as I crossed the street.

A new set of tire marks on the asphalt—did someone leave in a hurry? Or was there a near accident?

The front door looked normal, until I paused, my hand an inch from the handle.

No. Not normal. Rigged.

A wire, one only someone like me would notice, threaded from the inside of the glass door, along the top, and to the edge of the doorway.

Leading to…what? C4? That seemed too cliché.

Granted, whomever these people were, the stupid

sunglasses and dark suits made it seem like *cliché* might not be out of character.

Well, fine. There were other entrances.

The pane of glass off to the right, overlooking the lobby decorated with plain leather chairs and fake plants, had a small indentation in the metal section that separated it from the next sheet of glass. After a careful inspection to prove it hadn't been rigged, I pressed a finger into the dent and the glass slid back with a soft whoosh of air.

I'd thought the plan for that door was completely useless when they first installed it. Maybe I owed my weasel boss a bit of an apology.

Inside, the building was still. Far too still. At this time of day, everyone should be streaming in to work, the administrative assistants taking their places, the agents changing shifts, or if they were between jobs like I was, coming in to set up their next plans.

But all was silent.

I took a deep breath. A hint of smoke, probably from where they'd installed the charges.

I followed the ominous wire along the edge of the door to a small compartment off to one side. A quick inspection of the device in the breaker box there, and I snipped a line. At least the door would be safe to leave by.

Nothing "real" happened on the ground floor. It was merely where we attempted to look normal for our neighbors.

But going upstairs didn't sit well with me. Every last one of my senses warned against it—the smell, the strange scuffs on the ground, the way the top of the desk felt gritty against my fingertips. I should retreat somewhere safe and await news on how to proceed.

Except that call to the director didn't go anywhere.

So what if news never came?

I ground my teeth together and looked around again. No, I was determined to see what had gone down. There might be agents I needed to help, even if our whole organization had gone to hell.

After a quick study of the elevator, I decided to take the stairs.

Nothing could have prepared me for what I found on the next floor up.

CHAPTER NINE

I EXITED the stairwell and kept close to the wall, gun out, ears trained on the room around me.

Rounding the bend to the main floor of cubicles and offices—my desk among them, I stumbled to a halt.

The coppery tinge to the air spoke of blood.

The carpet under my feet squelched.

In three steps, I stood in front of the weasel's office.

He was slumped over his desk. A lurid smile sliced his throat, spilling blood, so much blood, across his desk and the stupid white carpet he'd installed.

His poor wife and kid. The thought went through my mind, remembering the exhaustion in his wife's voice when I spoke with her this morning. I set off to examine the rest of the damage.

Two more bodies, both agents, slumped at their desks.

Did I do this? Because of the photos? Was all this my fault?

A deep ringing in my ears grew louder as I went over the room, searching for clues, for anything that might point to motivation.

Nothing.

They were very thorough.

My stomach felt about ready to heave, so I made for my desk. The familiarity of it, despite the eerie calm in the room, settled some part of me. I took several deep breaths with my mouth, desperate to clear the scent of blood from my nose.

The sound of a footstep froze me in place.

From the doorway.

Someone tracked me up here.

My ears strained to hear where they might be headed, to get a step ahead. The buzz in my ears felt like it might take off and fly.

I stood, moving barely an inch at a time, every moment conscious, silence the ultimate goal.

One step in front of the other, I slid along the wall toward the back exit. Senses trained on where they might be next.

Ahead, the Exit sign glowed, even in the dim light of the room. No one had bothered to turn on the lights.

A blind corner of dull grey cubicle walls rounded off to the side.

Another footstep, muffled by the industrial carpeting. In front of me, to the side. Someone in the corridor I'd have to pass to get to the door.

Go back? Rush forward? Shoot?

My fingers were slick from sweat and the buzzing still haunted me.

I had to keep moving.

Breathing in once more, I made my decision. The calculated risks were lower taking this exit as the getaway would provide more cover. Even if someone was waiting around the corner.

In the single moment of hesitation, the long barrel of a riffle came around the corner.

With my gun up, I squeezed off one shot, wide, before the dark head came into view. And with it, a slam of pain that radiated up from my thigh.

"You shot me," I accused, not sure if I was more surprised or annoyed.

Both, I decided. And sleepy.

David mouthed, "I'm so sorry," as I crumpled to the ground.

CHAPTER
TEN

IT WAS odd how there was no moment of in-between. No grogginess. I went from dead asleep to wide-awake with a flick of a mental switch. With the cognitive switch came a rush of pain, primarily from my leg and head, but also from the bonds around my hands, which I found when I tried to sit up and rub my face. My stomach clenched and I ground my teeth together as panic swept through me. I pushed the feeling back, forcing myself to think around it—getting free meant keeping it together.

David's face peered down at me, concern etched between his brows.

"You fucking shot me." I spoke as if our conversation hadn't been cut off in the middle by me passing out.

"I'm sorry for that, but there wasn't any other choice. They were going to take you."

I scooted around, glancing at the interior of what could only have been a small RV, the kind people rented and could still fit in a standard parking spot, complete with lumpy narrow mattress beneath me and tiny stove/kitchen off to one side. With some effort, I managed to prop myself up into a sitting position.

"Just who the hell was going to take me?" Coarse rope cut around my wrists secured behind me, and the duct tape around my ankles. "Because it looks a whole lot like you guys beat them to it." I wiggled the bonds, forcing a deep breath in through my nose and out my mouth.

Even though I couldn't see him, David's father spoke up from the cab beyond the tiny cooking space. "That's what we're trying to explain."

"Well then, for fuck's sake, spit it out." There was probably a good reason for the bonds, since all I could think about was punching David right in his far too attractive nose. For a second, I debated whether I could nail him good in the gut or groin with my feet. At least that wouldn't mess up his face. The thought I wasn't completely helpless settled my stomach some.

I realized then that David's father was driving, the low rumble of the road vibrating the camper. He wasn't about to take me down. I could free myself if I could incapacitate David, but I needed a way to untie myself.

David settled back against the row of cupboards across from me. His features held tension in the fine lines around his eyes and mouth. As his eyes flashed to mine, then away too quickly, I knew he was anxious about the truth. That was probably his smartest reaction to everything about me, because I was damn well going to slam his head into the countertop.

"I doubt you'll believe me, but the company who's behind all of this—the head of the cloning division—has more money and resources than anyone, including the government and even the private security firm you worked for."

My mind caught and snagged on his words, teasing them apart and desperately attempting to piece them back together.

"Wait, what?" I almost laughed. Almost let the wild laugh at this utterly stupid story carry me away. Only the Game kept me quiet; I needed to keep playing until I got free. Then I could marvel at the stupidity of these fuckers.

David's flat-lipped smile was too brief. "The company who made us."

I rocked back and forth, his words hitting against me and nearly pushing me onto my back. It felt like a cold hand had gripped my stomach and squeezed. It took a heartbeat longer than normal to regain myself and start putting things together. I had to play along. Learn what I could. Panic wouldn't allow me to win this round.

"The other woman from the photos?"

"She's a clone, as are you. Your model has fifteen total, scattered across the States. Well, there *were* fifteen, at least."

I wet my lips, ordering my million questions into some semblance of a list. "And you?"

"There were only three of us. My brother and I, and one more. The source of our DNA is the person driving."

A ripple of disgust went through me, but I kept it in check. If David was telling the truth, the whole familial situation going on here was downright gross. "You said he's your father."

"He raised my brother and me. According to company specifications, of course, but for all intents and purposes, he's like my father." David shrugged as if this weren't terribly odd.

"So, why all this?" I gestured to indicate my bonds but implying everything that had happened since we'd met. Removing the ties was still very much a priority, despite his weird revelation. The latched drawers in the kitchen might have something inside that would allow me to free myself if I knocked David out, before the driver could pull over and catch me.

"They were going to kill you," a low voice entreated from the front, and David bowed his head. For a moment, I could have sworn a flash of agony ripped through his expression, but he was quick to hide it. Had he even felt anything? Or had he been playing the Game? Every indicator suggested his emotions were real, but he had the skills to fake anything as well as me.

For anyone else, this may have been a dreaded situation, but I'd had people intent on killing me more times than I could count. However, those had always been job related and this felt far more personal. These weirdos were acting like I was caught up in their strange little drama that rivaled any bad sci-fi movie. "I need more details than that." My tone took on the same iciness it had back in the café.

"When your guardian refused to take you out, a giant target was placed on your back. She was supposed to eliminate you when they said to. When she didn't, we didn't want to give her a chance to change her mind." The driver's tone was hard, and I couldn't quite tell if he was pleased my "guardian" hadn't done their job.

"Who?"

"The woman with you at the café? She's your guardian. Most clones have them, except when they're raised by their DNA source." David spoke carefully, like he knew full well the little bombs that might be set off.

And explode they did. I closed my eyes, processing. *Celine.* But how? She'd been my closest friend for ages. The one other human I felt comfortable around, the one who comforted me after my parent's deaths, who didn't judge me for the odd way my brain worked… No way would she be caught up in something so utterly ridiculous. Except, maybe I was wrong.

It was a little too perfect. Of course she was a plant. I did not have friends like that. I was just too weird, too observant, too much for others to really want to be my friend. I swallowed hard, struggling against the pain that settled heavy on my chest. Lesson learned.

"Then where are we going?" I asked with a small sigh. It

astounded me that I could get this much information out of them, though they were certainly playing some angle. More than likely, they wanted my help doing something.

"Sacramento." David stood and rocked over to the mini fridge, catching hold of the counter to keep his balance. He took out a water bottle and offered it to me.

I shook my head, not because I wasn't parched, but because I couldn't trust anything they gave me.

"I promise it's safe," David noted with a little smile.

I still wanted to kick him in the groin.

"So, are we going to meet my clone?" I surmised. Even with all my training, my voice caught on the last word. How strange to think there was someone out there with my exact DNA. That is, if David was telling the truth, and for all I could tell, they believed this whole farce.

Well, twins didn't think it was so strange to carry the same code in their cells, and I knew well enough that environment played a huge role in how lives were shaped, let alone how that same DNA was expressed through epigenetics. Still, it was odd. There was a woman who was my twin, family in some strange way, and I'd never even met her.

Even weirder was the idea that we'd both been manufactured. What did that mean? Just that we were the product of a petri dish? Plenty of IVF kids were born that way. Or was there more to it?

All of these thoughts spun out from the insanity that David spewed. None of this could possibly be true. Clones did not exist. If I had a twin somewhere in California, there had to be some perfectly reasonable explanation for it.

David settled back onto the seat across from me. "We're going to try and save her."

A few more pieces started to snap together—the assassins after me, David and his root clone on the run, the mopping up of anyone connected with us who might have information.

"Did the experiment end?" I asked warily. Something had

to have triggered all the madness that had happened over the last day.

David studied the water bottle in his hands for a long moment. "No, they just perfected the process. We're the extras, the failures, that need to be mopped up now that they have the results they aimed for."

His words settled in the back of my throat, hot and pointy. I had to cough to clear them. "But why bother? We could just continue on without anyone knowing about us." If I played along, maybe they'd untie me. Maybe I'd earn their trust. Maybe I could get myself out of his madhouse and figure out what had happened back at my company, back with my life.

David's father, and now that I knew it was supposedly his clone, spoke up with David's voice from the cab. "Because they plan to go public. That was always the end goal, at least overtly: to sell how to make a perfect child based on your own DNA, among other things. But they knew if anyone poked around too much, they'd realize there were early attempts, failures along the path. The public backlash at clones living among them, unregulated, for decades would be bad for business." There was a moment's pause and I thought he was finished, before his voice emerged again, this time with a small hitch. "They think you're not human. You're artificial."

"Artificial." I couldn't help repeating the word back. It may have been part of the scientific process, but that certainly didn't make me feel any better. Not that I believed anything they told me, but still, the whole idea was the mental equivalent of sucking on a lemon.

"It's best not to take it personally." David pitched his voice low so his 'father' couldn't hear. "It wasn't meant that way."

I shrugged. "It doesn't make it right."

"None of this is right."

I sighed and looked out the window, watching the trees rush by. We couldn't have traveled more than an hour or so, or the landscape would have opened up more. We were headed west, from the slant of the sun, and the road wasn't a busy one. Back highways would add at least eight hours onto our trip from the DC area all the way across the country.

The numbness in my arms began to turn to pain and I shifted, struggling to get comfortable and making more of a show than necessary. They were telling me all these details, all of this story, for a reason, and surely that couldn't involve leaving me tied up for however long it took. Not if I kept playing along at least.

After settling back against the side of the camper, I turned to David again. "How am I supposed to believe you? Because, to be frank, this sounds like a lousy sci-fi book."

David chuckled. "The pictures weren't enough?"

"You knew they wouldn't be. It's why you gave them to me—to get me curious." It wasn't a guess. His whole demeanor shouted his motive.

"True, but what other proof could we give you? After you witnessed the aftermath of your whole company falling, you were chased, and you found your murdered friend."

"Don't forget being shot and kidnapped by you," I added wryly. "And now you've told me an impossible story without anything to back it up, other than some photos that you got from who knows where." I wiggled around again, my eyes going back to the drawers, weighing the odds of a knife being inside one.

"I took the photos," supplied the voice from the cab, heavy and tired. "And if you'll hold up about ten minutes, I can show you more."

David didn't look at me as the camper came to a slow halt on a side road, under the bright sunshine and leafy green trees. I couldn't help mapping how I'd make a run for it—into the trees where it'd be harder to follow me, head southeast in hopes of coming across another road. Keep low and quiet. Both of these men probably hadn't spent much time in these forests, and I grew up in them. My dad had taught me how to track and navigate, skills that came in handy more frequently than I'm sure he ever considered.

The engine rattled for a few extra seconds after it was turned off; the truck had to be at least thirty years old. Could it even make a trip across country? Not with the way the back left axle rattled and swayed.

David's dad made his way back slowly, as if his knees pained him, and sat next to David.

Next to one another, the likeness was startling. They definitely looked like father and son, the same dark hair and eyes, slightly full lips, and they even held their shoulders the same way. It was uncanny enough that I shivered. This went beyond simple father-son resemblance, even if I had been primed to think that way by their tale. David didn't seem to have any visual aspect of him that was influenced by another party—like the mother he apparently didn't have.

"You can see it, can't you?" David's father asked.

I nodded, realizing for the first time I didn't know his name.

"It's Aaron," he offered intuitively. "David's twin was Corbin. There was another, although he didn't make it past eight months in the womb, but his name was Bruce."

"Are we all named in alphabetical order?" That would certainly make it easier to fake this whole thing.

Aaron nodded, seeming unsurprised I'd observed that. "The three before you have already been eliminated. If they follow their original plan, Eleanor should be next, but we're hoping to get there in time to save her. With your help, at least."

Eleanor. The next in the list. For a moment, I was boggled by the thought—the other ten of us/me/whatever who were out there. If there actually were others out there like me, perhaps it would be a good thing if we met. "They're going in order? One by one? Why not all at once?"

"That's been their pattern with the other cohorts," David said. "Probably don't want to arouse suspicions by having identical people all drop dead on the same day. They think they got me already, thanks to my dad, but there were fewer in my cohort."

"How am I supposed to believe this?" I asked, resting my head against the camper shell. As far as I could tell, they thought they were telling the truth. But that didn't mean they weren't excellent liars. I preferred to believe the simplest explanation, and this mess was anything but simple. Honestly, it was downright silly in some ways, though I kept that to myself.

Aaron stood and reached into one of the small square cupboards above his seat. He had to yank hard on the clasp to get it free, and then ducked as a collection of small instruments showered down.

A quick look between father and son told me this wasn't supposed to happen, but I just smiled. David reached down to gather the lighters, matches, a few small green army men, and candles from the floor.

So the camper had been theirs for some time, probably since David's childhood. Somehow imagining David playing in this place, another copy of him tagging along, brought the place into greater focus. It wasn't hard to envision two boys seated at the tiny table or sleeping on the foldout bed. My mom didn't like to camp, so it had always just been Dad and me, in a tent.

How odd it must have been for Aaron if this were all true.

The man in question pulled down a metal box and settled it onto the counter, popping open the lid and lifting out several thick files. With a motion to David, his son came to my side and helped me stand and take the two steps to the table where Aaron spread the papers out in orderly rows.

What stood out, though, were the photos.

These were older, reminding me of school photos from

when I was a kid, minus the horrible laser lines of color in the background.

One of the rows was all of me. My face. Staring up at me, wearing clothes I'd never seen. Different versions, in rows across each of the stacks of documents. The first photo was a newborn—wrinkly and indistinguishable. The second, at a year old, again nothing to really tell apart from other babies, just round cheeks and either a vague frown or red-faced cry. And on they went at roughly one-year intervals, until the age of five, where the photos seemed to jump in ages.

But it was my face that stared out of all of them. Some a little thinner, some carrying more weight, our hair styled a little differently but mostly left long. Fifteen sets of me, documenting lives so similar to my own that I couldn't breathe for a long minute.

The short column next to mine was that of David, Corbin, and a single blue-tinged photo of a tiny baby that had to be Bruce. Again, the series of photos for each of them, punctuating their lives as they grew up.

That wasn't the only column of files, though. There were three others, with other sets of clones. Another male set, and two females, each with about five individuals within each cohort.

This was an awful lot of work to go to try to fool someone into thinking they were a clone. An awful lot of work for no seeming reward, other than to get me to believe something so preposterous.

"These are the ones I know about, from the facility where I worked. There was another base in Germany, but I couldn't get information on those cohorts. I'm hoping somehow we'll find some data on them and at least be able to warn them what's coming." Aaron's voice was low, and a quick glance his way revealed deep wrinkles around his mouth and eyes.

"If it's not already too late," David added, a hint of bitterness sharpening his words.

The men's expressions told me there was more to this story, more to this mess that echoed personally between them, but I didn't want to know any more. This already boggled my mind too much.

"They could all be faked," I suggested, coming closer to peer at the H girl in my cohort. Heidi.

"They're not." David's tone was final, and our eyes met. His were clear, without a trace of guile or guilt. For the first time, I let myself consider the possibility that he wasn't lying—the impossibility of what it all meant. The whole situation radiated out in a thousand different directions, the implications splitting like a massive family tree. If it were true, there were some incredible ramifications.

I was a clone. I had duplicates out there, a whole lot of them. And the same company that created us was now attempting to exterminate us at any cost. Celine had been pretending to be my friend for over a decade, just waiting to murder me when the call came in. There wasn't much solace in the fact that she hadn't actually done it. And my parents... How much had they known? Had they been meaning to tell me before the car crash took their lives?

My parents' faces were replaced by more recent deaths— Ron, of my boss, of everyone I worked with—executed simply because I worked there. My skin crawled with the feeling of being dirty, contagious. I longed to bathe, as if that might scour away whatever taint I carried within me.

It took five full minutes to scan the details of my cohort, at least as best as I could without the use of my hands. Five minutes to let the potential truth of it all sink in. Why would anyone fake something like this? I had thought getting kidnapped would involve interrogations about the details of my top-secret cases. And while I had information certain groups might want, David and Aaron weren't likely to be looking into infiltrating African terrorist cells. They wouldn't have needed to spin this elaborate story.

I couldn't shake the gnawing anxiety that settled into my gut. The instinct that I couldn't fight the clues all stacked up in one direction. Every bit of me resisted any of this being true. That this was real. This had to be stopped. This could kill me.

I met David's eyes with my own resolved stare. "What do we do now?"

CHAPTER
ELEVEN

"FOR NOW, we move. As fast as we can. We need to get to California by tomorrow, but we can't fly from any of the nearby airports, since they'll be watching those." Aaron turned his dark eyes on me, looking me over as he spoke. "All I know is that there's one, perhaps two, clones there who weren't eliminated by their guardian."

When David stepped behind me, all my muscles tensed, ready to fight.

"You can calm down, I'm just untying you," David whispered in my ear, his breath hot against my cheek.

His fingers were quick with the knots and my shoulders and wrists ached with the return of circulation. I gingerly wiggled my fingers and massaged my joints, forcing myself to think around the pain.

"How much time do we have?" I asked. The part of my mind that was used to organizing and planning dozens of missions slipped deftly into place.

I could get us to California, near enough to my clone. It was possible to save her. This was just like any other mission, and I was damn good at missions.

"About twelve hours, based on prior cohorts," Aaron

answered. "But we don't have access to fake identification, nor do we have the funds for a private plane."

I frowned, mentally pinging between finding a way to get them false IDs—I knew useful people in every major city—or accessing cash I had stowed in safe locations. The bad guys couldn't know about those, I was certain.

"What's the name of this company, the one we're going to stop?"

"Future Solutions." Aaron didn't seem the least bit ruffled at my random line of questioning. Good. Because what we needed to do wasn't going to be fun.

"I need to know where we are, on a map."

I didn't think they'd drag out honest-to-goodness paper maps. With the sheets spread out across the miniscule table, I traced our route and plan. The boys were accepting of what I proposed, mainly because it meant much less time in the camper and a lot more leeway in arriving in Sacramento.

If all went well, of course.

With a plan in place, Aaron rattled the vehicle toward the highway and back the way we came.

"There aren't any other drop sites we could get supplies from?" David asked again, testing me.

I shot him a long-suffering look, swigging from the water bottle I'd retrieved. "Not unless we want to add a few hours' drive-time."

David nodded and looked out the window. I returned my attention to the maps of Sacramento and its surrounding areas, but David spoke up again.

"Thanks. For joining in on this with us, I mean. You didn't have to. We could have worked something else out."

I raised an eyebrow but kept my tone neutral. "Something else? Like not shooting me with a tranquilizer gun?"

"Well, that was necessary, given the situation. But we wouldn't have kept you, if you had really insisted."

Part of me wanted to say something cutting in response, to

remind him that I'd woken, bound, in the back of a moving vehicle, but I thought better of it. We had a lot of work to do, and they'd shared information I probably would never have been privy to otherwise. To be fair, they'd saved my ass from Future Solutions a couple times now. Which meant that I did kind of owe them. But "kind of" was the best they were going to get. The reality of all of this was that I wanted nothing more than to take down this Future Solutions company that had entirely stolen my life, murdered people I cared about, and apparently viewed me as less than human. If stopping them meant going along with these two strangers, so be it. I still didn't trust Aaron and David, but perhaps I could rely on the fact that our goals were aligned—for the time being.

"If you don't mind, I think we should keep ourselves focused on the task at hand," I said. "If you're really concerned about my feelings, then let me tell you that it's fine. I won't mention it again."

Another flash of emotion crossed David's face. I was getting better at reading them. This time it was one of regret, though for what, I could only hypothesize.

When we reached the drop site two hours later, I forced us to stop for food and supplies. I needed to change shoes at the very least, as mine were soaked with my boss's blood and the squelching between my toes turned my stomach with every step.

I spent the ride propped in the back on the bed, continuing to look over the paperwork Aaron had stolen about my cohort. There were so many lives that looked up from the pages, and my mind absorbed as much information as I could manage. The truth of what we were—all of us identical to one another, with the claim we weren't really human—ached in my chest. Someone, David I suspected, had made tiny red x's next to those who had been eliminated. Goosebumps filled my arms when I realized that I'd never know these women, even though we'd shared a face for their entire lives.

What all of that meant about who and what I was, I didn't know. Could anyone truly understand what it was like to be someone else? If I was born differently, did that make me something less? There had been religious objections to IVF when the science was new, but no one today thought twice about it. But did the process of my creation make me entirely different? Not human? Did all my memories, experiences, all of my thirty-plus years count for nothing?

After a quick pit stop at Walmart and a belly full of food from McDonald's, I started to feel a little more human. Well, as human as I could be, considering I'd been manufactured like the McChicken sandwich I ate.

But the food also helped me think about what we needed to do. I knew next to nothing about Future Solutions or how to stop them. My fingers itched for my work laptop and the ability to search the web, but all of that had to be forgotten now. I was forced to solve this like a civilian, even if that was setting up an unsettling David and Goliath moment. Hah. David.

"How did they choose the parents?" I asked David after an hour of contemplative silence.

Aaron was the one who answered. "It's different for each cohort. Some were under strict observation and regimen, like David and Corbin. Others, like your set, were given to adoption agencies with instructions to the parents to never reveal the adoption to the children."

I swallowed. It had been five years since their passing, and while the grief was no longer fresh, it was still sharp. Never would I have guessed I might not be their child. I even resembled my mother, or so I had thought. I longed to ask them for every detail they could muster, all the things they thought about my differences, and whether or not they'd ever regretted taking me on. But maybe it was better that I didn't know.

David, settled in one of the sideways facing seats, stared out the window. He was the identical clone of Aaron, and I wondered if biology really made any difference. My parents were wonderful and supportive, even when I was clearly different, and the years before I learned how to switch off my observational skills weren't easy. I knew things about them, always. There were no secrets. Except this one. This massive one about where I came from.

And, without having to really think about it, I knew it didn't matter. They were my parents. I loved them, and they loved me. They wouldn't have known about where I came from, and for that, I was grateful for the normalcy they had given me.

"Did you always know?" I asked, pitching my voice low so Aaron wouldn't hear.

David turned a blank expression to me, his eyes focused far, far away. "Yes."

"Did it bother you?" Perhaps it was too direct of a question, but I couldn't stop myself from asking.

David shook his head. "I've never known anything different."

With that, I turned back to the papers before me, the weight of them between my fingers reminding me of the cost they all carried. So many lives. So many deaths. I traced the small x's on the first three women in my cohort. My picture was next, and then Eleanor. Would we have x's next to out our faces next?

I had to stop this.

CHAPTER
TWELVE

THE SECURE SITE wasn't much to look at from the outside—a generic apartment complex on the outskirts of Philadelphia. The gray siding was new, but the parking lot showed its age in potholes and the landscaping around the building was mostly weeds.

After a couple trips around the block to ensure nothing looked out of place, I gave Aaron instructions on where to park: The last spot at the back of the lot, near the rear entrance onto a one-way street. It was as close to secure as we were going to manage.

"Keep the engine running. If I'm not back in five, get out of here."

Aaron narrowed his eyes. "And we're just supposed to trust you?"

I almost laughed. "Yes. That, and I'd never lead you here without planning on staying with you."

"I'm coming with you." David came up behind me, his dark presence over my shoulder like a looming thunderhead.

"Like hell you are."

David gave me one of his thin-lip smiles and shrugged. "Or else we leave now. We can drive straight through."

"You'd never make it before they kill her."

"Then we let Eleanor die and move on to the next one," he answered simply.

Fuck. I swallowed hard, thinking of the woman in the photos, the way her small children loved her. Their little smiles. I didn't know her, but I couldn't let her be murdered.

"Fine, but stay close. I don't want to have to protect your ass."

David chuckled, and with that, we left the camper, kept close to the wall of the structure, and made our way around the side of the complex.

I flipped my mental switch into high alert, my brain soaking up everything around us. The way David moved like a giant black cat, clearly focused on what he was doing. The window into an elderly woman's kitchen, where she tried to hide her daily cigarette from her grandkids.

And the silence. The strangeness of it.

"Something's wrong," I whispered to David.

He raised an eyebrow in question. I couldn't quite explain to him how I knew it, but regardless, we still had to take the risk of getting to the apartment and inside. The goods were worth the peril.

Up the stairs to the second floor. Down the open corridor on the side of the building to apartment two-two-seven. The door hadn't been damaged and the lock looked clean. No one had forced their way inside lately, or else they found another way in.

The keys from my bag slid into the locks. Tumblers turned and I pushed the door open an inch. Just enough to reach a finger through and type in the code to the alarm.

We didn't need anyone else showing up. Or the nasty, debilitating spray that would coat us if we didn't have the right set of numbers.

The alarm beeped the all clear and I let out a puff of breath as the door swung open soundlessly.

David's hand landed on my shoulder and pushed, and we both swung forward into the apartment's front hallway, then dropped to the floor.

Two shots sailed past our heads, the breeze from their passage rushing through my hair before they slammed into the stucco wall of the hallway behind us.

"Stay down," David growled, rolling to a crouched position in one fluid motion.

For a split second, I watched him. Based on his movements, he'd been trained in at least two martial art forms, and with his dark shirt and jeans, my brain conjured the image of a ninja.

But only for a moment.

Staying put was the fastest way to get shot. My ability to get into a low stance was nowhere near as graceful as David's, but I was able to look around the corner into the main living room area. There were three assailants. Their faces were covered, guns out. Two more shots were fired at David, but it's hard to get a bead on a target that could duck and weave like that. In two seconds, he was among them.

I rolled deeper into the apartment and into the fake kitchen area. A shot embedded into the doorframe behind me and I hissed in a breath.

I hadn't been shot at in at least five years. Well, other than this morning.

Aaron hadn't given me back my sidearm after they tranq'd me, so I dove for the knife block on the counter. I grabbed two and sunk down to peer around the counter.

David had one of the men in a headlock and was in the process of fending off the other with a kick that used headlock guy as leverage. Impressive.

Which meant the other one was tracking me.

Weighing the knife in my hand, I took a deep breath and peered around the corner again.

Another shot, this one taking out the kitchen window. Too close.

I grabbed a dish towel, wadded it up, and with a quick breath, threw it into the open doorway. The shooter didn't miss this time.

Neither did I.

In the split second it took the man to realize I'd fooled him with the towel, I dove forward and let the knife sail. It caught him under his chin, in the gap between his vest and his mask. With a wet gurgle, he dropped.

David caught my eye before catching the second assailant's incoming punch and twisting it back, dropping the guy to his knees.

"Who sent you?" David asked, his breathing heavy and sweat trickling down his cheek.

The masked guy struggled, fighting against David until, with a sharp jab, David broke the guy's arm. The sound seemed to take a long time to fade from the room.

"Next time it's your neck. Who sent you?"

"You know who," the man growled, his pain evident in his gruff tone. He howled when David twisted his broken limb.

"You *know* who sent me. Future Solutions. All I was told was that we were eliminating aberrations."

David gave me a look that was so clearly "See, I told you so," he might as well have spoken aloud.

All that rocked through my mind was *aberrations.*

With that, David took zip ties from his pocket and secured the man's wrists, then his feet. He did the same with the third guy sprawled on the floor.

"You didn't have to kill him," he noted, peering at the man I'd taken down. Blood still flooded from him in a creeping pool.

"Yeah, well," I sighed. Swallowed. "I didn't want to."

David coughed to hide his laugh. I just shook my head,

though a little grin worked through the adrenaline still humming in my veins.

"Damn it, these guys are serious, aren't they?" I groaned, staring at the demolition in the living room. There had been a couch and TV in there, but the gun fight had left the TV a pile of shards and the couch oozed stuffing from several slices.

David nodded, surveying the scene. "Yes. Yes, they are."

Something in his tone made me glance over at him, but he waved me away. "Let's just get the supplies and get the hell out of here before they track us any further."

I led the way into the back room, where someone from Global had put in a false back to the closets. I pulled back the opening on its silent sliders and took stock of its contents.

Guns, at least five of them.

A lockbox of cash, mostly dollars, but enough to get by for a few weeks in Europe or several Asian countries. And what I'd brought us here for: the spare IDs.

An envelope with my call number yielded a handful of driver's licenses and passports, already featuring my face and fake names.

But there were also several sets of blanks, just in case we needed to get someone important, or even family members, out of the country in a hurry.

Earlier in my career, I was given instructions on how to finish the mostly complete IDs, and all we needed now were photos of David and Aaron. Those could be taken and printed using the kit someone had carefully packed with special glue, laminate, and a card printer.

"Here." I handed David the heavy box of supplies, while I took a duffle from a cubby and filled it with as much as it could hold. David pulled down a couple boxes of ammo, and two minutes later, we were back out the front door.

"We're just going to leave them?" I asked, walking point back to the parking lot.

"I'm sure they have backup somewhere close," David

answered, trying to juggle the heavy box and keep an eye out for anything suspicious.

"Where did you learn to fight like that?" I asked. David seemed tightlipped around Aaron, so maybe without him around, he'd be more talkative.

"I already told you I used to work for a company a lot like yours." His attention was elsewhere, too busy scanning our surroundings.

I rolled my eyes, even if the effect was lost on David behind me. "I know, but even *I* wasn't given that kind of physical training. Enough to defend myself, but nothing like what you did back there." Granted, I had always been more of the brains of my operations, the one who could blend and disappear, allowing others to do the physical work.

"My dad put Corbin and me into lessons at a young age. We were always good at that kind of thing, Corbin much more so than me. Not that it did him any good."

The bitterness in his tone stopped me halfway down the lower level corridor. I peered back at him over my shoulder, surprised at the raw honesty in his tone.

"What happened to Corbin?" I assumed he was dead, and that Future Solutions had something to do with it. But the details to fill in the gaps were… of interest.

"That," David sighed, "is none of your business. We need to move. Their backup will be here in less than a minute."

He was right, and I ran as fast as I could, laden with at least a hundred pounds of gear. That did nothing to keep my mind from pondering about what had happened. David's grief was still fresh, and my heart went out to him. I knew that kind of pain from losing my parents, and I wouldn't wish it on anyone. It often stung at the most random times, a heart-rending blast of hurt while doing something innocuous, like brewing tea. No wonder David wanted to stop Future Solutions.

Aaron already had the engine running, and as we got in

the camper, I saw that all the color had drained from his expression. Before the door was fully shut, he was screeching out of the lot and away from the apartment complex.

"What happened?" he barked, merging onto a busier street. I settled into the passenger seat, scanning out the window, my gun held below the lip of the door handle. No one was obviously following us, but that didn't mean much.

"They were waiting for us," David bit out, his tone so dark I had to look at him.

So, he must blame Aaron for this mess. That made some sense. Aaron was the one who brought him into the world, in some twisted way. Just what Aaron's role had been with Future Solutions still hadn't been discussed, but from his hands and posture, I assumed he was one of their scientists. He clearly loved David. So how did Corbin die?

Aaron muttered a few choice words under his breath. "You neutralized the situation?"

"Diana took one of them out."

Aaron looked over at me, glancing over the top of his sunglasses. "That'll provoke the beast."

I shrugged. "He was shooting at me." The comment was far more nonchalant than I felt, but better to let them think I could be heartless. It would make them take me more seriously.

"But you got the supplies?" Aaron asked.

I shot David a confused look. Hadn't he seen us enter the RV with all the gear? But David didn't look at me, just said, "Yep. I'm going to go work on a set of IDs," and disappeared into the back of the camper.

I returned my attention to the road. Our route toward the airfield would take an hour or so, and I didn't want any of the goons knowing where we were headed. I scanned license plates, memorizing them, along with the faces of the drivers I could make out in the sun's glare. It was tedious but kept my brain from wandering down the rabbit holes of all that went on around me.

"Thank you. For getting the supplies," Aaron volunteered suddenly. "And for, er, joining up on this windmill joust." He looked over at me while we waited for a light to turn green.

I met his eyes, his words rattling around in my mind. "Those men, back at the apartment, at my office, at my house… they weren't fake. I'm not imagining this. Thank you for providing me with information about where I come from. About what's going on with me. I always assumed I was just terribly odd." I almost added that I was also grateful to have the opportunity to take out this company trying to kill me, but seeing as how I didn't quite trust his relationship with the people we were running from, I held my tongue. It wasn't that I didn't want to trust Aaron and David, but there were far too many contingencies on that for the time being.

Aaron laughed. "You *are* odd, if only in the sense that you aren't like anyone else. But that was on purpose. You have skills that many would kill for, and some will."

I swallowed, thinking again of the man I murdered back at the apartment. My third kill. As utterly unscientific as I knew it was, I felt like their souls took a piece of mine with them.

CHAPTER
THIRTEEN

THE INCREASINGLY HEAVY traffic of the afternoon rush-hour slowed our progress to a crawl. I kept up my tabs on the cars around us while my mind continued to piece together all I could about Aaron and David. What they knew, what they'd told me, and what they hadn't meant to tell me. So when Aaron spoke up again, his voice so low I could barely hear him over the engine, it caught me by surprise.

"He's not going to forgive me. And I don't blame him."

For a moment, I wondered if the older man was talking to himself, but then he swung his dark gaze to meet mine. "I know he won't. He and Corbin could always hold a grudge. Must have picked that up from someone."

My jaw sagged. He had made a clone joke. It caught me so off guard, I couldn't help giggling. There was someone out there who I shared traits with, and our identical DNA meant, what? We liked a certain kind of music? Laughed at the same jokes? I wanted to find out… and put a stop to our murders.

"But you have to know that I never thought this would happen. Never. I never would have put them in danger," Aaron continued.

I managed a nod while questions flooded my mind, but

this wasn't the time or place to pry into these people's lives. Not when so much of their privacy and relationships had already been mined by a murderous company.

For a fleeting moment, I wondered if Aaron was as good an actor as his son; if his sincerity was a ploy to ensure I trusted him. But even as I thought it, I squashed the idea. Even if Aaron could play-act emotions as well as his clone, or even as well as I could, the level of this venture still couldn't be faked. This may have been a gut-level assumption, but I knew it to be true.

I turned back to the road, snapping together what pieces I could from this whole insane scenario, and noticed the car.

What was it with Future Solutions and cliché black sedans with tinted windows? Didn't they have enough money to find something that blended in better?

The plate was one I'd seen about ten minutes before, crossing an intersection going another way, but now the car was just ahead of us. A longer look revealed cigarette ash that had trailed and stuck to the side of the driver's door. Someone had spent a long while sitting and waiting for something, or someone. Likely us. And now he'd been sent to tail us.

"We need to make a left as soon as possible," I ordered. "We've caught a tail."

Aaron grumbled again and with a loud "Hold on!" We took the closest exit, just behind the tail, and the whole little camper swayed with the sudden motion.

Several things rattled and crashed in the rear of the camper and David swore. "Thanks for the warning!" he called.

"I *did* give him a warning." Aaron pitched his voice just loud enough for David to hear.

A huff came from the back.

Ignoring Abbott and Costello, I turned back to the road, trying to see if we'd lost the other car, or if someone new had replaced him. Not that this was a simple process. Aaron took the first side-street beyond the exit, cutting people off and racing along in what was definitely not a safe speed in the ancient RV.

David swore from the back seat again, and then I heard him sweep everything into the cardboard box.

"Your photo's crooked," he called up to his father.

"That's fine. I'm old. No one looks at that kind of thing for me."

I doubted that but held my tongue. Another car came into view, this one a little more inconspicuous, but still with plates I'd seen recently.

"We've got to ditch the camper." I didn't want to, but now that they knew what we were driving, it wasn't like it would be hard to spot the rogue RV driving recklessly on the city streets. How long until they brought out a chopper?

"Hold on to your hats!" Aaron shouted, taking a sharp right that tipped the camper onto two wheels for a moment, before we thudded back onto the cement and squealed away.

"Quit showing off!" David snapped from the depths of the rattling mess behind us.

Aaron chuckled, then took a hard left, and two more rights. Once I hadn't seen anyone following us for a couple of blocks, he whipped into a parking garage and managed to wedge the vehicle into a top corner near the exits.

Only after we'd been stopped for a full thirty seconds did any of us move. David, hobbling through the wreckage of maps, water bottles, and anything not tied down, came to stand behind his father in the cab. "You enjoyed that far too much."

Aaron laughed, real, deep, and rich—the first time I'd heard him do so. He sat there enjoying his mirth for almost a minute. "Well, it's been too long since I had an opportunity to try that out."

David cast me a look. "*Too long* being about a month since

he went joyriding in his Porsche. Want to tell her how I had to haul you out of a ditch?"

Aaron hushed and tutted, the adrenaline seeming to make him a bit giddy. Still, a part of me enjoyed the interaction of these two, their banter and obvious affection, despite whatever had happened that led to David blaming Aaron for Corbin's death.

The three of us made quick work of the camper. Necessary things were packed into bags and boxes. Surfaces were wiped down in hopes of catching most of the fingerprints, or at least mine. Not that it would do much good since they saw us together, but it was better to take precautions.

David left us while Aaron and I finished up and returned a couple minutes later, driving a minivan that had seen better days.

"I think my parents had this model when I was a kid," I said, opening the side sliding door and hefting my personal bag, along with the duffle of supplies, into the back. I remembered rides to school in the old van with my dad, while he grumbled about how unstylish it was.

As I slid onto the bench seat, the smell hit me: cat piss. I gagged and pressed a hand over my face. "Open a window!"

David rolled both the front ones down, and as soon as we started moving, the air cleared some. Still, the smell left my stomach roiling.

"We're really doing this person a service, getting rid of this thing," David muttered darkly.

I nodded my agreement. The van needed to be scoured with a blowtorch.

While David merged into traffic, Aaron took over ensuring we didn't have a tail. I grabbed the IDs David had created, noting they weren't half bad. Yes, Aaron's was a smidge crooked, but considering it was from North Dakota and wasn't terribly complex, it didn't look horrible. A quick scan from a normal individual wouldn't turn up anything odd. That was all we really needed at this point. The second thing I grabbed out of the bag was a cell phone. One from my company, not linked to anyone, and encrypted with several levels of protection to keep anyone from hacking it or my data stream.

Finally, the internet.

Not that I could get onto the work databases, which was what I really wanted, but that would flag someone for sure. Still, the web in general would be essential in getting us where we needed to be. Which, right now, meant across country.

Pulling up a browser, I searched for a private jet service my office had used several times. If work could trust them, I assumed I could. After a ten-minute phone call and the assurance of cash, we had a flight departure time in a little over an hour. Now we just had to make it to the airport without anyone following us.

"We still looking safe?" I asked Aaron, peering around us and taking quick stock of any cars I could see. None looked familiar, and David had routed us farther from busy streets to keep potential sightings and traffic to a minimum.

Both guys answered in the affirmative. I felt better after checking for myself.

"Then let's gun it," I charged, patting David on the shoulder.

He caught my eyes through the rear-view mirror and shook his head. Still, I could see his spark of amusement, which settled some of the creeping nerves in my gut. For a moment, I thought about all those emails we sent back and forth, the banter we'd had. It had been so nice to finally be that open with someone. But now I knew he'd had a motive far beyond getting to know me. Which in some ways was good—I needed to know what he knew. And also, it deeply bothered me. Trusting either of these men beyond taking down Future Solutions was impossible.

As I settled back in my seat, fleetingly wondering if the cat-piss smell would seep into my clothes, I caught Aaron's watchful stare. His mouth was set in a funny half-grin as he looked to David and then back at me.

How much did he know about David's and my emails? I certainly hoped not too much.

CHAPTER
FOURTEEN

WE MADE it onto the private jet without any problems after we ditched the van in the giant long-term parking lot, and after handing over most of our cash from the safe house.

"Do I still smell?" I asked, sniffing my sleeves and hair as the pilot went about his pre-flight inspection.

David, in the seat next to mine, drew his brows together. "Does that really matter?"

"I'm not really a cat person. And that smell…" I shuddered. "I just worry I have nasal fatigue and it's still lingering. It would also ensure that people remember us." The memory of smells was one of the strongest, and I did not want to have anyone paying us extra attention now.

"You don't smell. At least, not any worse than the rest of us," Aaron said from behind us.

Despite the cost of this flight, the plane wasn't posh. No reclining chairs or open bars or any of the other things the movies hyped about private travel—although those who could afford them certainly enjoyed that kind of thing. But this was nothing more than a normal-looking small plane with two rows of two seats each and an open cargo area at the back where we secured our things. Thankfully they didn't search those. Our cash ensured we could travel with weapons. And no one looked too closely at our IDs.

I held my breath as we took off, a strange habit I picked up as a kid. My mom, who had always hated heights and hadn't been terribly fond of flying, held her breath during take-off and descent. For some reason I copied her, knowing it did nothing but conjure memories of her. When we leveled off, I slowly released all the air in my lungs and relaxed back in my seat.

"You sound like a flat tire," David quipped, a little laugh in his words.

"Thanks." I rolled my eyes and looked away. I wasn't upset that he pointed it out. I *did* sound that way and knew, rationally, that my silly habit was ridiculous. Yet some silly habits allowed me to blend in better. If they mattered, I certainly wouldn't be doing anything like that in front of people I barely knew—I played the Game better than that.

"Good grief, the way you two flirt makes me marvel that you ever managed to meet in the first place," Aaron muttered.

My jaw dropped and I pushed myself around to look back at Aaron, narrowing my eyes over my seat. "You're mistaken about the situation. Deeply." Okay, so I sounded like a petulant child... but we had not been flirting.

"I'm just saying you'll have to kick it up a notch if you ever hope to emulate your brother." Aaron peeked between the seats and poked David in the arm.

David's mouth opened, closed, and repeated the process once more before he turned to look out the window.

So, Corbin had dated? Or more? From the way Aaron spoke, I suspected more. "Corbin was married?" I asked. Somehow that seemed strange, considering what I knew of the two men. While David could manage a smooth email, he certainly didn't come across as flirty in person. Or interested. Definitely not interested in me—which stung. All of his emails had been a ruse to lure me out to meet with him, nothing more.

Granted, I wasn't interested in him either, so that was probably a good thing.

"He and his wife were expecting their first child," Aaron confirmed. His voice had gone soft and I didn't have to look at him to know the depth of how horrible he felt.

"They killed them all." David choked out the words, his hands gripping the armrests with white knuckles. "It was senseless."

Another piece of their puzzle snapped into place, the force of it rocking me back against my seat. "That's terrible."

David just watched the expanse of blue out the window.

It was Aaron who spoke. "You can see why we have to stop them. They'll do anything. Eleanor's children…" He trailed off, not needing to complete the thought.

Those little faces in the photos. I didn't study them closely because Eleanor was the one who captured my attention, but in some strange way, I knew them. I'd do anything to save them.

The three of us fell silent for the next couple of hours. I managed to doze, the stress and exertion of the last few days having depleted me. I dreamed of entering an auditorium filled with people, and they all turned to look at me. As the rows and rows of people faced me, I realized with a kick to the gut that they all wore my face. The entire place was filled with other clones.

Eventually, I woke to find David still staring out the dark window, lost in thought. The lights had been turned off in the cabin and it was possible to see the landscape below, lit by the moon and the twisted tangle of city lights we crossed over.

I twisted around and caught sight of Aaron, sprawled across two seats, snoring lightly.

"Is that how you generally sleep?" I asked, motioning toward David's sleeping father.

David glanced back and shook his head, the hardness still evident in his features. "Just because I'm his clone doesn't make us identical."

"Well, obviously. But some things, certainly, are similar. I imagine Future Solutions had Aaron raise you both in a way that ensured your qualities emulated those of your father as much as possible." I assumed the company wanted to get David and Corbin to act like their father, and a similar upbringing would help to guide the other half of heritability: the environment.

David nodded. "Well, as best they could. Things are certainly different than they were when he was growing up in the sixties."

"Obviously."

David's eyes met mine and finally the stony quality there seemed to slip away and he grinned. "Yes, well, most people don't understand."

"You know who you're talking to." Okay, so maybe it was flirting. Just a little. But who could blame me? A few extra blinks and licking my lips always helped to get information out of people.

"That's true. I do." David settled back against his seat, angled to look at me.

"Tell me, how much of what you surmised about me was real, and how much did you gather from your dad's files?" I asked, keeping my tone light. It wasn't meant to be an accusation, but I couldn't resist asking.

"All I knew was your name. I found you on the train that way, but the rest? All of that was me. Your file has gone very quiet since you joined Global."

Well, that was a great answer. At least working for Global offered me some protection—something I'd figured was nonexistent after the last few hours.

"You're still better at it than I am," he continued.

"Whomever you're the copy of, she must have had an incredible mind."

His words rattled through me. I was a copy. A duplicate. Someone else was the original. Did that make me any less? Diminish what I was and what I'd done? The company that made me must have thought so, but I couldn't see things the same way. I was still a person, human, with emotions and dreams. Even if they were nightmares of others wearing my face.

"I know it's a strange thought, but I don't mean it in a bad way," David assured, his hand coming to rest on mine on the armrest between us. It was a friendly move, the kind meant to reassure more than anything else. "It doesn't mean you're less of you."

I swallowed, staring at where our hands touched. "I know, and it makes sense. I've lived for the last thirty-five years being me, and only me, but it still feels odd to realize that someone out there was me *before* me."

David shook his head. "Not you before you, just someone who shares many of your traits. An ancestor, if you want to think of it that way. But instead of getting your DNA from two people, you got yours in a direct line."

I cocked my head to the side, thinking about what he proposed. "That's pretty good, actually."

David's grin was real, his full lips even more attractive. "I've had a while to work it out for myself. The least I can do is pass along what's helped me."

I laughed and clapped my free hand over my mouth to keep quiet. Aaron snorted and resumed his snoring, David and I both grinned, and I felt like a kid caught laughing with friends well into the night at a sleepover.

"What was his role at Future Solutions?" I asked once we'd settled down.

David peeked back between the seats at his father. "That's… complicated."

I checked my watch. "We have a couple hours until we land," I commented dryly.

"That's not exactly what I meant."

"What, you can't tell me?" The edge in my tone was completely intentional.

"No..." David paused, looking back at his father again. "It's not my story to tell."

That, I could understand. I slumped back against the seats and rubbed my hand across my face. David's hand still rested over my other, officially crossing into more than just being kind and reassuring. I slid my hand free and clasped them together in my lap. His touch had felt wonderful, but he was not to be trusted.

"I'm not trying to be difficult," David offered apologetically.

"I know that, really, I do. I'm not upset. It's just a lot to process."

There was no response to that, so David turned to look back out the window for a long minute. Then he sighed and turned back to me. "He was a scientist. One of the top ones. I know he acts a bit goofy at times, but when it comes to the science of cloning, there's no one smarter. He's the one who figured out how to create... us, to ensure we had longer lifespans than the earlier versions."

"Earlier versions?"

"You didn't think we were the first?" David asked, a pained smile marring his features.

"In truth, I hadn't thought about it," I admitted. "I was still attempting to figure out what it all meant for me."

David nodded. "The earlier versions only lived a few years. Their DNA was old, as old as the donors, and the process sped up its degradation. My father figured out how to reverse that."

About a million detailed questions lined up in my mind, not the least of which was the implication this had for normal aging in everyday people, but I just nodded. I'd bug Aaron about that at some point.

"Anyhow, he was the first volunteer to attempt our version of the clones. After seeing how the earlier clones were treated, he insisted on raising us himself."

That thought left a bitter taste in my mouth. "How can they do this kind of thing to people?" I asked, letting my mind run ahead of itself.

It was only when I looked up and saw the look in David's eyes that I realized something: I'd been speaking openly, with no thought to how I wanted my conversation to make the other person feel or think. I couldn't remember the last time I managed to do that. The feeling was both liberating and frightening. I had to be careful around this man.

"Well, that assumes that we *are* people, and I'm fairly certain most of their scientists don't think we are."

I wrinkled my nose. "What? Of course we are."

"We're clones. We were made. Manufactured. Not born. For most of their scientists, that made the difference between seeing us as people or a biology experiment."

"How?" I shook my head and attempted to phrase my question better. "What do you mean, *not born*?"

"I don't know all the details, but I guess they worked out some artificial system to nurture and grow a child. Dad never told me much about it, but I think that was because it wasn't his specialty."

My mind flashed through several movies where I saw fetuses grown out of the womb, and my stomach flipped. It was one thing to learn I was adopted—that was enough to rock my foundations—but this rattled my very core.

"You okay?" David asked, leaning in closer.

I shook my head. "I have about three thousand questions and can't even begin to answer them because I'm both running for my life and trying to bring down the corporation that *created* my life."

David settled back against his seat, his deep sigh telling me everything. He knew what I meant, agreed with me, and wished he had some better news. "They're not invincible. No one is. We will work out a way. They'll wish they'd cloned a few people with average intelligence afterward."

My laugh caught me by surprise and David joined in. My stomach ached and I had to wipe my eyes by the time we finally let the moment pass. Damn, did it feel good, even if I knew at its root, my laugh was only because I was scared out of my mind of what this new reality would change for me.

"What's so funny?" Aaron asked from behind us, groggy and moving like, well, like he'd just slept slouched on an airplane seat.

"Nothing, nothing," David insisted, waving off his father.

Aaron glanced between us as we peered back at him over our seats, and a small grin snuck across his features. I didn't have the heart to tell him that nothing was going on between David and me. We had bigger concerns.

"So, we'll land in a little while. What then?" I voiced the inevitable question that sobered us all up quickly.

The response occupied the rest of the flight into the Sacramento airport. In all the many meetings I'd taken part in over my life—school, grad school, work—I never once had truly collaborated. Either I didn't participate, or I guided the others towards the decision I wanted.

Not with David and Aaron. It was something we did together, arguing over each detail, eventually coming up with a consensus and contingencies.

It was actually kind of fun. Except for the part where people were trying to find and kill us.

"AT LEAST IT doesn't smell like cat pee." I settled behind the wheel of the compact car rental. I used another of my IDs, different from the one I used for the plane, and picked the boys up from where they waited in the small lobby of the private jet's office. It had been the only model available at the rental desks, and it was going to get uncomfortable when we picked up Eleanor and her kids.

It was really late, or rather, very early when we landed, the bright lights of the airport in stark contrast to the dark of the countryside all around. While different from the humid heat of Philly, it was still enough that I cranked the AC.

"Just cigarettes," David muttered, taking a deep breath from the passenger seat.

"Rentals always smell like cigarettes," I noted, and David shrugged.

"Get on the I-5 North," Aaron instructed from the back seat. I watched him look between David and I for about the tenth time. He really needed to give up on that idea. Yes, it was fine to take down the clone-makers with them, but just because I enjoyed David's company didn't make me eager for anything more. He *shot* me, for Christ's sake! That did not engender any confidence in either of them.

Aaron directed us the rest of the way—about ten minutes to a nice development in the western part of the city—using my untraceable phone. David prepared weapons in the passenger seat, ensuring each of the guns was tended to and fully loaded. He even put the tranq gun into a holster at his hip.

"You know, they could still shoot you a few times, even if you hit them with that," I offered, nodding to the weapon.

David just shrugged. "I'd rather have a non-lethal option."

In other words, he'd already killed his fair share of people and didn't want more blood on his hands. I added that to my list of things to ask him about at some point. If we survived getting Eleanor and her kids to safety.

I recognized the neighborhood from the photos as we drew nearer. It was in a newer development, with houses so close together that it was possible to stand between them and touch both. The yards were tiny, but large expanses of parks with brown lawns, complete with jungle gyms, opened up every few streets. Most of the windows were shuttered against the night and heat.

"Very Californian," I muttered, following Aaron's directions through the maze of houses.

"It's the last one up here on the left," Aaron offered.

We drove by, a little too slowly to pass for casual, but the street appeared deserted and I doubted anyone would think much of it, if there were even anyone awake to notice. We resembled people looking for a friend's house in our bland blue rental.

The house itself was just as it appeared in the photos. Two stories, light tan stucco, with a tiny front porch that no one could legitimately sit on. Lights filtered through the slats of blinds on the second story.

One of the children's toys—an action figure—sat in the

middle of the walkway. The front door stood ajar, the rug from the inside hallway peeking out. Just a few inches, but enough that all three of us drew in a collective breath as we passed.

"They couldn't have gotten here this fast. Not after how we left them in Philly," I reasoned, but I knew that wasn't the case. There undoubtedly were more of their agents on this case than those we left incapacitated, or dead, in the safe house. Who knew—maybe Eleanor's guardian had been coerced into changing their mind and had come back to do their job.

No one said anything. We all knew I was trying to be optimistic, when the truth could be far worse.

"Looks like we're jumping to plan F," Aaron stated from the back seat.

And with that, I hit the gas, my heart hammering in my chest.

Eleanor. Her kids. I didn't know which one I worried more about, but their faces kept flashing through my mind. As I pulled into an alley behind the house, into one of the free parking spaces almost a block from Eleanor's, I went over the details I'd gathered from the front of her house, trying to see if I could come up with some other explanation for what might have happened.

It didn't have to be that something was wrong. Someone could have accidentally left the door open, strewn the toys outside, and left the front rug half dragged outside, but something about the situation felt off. I wasn't the only one to sense it. Aaron and David both got the same impression. Our emotions had us strung tight, and lack of sleep didn't help. Something more gnawed at me, but I couldn't place it. For now, I'd have to go with the supposition something terrible had happened, and hope we were wrong.

Quickly and efficiently, Aaron handed us weapons from the duffle on the seat next to him, then we each put on a hat.

Aaron went over which entrance to take into the house, and we reviewed where to go if we had to run, and where we'd meet back up.

As we got out and slinked along the back alley, keeping out of sight from the rear windows on either side or from the houses looking down on us, I wished for a moment for the communication earpieces we had at work.

At the edge of Eleanor's house, we opened the gate to their slip of a side yard and edged around the outer wall. The windows weren't covered and I had a direct view inside.

The sight almost stopped my heart.

The kitchen table was overturned, one of the chairs broken. The remnants of what looked like dinner was smeared across the floor.

I didn't look too close for long but gave the signal to Aaron and David to go to their entrances, while I made my way to the side door.

"Please, please let them be okay," I whispered to myself. All the signs pointed against it, but I still hoped that nothing had happened to her or the kids.

The side door was locked, but I had the simple latch open in less than a minute and stepped inside. The television lit up the living room with the sound muted, but the bright colors of the home shopping network swam across the screen.

My brain flicked into high gear and I took in the scene around me. One glass shattered. The others lying on their sides.

Food in an almost artful sweep on the floor.

The chair had been broken before today—the edges of the leg sported a healthy amount of glue from where it had been fixed.

The stove was a mess of food and crumbs, but nothing was burned.

The AC blew cold air, despite the open door.

No footsteps went through the spaghetti sauce on the floor. No smears that implied anyone being taken.

Something was off.

Aaron entered by the front door and I held a hand out to him. He paused inside the shadows of the living room.

I could hear David upstairs, a faint scraping of the window sliding open in the alcove over the garage, where no one would notice his entry.

"Something's really strange," I whispered to Aaron.

He frowned and looked around.

I went to the door that opened off the short hallway next to the kitchen. A discarded toy doll, its dress flung up over its head, sat in front of the door. Opening it to darkness, a muffled scrape made it obvious someone was in the inky black of the garage.

"Eleanor?" I called into the gloom, feeling along the wall for a light switch.

Another thump, but no reply.

"We're here to help. Really. Please, I'm going to turn on the light now. Just—" But before I could finish, the garage door started to rattle open.

A car engine started.

I found the light.

As the bright light flooded the space, Eleanor stared out at me from behind the wheel of her black Corolla.

Our eyes met and I held my hands out wide to show they were empty.

The garage door only took a second or two to slide open, but Eleanor sat in her seat, frozen, staring at me. I swallowed and reached for my hat, pulling it off and letting my long dark hair fall around my shoulders. Hair that was identical in shade to hers, and much the same as she'd worn hers in college. Eleanor's hair had been cut short, but there was no denying how much we looked alike. Her expression was like looking into a mirror. Shock widened her eyes, then slowly anger took over. Like she couldn't believe someone would do this to her. That made two of us.

It only took a few seconds for her son to start to cry.

She yanked her car into reverse and started to peel out of the garage, but David beat her to it. He dropped behind her car, hands out, his presence enough to hem her in.

She wasn't the kind of person to mow him down. I would have. What did that say about me? No time to worry about that now.

Eleanor swore from inside her car, and her little girl looked at her with wide eyes.

"Eleanor, turn off your engine. Please. We're here to help you stay safe." I hoped my voice could be heard above the sound of her car and her son's mounting screams.

All the noises rattled around in my head, coupled with the telling details from her garage: They went biking last weekend. She'd canned beans two summers ago. Her son's height made it hard to find clothes. A million other little things seemed to pound in my head.

I closed my eyes and rocked back on my heels.

Never, ever, while on a mission had I let my brain get the better of me. I was always in control of my senses. But now, seeing Eleanor in person, seeing my face, my expressions, all of it, the truth about where we came from, it all hit. I had to stand there, taking deep breaths, until I was able to force the internal switch off. So I could keep it together. So I would not lose it. So I could help her.

After what seemed like an eternity, Eleanor's engine switched off. Her son's wails trailed off. Her car door opened.

"You have to do that, too, don't you?" she asked as she stepped one foot out of her car. Her voice. My voice. Our voice.

I opened my eyes, staring down my twin, my clone, and nodded. "It overwhelms me sometimes."

She nodded. "It's not easy to control." Eleanor sighed and

closed her car door, leaving her kids inside. "If you're going to take me in, could you please let me leave my kids with my mother-in-law? I don't want them involved in this."

The resignation in her voice, like she couldn't even begin to think how she could fight back, caught me off guard.

"Eleanor," I said slowly. "We're here to get you all to safety. But we need to know what you know."

IT TOOK precious minutes to convince everyone to go inside and for Eleanor to nestle her kids onto the couch with a movie that they'd both clearly watched a thousand times. Eleanor met us in her living room, dark circles under her eyes, eyeing us as though she were gauging the best way to escape.

I'd done my best to wipe up the food on the floor and clean some of the other mess, and she looked around with a grin that twisted her mouth to one side. "Well, at least I know you're not *totally* my evil twin."

I laughed, though the boys didn't budge. Apparently, that was a clone thing: similar sense of humor. Good to know.

"What tipped you off?" I asked as Eleanor settled into a non-broken kitchen chair like she wanted to sink through it and disappear.

"There have been a few odd things over the past week. At first, I didn't think much of it, but there's been someone tailing me. And then tonight, a few strange cars kept going by. I decided to make a break for it. I had been about to leave when I saw your car and stepped up the plans I'd been laying." She gestured around the house. "I wanted people to think we'd already been abducted."

I think all three of us raised our eyebrows at this. She'd known something was wrong and had been in the process of getting the hell out. That certainly made sense, and I couldn't help being grateful we'd interrupted her plans first. Finding her after she'd run would have been far more difficult.

"I guess the front door open and all of that probably looked suspicious?" she asked, a half grin ensuring me she'd planned just as much.

I nodded, still smiling. "It scared me to death."

"So, are you going to tell me who you are, or do I have to keep guessing?" She crossed her arms and settled further into her chair.

After a quick look at Aaron and David, I started in on the story. "You may not believe this, but there are some vital things you need to know about where you, and we, come from."

It took a scant three minutes to fill her in on our story, my job, and how I met the boys. She frowned, listening to most of it, but an increasingly intense look of frustration and fear settled in as I explained what brought us here.

"You mean to tell me there are people out there who are willing to kill all of us, including my children, and we're still sitting here?" she asked after a ringing moment of silence when I finished.

"Oh, no, we're getting the hell out of here now. But would you have come without some of the details?" I asked, already knowing the answer. Well, knowing enough about how she would operate if it were me—and she was as close to me as it got.

Eleanor rounded on Aaron and David, her gaze going from head to toe and back again. I recognized that look. She'd basically just x-rayed them, gleaning every detail she could muster.

So that was what it looked like from the outside. I'd always wondered.

"My children will always come first. Do I make myself clear?" she answered. "Now, Diana, come with me. We're going to be quick about this, and then we're getting the hell out of here. You two," she pointed to the boys, "are going to pack some food and water for my kids."

I grinned, instantly liking this whole situation infinitely more. With a little laugh at David's expression, I followed Eleanor up the stairs at a run.

"They're going to regret having two of us around," I snickered as we headed into Eleanor's daughter's room first. Despite everything, I couldn't help the giddiness I felt at finding her alive. It went beyond that though. I almost couldn't understand it, but I *trusted* her.

Eleanor grabbed a bag from the closet, and we loaded it up with clothes and an assortment of things to keep the girl occupied and clothed. We then moved on to her son, doing the same so that the bag bulged with diapers and all sorts of other apparently essential things for a five-year-old and a just barely one-year-old.

How smart would her kids be? Would they share the same strange tendencies Eleanor and I did?

"Where's your husband?" I asked as we stepped out of her daughter's room and headed down the hallway. There was one family portrait on the wall in the stairwell, which I thought was a little strange. Didn't families usually have far too many photos on the walls? My mother had been religious about family photos, although only one hung in my house— the one that wasn't too painful to look at.

"Deployed. Engineering project for the government. I expect he's somewhere in Dubai, but he can't tell me. Nor are we supposed to have too many photos of him around, in case he's compromised."

"Okay." I had so many more questions, a million things I

wanted to ask her, to see what we shared so I could understand about what made us similar. Did we like the same snacks? The same colors? The same hatred for heels? Maybe even more interesting, what made us different?

"Did you ever read about the Jim Twins?" she asked once we were back downstairs, as she gathered her son in her arms, despite his protests to continue watching the film.

I followed her train of thought instantly. "Of course. Twins, separated at birth, and when they were reunited, they had a lot of very striking similarities," I recited from some reading I'd done years ago. At the time, it was no more than an interesting tidbit on a nature versus nurture vein. Now, it meant a whole lot more.

"Something tells me we could beat them at that game. But how much of that is engineered? It's not like they can make us more genetically similar, or control every aspect of our environment."

I paused in the kitchen, holding both bags, running through her words in my mind. "How do we have more in common than the Jim twins?"

Eleanor gave me a *duh* look over her shoulder. "I just watched you go through my kids' things and instinctively know where I'd stored everything, without having to say a word. It was like you were reading my mind."

I shook my head. I hadn't even been thinking about it. "I just notice things. Everything. It's clear once you know what you're looking for."

Eleanor nodded. "I know, which is probably why we have a lot in common. We'll have to talk about it more later."

I grinned. Having Eleanor and the promise of a conversation where I didn't have to hold myself in check was enough to get me positively giddy. Even if someone was chasing me down to kill us all, I longed to know this woman. This separate part of myself, who had lived a life entirely different from mine, but possibly also craved square cheese crackers just as much as I did.

The little girl, dressed in a nightgown with her hair pulled back in a braid, sat on the couch looking up at me. Eleanor gestured for me to pick her up and there wasn't time to argue about it. Instead I looked down at the small human on the couch, who watched me with giant brown eyes that were definitely not sure what to make of her mother's doppelganger bursting into her house in the middle of the night.

"Who are you?" she asked, drawing her knees up to her chest protectively.

Well, if that wasn't the question of the day. I didn't know who or what I was any longer. Not really. "I'm your mom's sister. Can't you tell we look alike?" I smiled and dropped to my knees at the edge of the couch. We needed to move, but the girl would be far easier to manage if she came willingly.

She flinched back, like I'd invaded her personal space. "My mom doesn't have any sisters. My only aunt is my dad's sister." For a five-year-old, her diction sounded more like an older teen. Of course, what else could I really expect?

"We didn't know about each other until very recently, and I'm here because there might be some danger. We've got to leave now, but I promise I'll answer the rest of your questions."

The girl frowned, her young face screwing up into the most impossible expression. "You really promise? I hate it when people don't tell me stuff."

I smiled to bite back a laugh. "I completely understand that. I'll show you how to work out what people don't tell you, too, if you want."

She cocked her head to the side, her braid flopping across her shoulder. "You can't read minds, can you?"

This time I did laugh, but the girl just looked relieved. "No, not really. But good enough. Like, I know you snuck a cookie before bed."

A flash of worry drew her brows together. "Just one."

"I won't tell, promise. But right now, we've got to get going."

She hesitated a moment, and a burst of noise from outside made her curl tighter in on herself.

"Diana, we've got incoming!" David yelled from the kitchen.

A swear word hung on the tip of my tongue, but the expression on the girl's face forced me to swallow it back.

"We have to run. Where are your shoes?" I asked, already searching for them.

I found them kicked off on the floor nearby, and she stepped into them while I found myself planning through the best way of getting her out of here.

Another crash outside.

David's face appeared at the corner. "We've got to *move*."

I bent and snagged the little girl, her body surprisingly lighter than I'd expected. With the bags swung around my shoulders, my gun in its holster under my arm was about as useful as if I'd left it in the car.

"I'll cover you," David murmured, motioning me toward the garage door as he hurried toward him. Ahead of me, Eleanor and Aaron headed in that direction.

Surely someone would be covering the garage. And David and I were the best with a weapon. Making a quick decision, I rushed to Aaron's side and pushed the little girl into his arms.

"Make sure she stays safe," I hissed, sparing a second to smile down at the girl's face. White shone all the way around her irises. But she managed a small nod, as if she understood that now was not the time to panic.

I grabbed my weapon and went to the door that led to the garage. We'd left it open, which created a terrible strategic scenario: a tiny opening and all the space in the world for us to be picked off as we made our way outside.

Not going to think about that. I motioned for the others to get down, and standing off to one side, I cracked the door.

Two shots splintered through the door, embedding in the wall above everyone's head.

Eleanor shoved her fist against her teeth to keep herself from screaming.

I calculated the angle from where the bullet had come through, and before the guy could move, I slid my gun through the crack in the door and fired.

A muffled thump said I hit my target. There would be more.

I opened the door a little more, edging a foot into the space and scanning what I could see in the dim light provided from a neighbor's back door lights. A dark form to the left. A bullet, and it toppled.

Racing toward the opening to the back alley, I took a deep breath and slid around the edge into the open space.

Two more black masks. I didn't hesitate. For a fleeting moment, I wondered why they did. But I didn't care enough to worry. Instead, I dropped them both, then ran back to the door to yank it open, ducked so David didn't shoot me, and grabbed Eleanor's arm.

Tears glistened in her eyes and she was sluggish getting to her feet, a hand firmly clapped over her son's mouth to keep him quiet. But the little boy only watched, eyes as wide as his sister's, as if he somehow sensed the imperative to keep silent.

At the garage opening, I scanned again, making sure no one had shown up in the few seconds since I doubled back, and leaned in to whisper in Eleanor's ear, "Run like hell. The little blue car at the end of the alley. Go now!"

I pushed a solid hand in the middle of her back and signaled for Aaron to go with her, while David took point, his long legs outpacing them. Following behind, I kept careful watch all around, ensuring no one followed us. The alley remained dark and silent.

Too dark and silent.

Surely an organization that good wouldn't just let us slip through their fingers so easily. The thoughts barely had time to run through my mind before I heard the crash behind me where David must have reached the car.

Damn it, they couldn't have disabled our car, could they?

I cursed my own stupidity. Of course they would have. It wouldn't have been hard. In fact, if it had been me, that would have been the first move I made, ensuring I knew where they'd go and hanging them up there.

Breaking into a sprint, I caught up to the others a few seconds later, surveying the scene while my heart pounded in my ears.

David was wrestling a man at the front of the car, both too close to draw a weapon. Aaron was getting into the back of the small car, his arms full of little girl. In the second it took to assess the situation, David took a hard blow to the head and wobbled on his feet.

Without even thinking about it, I raised my gun and shot once at the assailant who stood ready to land a kick at David. The man fell and David looked over at me, blood dripping from his nose and mouth.

"Get in!" I shouted, rounding the nose of the vehicle to the driver's side.

David held up a hand and yanked up the hood to do a quick inspection. He reached in, pulled out a small piece of metal, and crunched it under his boot.

I watched, halfway into the driver's seat, a question plastered over my face.

"A tracker," David answered grimly, already to the passenger's door.

"Fuckers," I grumbled, sliding into the seat.

A soft giggle from the backseat reminded me of the small children present.

"Sorry," I confessed, glancing over my shoulder at Eleanor as I backed out of where we'd parked.

She waved me off, too busy scanning the shadows for more boogeymen.

Grateful for the extra eyes, I sped toward the closest exit, praying the suits would have assumed we wouldn't make it past them this far and wouldn't have set up a roadblock.

But who was I kidding? Fifty yards from the end of the alley, two guys emerged, guns drawn. Two shots pinged off the car; one of the side mirrors suddenly hung by a wire.

"Stay down!" I yelled.

Eleanor whimpered as I dodged and weaved as best I could in the narrow space, making a clear shot difficult.

Aaron, through a slit in the window, managed to nail a shot at one of the men. Another shot shattered the windshield, and I felt myself slammed into the seat with the force of an elephant sitting on my chest.

All the air raced from my lungs. I couldn't see past the spider's web of glass in the windshield in front of me and the blackness that seemed to seep into the corners of my eyes.

The last guy shot twice more before I reached him traveling forty miles per hour. His body flipped over the hood with an audible crunch of bone.

Cranking the wheel to the left, I raced down the street, two rights, a left, and across a busy street against the light.

I couldn't breathe; nothing came into my lungs each time I tried. The blood in my ears kept everything at a dull roar, and it wasn't until we were several miles away, on a frontage road next to a giant field of tomatoes, that I realized David was shouting.

"Pull over, Diana! For shit's sake, pull over!" He grabbed the wheel over my hand, forcing me over to the gravel on the edge of the road. His touch felt nice—a strange errant thought in the middle of trying to gasp.

Instinctively, I applied the brakes and we ground to a stop. David threw it in park, and before I could figure out what happened, he had my door open and was pulling me out of the car.

"She's been hit," he informed the group.

It was the last thing I heard before passing out.

CHAPTER
SEVENTEEN

"HOLY FUCKING SHIT, THAT FUCKING HURTS."

A small giggle met my words as my eyes fluttered open.

Oops. The girl looked down at me, still dressed in her white nightgown and tennis shoes, her hand pressed to her mouth.

Eleanor sighed. "We need to have a little talk about your language if you're not dead."

I groaned and managed to get myself into a seated position, with the liberal use of David's help. "I'm not dead, but damn, I forgot how much that hurts."

"You're lucky you had the vest on." Aaron spoke up from where he cradled the sleeping boy in a corner of the room.

A quick glance around told me we were in a rather dingy hotel. Two beds, covered in atrociously patterned bedspreads, were lined up next to mine, and from the way the place smelled, it had been a smoking room at some point in its recent past.

"Where are we?"

"About thirty miles away, which was all the gas we had in the car we stole," David asserted, his tone far too matter-of-fact.

I glanced at him and my breath caught at the concern for me I saw in his face. For just a moment, a hundredth of a second, the room stilled around us. Did he care, for real? Was there more there than just taking down the company that made us?

I forced myself to look away. There was no trusting this situation, not any more than I could throw him, and right now with the hitching pain in my chest, that wasn't far.

"You alright?" David asked, rubbing my back as I fought to keep from coughing, breathing, or doing anything that would bring back the ache.

"Well, considering I've been shot twice in the last twenty-four hours, I'm not so sure," I retorted, struggling to maintain a bit of levity in the situation.

"Twice?" Eleanor piped in.

David groaned and grabbed some pillows to prop me up. "If you're feeling well enough to bring that up, then I'm going out to get us some food."

I grinned and shook my head. "Oh, that's right, I wasn't supposed to mention it again."

"Wait, *he* shot you?" Eleanor asked, glancing between the two of us, a spark of amusement shining in her eyes.

"Yes, but just with a tranquilizer gun," I explained hastily as David made for the door. "So we could escape." Looking over at him as he opened the door, I added, "If you're not back in twenty, we'll come looking for you."

He made a dramatic eye roll that elicited another laugh from the little girl. "You need to rest. I'll be fine."

"I'm just saying," I taunted.

"You'd better stay there and stay resting." With that, the door closed behind him.

"Well, that was bossy." I pulled a face of mock annoyance for the girl's amusement.

"Takes one to know one," Aaron muttered from the corner.

I let that ride. Yes, I was bossy. But I had my reasons.

After another stab of pain as I breathed in, I gingerly touched my chest. My button-up had been removed, leaving me in my undershirt—better than just my bra—and I pulled it away from my chest to peek at my wounds.

During training, we had to be shot by one of our instructors while wearing the vest so we'd know what it felt like. Of course, that was a lower caliber bullet, and from a greater distance than just a few yards. The vest had worked like it was supposed to, and to the left of my sternum a bloom of angry red and deepening purple spread from the impact point. A kill shot. If I hadn't been wearing the vest, the bullet would have done me in.

I felt less guilty about mowing the guy down.

"So, what happened?" I finally asked after my cursory self-examination.

"David stole a car from a grocery store parking lot." Eleanor's voice trembled as she spoke. "You were out cold, and we made it here just a few minutes ago. It was frightening. I really thought you might be dead."

I managed a small smile, weirdly grateful for Eleanor's concern. Not that I wanted her to be upset, but because it showed she cared, showed we shared some kind of connection, as new as it might be. She was my clone. Twin. Whatever. It still seemed so very odd. But, deep down in a place I couldn't question, I trusted her. I had never felt that immediate bond with someone, and certainly not with either of the guys. Anything I felt for David I chalked up to hormones, even if some part of me really wished it could be more than that. Whether the bond between Eleanor and me was a product of our shared status, DNA, or what, I wasn't entirely sure, but it felt so good to be around someone who I didn't need to constantly analyze or watch myself around. Like I could breathe freely—except for the bullet bruise.

Eleanor's daughter came closer and reached out to touch

my hand. "You promised you'd explain everything later. What's going on?"

I leaned back against my pillows and smiled, despite the wave of pain that raced up my back. I had promised, and if this girl was anything like me as a child, she'd want to know everything.

Eleanor caught her daughter's hand and pulled her away. "Auntie Diana needs some sleep. Did you see her bruise?"

"I did, but can't you tell me *something*?" Her small forehead creased with frustration.

"I just realized something. Your mom hasn't told me your name. Or your brother's name. Why don't you tell me that?" It wouldn't distract her much, but it was the best I could do. Sleep already called to me.

She turned her frown on me. "How can you be my aunt without knowing my name?"

"Because we only just found out about each other," I explained. "We didn't know we were twins until tonight."

"But, but how?" she asked, slumping onto the bed next to me. Even the slight movement made me wince.

"That's a very good question," I answered, taking a moment to think through my response. "You know the bad guys who were chasing us tonight? They're the ones who kept us from knowing about each other, which is one reason why we had to escape them. We want to learn more about each other and make sure you have lots of cousins to play with."

She pressed her lips together, clearly not sure she wanted to play along with my simplistic description, but finally she sighed and nodded. "Okay, fine. My name's Sarah. And my brother's Joey."

"Joseph, like his grandfather," Eleanor added.

"Nice to meet you, Sarah." I extended a hand, which she shook like she wasn't quite sure it was the right thing to do.

The sound of a key card sliding into the door had

everyone freezing, but it was just David with several fast food bags from Wendy's in his hands. He spread them out on the tiny table next to the television. He got a little bit of everything, and I managed to choke down a few fries and half a burger, along with some water, before swallowing a few generic pain pills and slumping back against the pillows.

We were all exhausted, the adrenaline high having worn off long before. Eleanor looked like she still wanted to pinch herself and wake back up in her own bed in her own house. I didn't blame her. I wanted that myself.

After a few chicken nuggets, Sarah settled in next to her mom on the bed farthest from the door. Once she voiced a few random questions about what tomorrow would bring, which none of us knew how to answer, she fell sound asleep. Aaron set her brother next to her, smiling gently at the sleeping boy.

"We'll figure something out in the morning. We'll be safe here until then," I added, accurately gauging the half-hidden panic in Eleanor's eyes.

"Those men..." Eleanor asked in a low voice. "If you hadn't gotten there first, what would they have done?"

"You know what they would have done," Aaron intoned.

Eleanor stared at me for a long moment, panic flaring in her eyes. "Thank you for getting us out. We never would have made it."

I just nodded, and after another moment, she slid down on the ugly comforter and turned to curl around her family.

Aaron settled onto the middle bed, clicking off the lights so the back of the room was plunged into darkness.

David settled into one of the chairs by the window, a gun resting on the table in front of him. He reached over to turn off the lights and caught me watching him. A little grin lit his features.

A small flutter of pleasure bloomed in my belly, reminding me that I had been drawn to this person before my life fell apart. That I had been planning on meeting him before he asked to get together. That, at one point, I'd been entirely happy thinking that I might be able to trust him, as foolish as that seemed. Now that our lives had narrowed to survival, I merely nodded back and fought to find any possible comfortable position in which to get a few hours' sleep.

CHAPTER
EIGHTEEN

I JOLTED awake with no idea where I was or what was going on. My chest ached like I'd swallowed a hot ember and it was lodged in my throat.

I rolled over and knocked against something solid. Cracking one eye open, I stared straight into the chest of someone. Daring a peek higher up, I realized it was David and my heart froze. How the hell did he end up in my bed? A few other less than chaste, very irrational thoughts rattled around in my half-awake brain before Aaron cleared his throat.

"I woke to take my shift and saw him passed out. I couldn't get him to our bed, so I just left him there."

"Oh." I struggled to put a little distance between David and myself, and with a whole lot of wincing managed to get to my feet.

"How are you feeling?" Aaron's face was lit by a strip of weak sunshine that came through the opening in the curtains. His expression carried more than a little amusement, and I knew he thoroughly enjoyed watching his son interact with me. He probably thought it was some kind of science experiment.

I stretched, winced, and tried again, managing to get my arms over my head. "Fine, I guess. Not dead, which is the best part."

Aaron chuckled. Behind me, Eleanor stirred and rolled over to look at us.

"What time is it?" she asked, her voice thick with sleep.

"Eight," I answered. We'd gotten into the room at three in the morning, so there certainly hadn't been much time for rest.

"Oh, heck no. Wake me in another twelve hours."

I smothered a laugh. Sleeping for a few days would have been easy if I had the luxury. My bladder, on the other hand, was what woke me. After a quick trip to the restroom, with a long look at the darkening bruise on my chest and a few attempts to smooth my hair into a somewhat presentable state, I returned to the room.

David still slept, his face smashed against his pillow and a dark halo of his hair spread around him. How stupid I had been to allow myself to trust him.

"How long have you known about me?" Eleanor asked from where she remained in her bed, still fully dressed and looking distinctly rumpled. Her kids slept curled about one another.

"A couple days, I guess." I settled on the middle bed to talk in hushed whispers. "David and Aaron tracked me down and told me about what's going on. Then the person who was supposed to take me out didn't do her job." The thought of Celine made me grind my teeth. "Which led to a whole lot of people getting killed." I swallowed, thinking of Rob. My entire office.

She nodded. "And before that, you worked for the government, or the FBI, right?"

I shook my head. "I can understand why you'd guess that, but no, I didn't. I worked for a private espionage and human-itarian aid organization."

"So, basically a spy for hire." Eleanor grinned. "I always thought I'd be good at that kind of thing."

"You would be, with some training," I agreed. She'd be just as good as me. Maybe better. Who knew? It was all so strange to think about. "My job used to be focused on trying to keep humanitarian disasters from happening."

"Ah, so a good guy, or gal, for hire?"

"Something like that." I shook my head, the image of the two us working on such a project together making me laugh. We'd be unstoppable.

"So this group, Future Solutions, they're coming after all of us?"

I nodded, swallowing hard. Eleanor and her kids came uncomfortably close to meeting their end last night. Too close. And what about the rest of our cohort? How many more could we save?

"Why?" she asked in a soft voice.

I frowned. I hated the answer I'd learned from Aaron. "Because we were mistakes, no longer needed, manufacturing prototypes." The answer still sat poorly with me. "They want to make sure that when they unveil their public prototype, no one thinks about the really unethical shit they've done to get there. They want to avoid us 'stains.'" I nearly spit the final word.

"But that seems so wasteful and ignorant of the possibility that we might be useful in the future," Eleanor argued, matching my frown. "How do we stop them?"

I kind of wanted to hug her for her plucky response. We needed to stop them, and I loved that she was willing to help.

"First of all, we get you and your kids someplace safe."

"In other words, you get rid of the dead weight?" She managed a smile.

"No, we maintain the ground we've gained against them." I spoke firmly, wanting her to know it wasn't that I didn't want her help, or that I didn't want to sit in a café somewhere and talk for days, but we couldn't. The next name on the list beckoned, and we couldn't risk it. Sure, I could show her how to defend herself, how to shoot and hide and help, but Sarah and Joey needed to be kept safe, and their mother offered the best protection.

Still, in the funny way of being an only child, I wanted to get to know my sister so badly I couldn't ignore the ache in my chest. My mother would have loved Eleanor—she'd always hoped I'd have a full life. The kind that involved home and hearth. And I longed to talk to Eleanor about all of it, to share in some of my grief.

So strange, really, that ache. I'd spent years and years being the perfect spy. I had the ability to make others perceive exactly what I intended them to, making sure my emotions were hidden. By this time, I thought most of my true emotions were gone, or else so shallow, they wouldn't hold a reflection. However, in the last day, they felt as deep and fathomless as the ocean. The experience of finding out I wasn't "fully human" made me feel more so than ever before.

Did being clones mean we weren't human? Did being *born* somehow confer a level of humanity that couldn't be granted by a machine? Whatever made Eleanor and me, made part of her children, all of it was something different. Something unique, not a mistake. Just because I wasn't what Future Solutions wanted, it didn't make me an error as a human, to be human, to exist.

Eleanor seemed to sense the conflict flickering behind my eyes and reached over to grab my hand. "We'll figure something out."

I managed a small nod. Yes, we'd work something out, and with some luck, might live to see it, but that didn't mean there weren't a hundred million questions lurking in my mind, and none of them had answers, other than the soul-deep knowledge that we didn't deserve to die because others thought we were a failed experiment.

"So where are we going?" Eleanor asked.

I twisted to look at Aaron and groaned as my bruised chest flared to violent life.

Aaron, invited to enter the conversation, stood and stretched. "We rented a cabin a few hours from here, and we'll get you settled there today. The next clone isn't far, just in San Jose. When we retrieve her, we'll bring her to you at the cabin."

Huh. When had they rented a cabin? And why hadn't they told me until now? I filed it away to ask about later.

Eleanor shook her head like she couldn't quite believe the idea that even more people in the world were identical to her. "What's her name?"

"Faith." I gave a little laugh. "Alphabetical order, remember?"

"Well, that's better than Fanny, I suppose."

We both snorted with laughter.

David rolled over at the sound and I clamped a hand over my mouth.

Our eyes met and Eleanor and I had to suppress our giggles, which resulted in the two of us sounding like some kind of strange, snuffling animal. It wasn't really funny, but it felt good to laugh a little, despite all the insanity.

David's eyes opened and he pushed himself to his feet with a groan. A funny little part of my mind wanted to reach over and smooth down the little curl that had fallen across his forehead. Which was, of course, utterly ridiculous and I instantly squelched the thought.

While David padded to the bathroom, Eleanor and I tiptoed around, cleaning up after ourselves, and otherwise attempting to keep the kids asleep as long as possible. Eleanor shrugged when I told her that her kids slept like the dead. "They get it from their dad. He sleeps through mortar strikes all the time," she explained.

I wanted to ask more about her husband, learn more about

her life, how she ended up staying at home with two kids when I understood the ferocity with which her brain operated, but it would have to wait. We needed to keep moving, with the hope that whatever cabin we were heading to would afford us a bit of time to get acquainted beyond the odd similarities that kept popping up.

When we'd packed everything up, David gently patted my shoulder and motioned me toward the door. "Come with me to grab us some food. And a car." He added the last part in a low voice.

I nodded. Hot wiring a vehicle would be easier with two of us.

As we stepped out into the warm morning light, it felt like walking into another world. I hadn't been conscious when we entered, so seeing the dingy place from the outside made my skin crawl.

"Nice motel choice." I stood in the parking lot, looking back at the two stories of peeling paint and ugly green doors.

"There weren't any recording devices in the lobby, and it's got a back exit if we need it," David explained with a wave at said exit.

Good points. I shrugged. "But if we get bed bugs, I'm still going to be annoyed."

David chuckled. "You won't be the only one."

The nice thing about the location was that we were within walking distance to several fast food joints, and after sizing each of them up, we headed to the McDonald's. We couldn't go back to Wendy's without being remembered later, but the crowd at the McDonald's drive-through was enough to ensure we both had cover. Plus, I adored egg McMuffins, though I wasn't about to tell David.

As we walked across the pitted parking lot, I took a moment to mentally process the two cars in the lot (single man traveling to see family, recently divorced woman looking for a new apartment). Nothing I couldn't readily identify as benign, or at least not suspicious. We seemed to have eluded our trackers for the moment, which was a tiny relief.

As we walked, David's hand brushed mine. It could have been an accident, and I glanced up at him while pulling my hand away. Not that his touch repulsed me; I just didn't know what to make of it all. Damn hormones making me think that because I was physically attracted to him, I should open my heart. David and Aaron had to earn my trust. So far, all they'd done is shoot me or gotten me shot at.

David met my gaze with a grin that was similar to last night's. Friendly, warm, and left me blushing just a little, while I quickly looked away. Well. That was absolutely not what we needed, but the tiny twang of my heart let me know I may not have full control over it, no matter how well I played the game.

David opened the door to the restaurant, letting out a blast of greasy hash brown smell. My stomach rumbled, letting me know it had been far too long since I'd had anything substantial to eat.

He kept silent as we waited for the extra-large order to be ready. I scanned the place, ensuring no one looked suspicious, which wasn't terribly difficult to discern. There were only three customers, and none of them were employed. The cars that went through the drive through were a little more difficult to read, but I took careful stock of each. A contractor. A school teacher. A soccer mom.

"Why isn't Future Solutions sending more of us against ourselves?" I asked as soon as the door closed behind us and we started back to the hotel with our hands full of greasy goodness. The question had hit me while we waited and I thought about the tactics I might use to come after myself. Someone with equal intelligence and ability to blend would be incredibly useful.

"Because they don't intend to waste the next generation on things like this, and they can't convince any of us to work for them. Not once we know the truth." David met my eyes, clearly thinking along the same lines as me. "At least, so says my dad."

"Why wouldn't they just lie? Maybe have one of my cohort take the rest of us out? A few careful half-truths, and it wouldn't be so hard. Our enhanced skills would make the process go a whole lot faster than using normal people."

"Would you be able to kill someone with your face? Your personality?" David asked, his tone changing as if he were attempting to size me up.

I opened and closed my mouth a few times, thinking it over. The obvious answer was yes, I'd do what I was told and complete my assignment. I'd had that knocked into me a million times. But the reality? No, I couldn't have executed Eleanor or her kids in a million years.

"I could've been assigned a different cohort to kill," I pointed out.

"True. Heaven help me if I ever end up going against a whole group of you."

I laughed, trying to picture it. "Who knows, you might actually like it," I teased. A small action, vestige of my normal life, to draw him in and get him to trust me. Not that he ought to.

He shook his head. "Nope. It doesn't work like that. Yes, you might all look the same, and have the same funny way your brain works, but you are definitely you—not Eleanor, not Faith, not any of the others."

The intensity of his tone burned my insides and heat curled low in my belly. I ducked my head to keep him from seeing it reflected in my cheeks. Something about the way he spoke felt like he understood—even all the mismatched parts of me still attempting to figure out what the hell it meant to be a clone.

I catalogued that away as another reason why being just a copy of someone else didn't mean a thing when it came to defining who I was. No matter what, I was still human, and fuck anyone who thought I didn't deserve to live.

"I think we have a car to steal." He paused and leaned in a little to speak in a whisper. Not that anyone was around, but I could smell coffee and the faint remnant of cologne he wore, and couldn't help but think it was delicious.

"We should take the john's car," I suggested, motioning toward it. "It's the nicest one, it has more seating, and he's not going to report it stolen for a while. Just don't shine a black light around. Plus, it has a full tank."

David, watching me closely, nodded. "That's true."

Without thinking more about it, we had the back door to the small SUV open in a minute, and the food placed inside. This was followed by me sitting behind the wheel and getting the ignition wires ready while David went under the hood. Within a minute we had the vehicle running, and I pulled it around behind the side of the building, knowing that the others would be ready to load up promptly.

David, coming to open my door for me, gave me another of his little grins, which this time I enthusiastically returned.

NINETEEN

DAVID and I entered the hotel room, calling for the others to get ready and out the door. Eleanor watched me with a smirk. I could tell from the way she almost bounced on the bed that she knew something was going on, but held herself in check. Funny thing, finding out you had a clone: all those odd little sisterly things seemed automatic. I'd always wanted to have someone to share them with but never had a face to go with the urge. Now I suddenly understood why girls would huddle in packs and whisper incessantly like their lives depended on it. I certainly never understood that desire when I was younger.

Joey was dressed and attempting to nibble on his toes on the bed. Sarah emerged from the bathroom with wet hair. Aaron nodded. And with that, we went about gathering the scant belongings we'd left in the room. Aaron and David disappeared downstairs to keep an eye on the john's car while I wiped down as many surfaces as I could recollect us touching.

A quick check under Aaron's bed revealed a small, dark shape. I had to get down on my hands and knees, stifling a groan, to fish it out—a cell phone. It was nondescript, lacking even a brand name, but pressing the power button revealed the faces of two identical Davids and a lock screen. Aaron's or perhaps David's.

Closing my eyes for a moment, I thought about what I knew about Aaron. My second try—Corbin and David's birthday gleaned from the files yesterday—unlocked the device. The phone opened to a notes application, typed script flowing down the page. Why he'd even kept a phone around baffled me—they were easily traceable. It had at least been disconnected from service, but that didn't sit any better with me. My eyes drifted over the screen, my stomach twisting down tight.

The subjects are compliant. Forgiving, and willing to believe any tale I tell about their origins. It's truly a marvel they haven't become more jaded with the partial truth they've learned. The time stamp on the note was early this morning, before the rest of us woke.

"Are you okay?" Eleanor asked, a light hand on my arm.

I angled the phone away from her eyes, not ready to share it.

"The subjects?" I whispered. He meant David, Eleanor, and me, no doubt. And if I thought about it, probably Sarah and Joey too—the second-generation clones.

The implications of Aaron's thoughts on us made my mind whirl; they stacked up in tidy rows to the horizon like a long line of dominoes. And I'd just tipped the first one over.

Aaron. What was he doing here?

Did David know?

Somehow that question soured my gut more than any of the other horrific possibilities. David's attention suddenly rang false. Surely he knew about what his father was up to. That brief moment of warmth, the thought that maybe there was a chance for more than the Game with him, curdled with the smooth plastic device in my hands. I longed to throw it at something and let the glass shatter.

I knew better than to trust either of the men. I'd thought I was capable of outmaneuvering them. It was going to come back to bite me in the ass, too.

Pushing the thoughts away, I looked up at Eleanor's carefully crafted blank expression. The one I knew hid her concerns, because I used it myself.

"It's Aaron's," I whispered, holding the phone out to her.

She scanned over the entry, her breath catching as mine had. "He's playing us?"

Sarah perked up behind her mother, and I shook my head in a quick "not now" gesture. This was something we'd have to look over more. Later. Alone.

How the hell were we going to find time alone?

I tucked the phone into my jacket after hastily powering it down. Part of me wanted to launch on Aaron as soon as he walked in the door. Most of me knew that was a terrible idea. No way could I trust either of the men outside, but I could still use them for taking down Future Solutions. After ushering the others out, I wiped down the last of the surfaces rapidly as we emerged into the bright morning sunshine.

David sat behind the wheel, casual, but with a vigilant eye on our surroundings. Aaron opened the back door of the mini SUV and helped Sarah crawl over to the jump seat in the back, while Eleanor carefully arranged Joey. I settled into the passenger's seat, inspecting the parking lot to ensure nothing had changed during the last five minutes.

David's eyes met mine and I managed a tight-lipped grin. He frowned for a moment before turning away.

Please, for the love of everything holy, don't let him be in on whatever Aaron's up to.

Stupid of me to even hope that was the case, but I did.

Less than a minute later, David merged into traffic and we left the hotel behind. Under the guise of inspecting our surroundings, I peered between the front seats and past

Aaron. Nothing seemed different. He was busy keeping Joey occupied by playing peekaboo.

Then Aaron patted his jacket pocket. If I hadn't been paying attention, I would have missed it, chalking it up to an unconscious tap for keys, a phone, change, or something along those lines. But the flash of dismay made it clear something was up. His eyes widened and he paused in his play with Joey to pat his other pocket.

He knew he'd misplaced his phone. The phone he'd pretended not to have yesterday. The phone that now sat in my pocket, full of secrets and terrible words.

I settled back in my seat before he noticed I'd been watching, feeling a nasty twist in my gut. Aaron was hiding something, something big, and it wasn't just about what we were. It was about what we were doing.

TWENTY

"I NEED to know more details about where we're headed," I announced after eating a McMuffin.

The decision to stay in a cabin had been made behind my back, and I wasn't thrilled. I needed to know everything about the place we were headed. Most especially if I was getting Eleanor and her kids messed up with it. Silently, I debated escaping, but knew there was no real way out. Not for the long term, at least.

"A former business associate owns it. He got out of the work when we started creating humans," Aaron explained in a low voice. "He began working on cloning technology for replacement organs and has done well for himself." I could sense his distraction, and knew without turning around that he was trying to look around for his phone without drawing attention.

Also, his reply had given me anything but answers. "So, this place is located where? How close is it to other towns? Houses?"

"It's about thirty miles from South Lake Tahoe, up in the mountains. It's about as safe a place as you can get. The guy used to do some of the security work at the labs, keeping people out. Now his place is entirely enclosed and guarded. No one's making it onto the grounds to harm anyone." Aaron's tone clearly meant that to be the end of the discussion.

"Have you ever been there? Is there anything you could tell us about the layout?" I asked, by no means about to let the subject drop.

"No, I just called him yesterday on your phone while you were out. He volunteered the spot for us to lie low while we figure out how to rescue Faith." His expression attempted to show that he was totally happy with these turn of events, and that I ought to be too. Except he seemed too careful with his words which made alarm bells ring in my head. Knowing what I did, I was on high alert as we drove. A place to lay low would have been an excellent way to regroup, if I wasn't pretty sure Aaron had other plans.

Aaron changed the subject, and when none of the adults were in the mood to talk, he started up the alphabet game with Sarah. Then the scenery lost signs and other ways to get letters, and Sarah nodded off.

I caught Eleanor's eyes through the side mirror, the two of us processing our best possible next move. So many questions, so many things I wanted to know, and all I could do was snatch glances of her through the mirror. It was almost physically painful.

All the while, my mind churned over what else the phone tucked into my pocket could contain. A brief pitstop for the baby afforded me thirty seconds in the bathroom stall to scan a little more. Several notes were filled with technical outlines about the process by which we were created. I would need more time with those, since some of the information was in jargon I hadn't seen since my years at Oxford.

Another note outlined David's progress over the last few weeks.

He's taken it well, because he knows the truth about himself. His brother's death was a shock, surely, but one I think he understands on some level, as to why it had to occur. I swallowed hard. David knew parts of the truth, but not all the details. What else could there be? What other horrors did Aaron know about us? And how safe could we possibly be with him?

Yet, I wasn't about to let Aaron out of my sight. Whatever he was up to, I'd catch on soon enough.

TWENTY-ONE

WHOMEVER AARON'S contact was with the cabin, they clearly had money, and a lot of it. We snaked up Highway 50 into the Sierra Nevada mountains, emerging into the city of South Lake Tahoe, then skirted north again. The road wove around the lake, twisty and congested, but David drove like even the hairpin turns only took a fraction of his brain. It probably wasn't far from the truth.

The driveway to the house started with a wrought iron gate that looked like something better suited to Beverly Hills than a side road in the middle of the mountains.

"The code is seven-seven-six-five-nine-two-eight," Aaron offered as David leaned out the window to type into the keypad.

Cameras lined the drive, spaced just far enough apart that every single foot was covered by their watchful gaze. Lights positioned to shine on the road flipped on as soon as we passed the gate. The afternoon sun hid behind a mass of thunderheads accumulating on the horizon. The grounds themselves were perfectly groomed, with a neat lawn and blooming flowers that traced through the hills as we meandered another quarter mile to the main house.

And what a main house! Three stories. The bottom floor made from stone, with the top floors in rough-hewn logs that gave the place a cabin-like feel. Of course, the giant windows and five chimneys didn't exactly convey cozy.

"This is owned by someone who used to work with you, Dad?" David gave his dad an appraising look. Apparently, David hadn't grown up in a giant mansion with a million windows and eight thousand square feet of space. Based on the files, none of us had—all the clones had been placed into relatively stable middle-class families.

I glanced at David, reading the honest curiosity in his eyes. There was no hint of deception, which would have played well with Aaron's duplicity. But David easily could have been playing the Game, and I wasn't sure I could tell.

The giant house also apparently included the luxury of servants. A man dressed in a neat dress shirt and dark jeans hopped down the front stairs and opened my door.

"Welcome, miss, to the Fireside Cottage," he greeted with a hint of a Southern accent, waving a hand at the building behind him.

"Cottage," Eleanor muttered under her breath, and I fought against a grin.

"Thank you." I accepted his hand and exited the car. The man then turned to Eleanor and with practiced ease, got Joey settled in one arm and carried the sleeping Sarah in behind the rest of us.

"Can I keep him?" Eleanor whispered to me as we stepped into the foyer.

A large chandelier made from tasteful antlers (something I would have normally considered an oxymoron) lit the room with a warm light that made me think of candles and evenings camping in the woods.

Not that we would be camping here.

"I think we get to if we're staying here. Wonder if he

cooks?" I returned the sotto-voice commentary and Eleanor laughed outright.

"Rooms have been prepared for you upstairs," the pleasantly efficient servant inserted. "Would you like to see them now, or would you like something to eat first?"

My stomach rumbled with the mention of food. The morning's fast food buffet didn't last more than an hour, and I was distinctly curious about what the promise of food entailed in this place. But a quick glance at Eleanor made me decide differently.

"I could use some time to freshen up," I answered.

The others nodded and followed along as we mounted the curved staircase to the next floor and were led down a cozy hallway, decorated with Ansel Adams photography and several other artists' work I didn't readily recognize. The corridor itself extended further than seemed necessary, but as we made our way down, our host ignored the first few doors.

"This is for you and your children," he instructed, pausing with Sarah still tucked into his arms. With a nod to the key-code box on the outside, he motioned for Aaron to type in the digits. "You're welcome to set your own code from inside. It's one of the most secure rooms on the premises."

A nice touch. I glanced at Aaron to see his reaction, but nothing about him suggested this might be out of the ordinary or excessive on any level. I inspected the small screen as we entered the room, wondering how to override it if Eleanor needed to escape. A small camera lens blinked back at me and a shiver went up my spine. Aaron had mentioned this place was secure, but this felt more like a prison.

The room itself was fantastic. Two queen beds were lined against the wall with a massive picture window and private balcony. In the distance, over the treetops, I could just make out the tip of Lake Tahoe.

Sarah curled up on one of the beds, and after quickly scanning the room to ensure all looked as safe as our situation allowed, the rest of us left Eleanor to tend to Joey and use their palatial bathroom.

The next rooms we were assigned were no less magnificent, though a bit smaller for single occupants. All came with standard security features.

"Food will be served in a half hour in the dining room. Join us when you're ready," the servant added formally as he left me alone.

I nodded absently, waving my thanks as I wandered to the window. Situated on the opposite side of the hallway from Eleanor, my room overlooked an expanse of trees and the wide break of mountains that spread out from the lake.

First things first. The security system.

The inside panel had a small drop-down keyboard that allowed me to access the system. A quick run-through of the menus told me what I needed to know: while I could set my door to admit only me, it was also remotely accessible and could be locked down from the outside. The more troublesome part was the cameras. Those required a bit of effort to shut off, or at least loop as blank back to whomever monitored them. I felt certain that the monitoring wasn't constant, so if someone—likely the servant guy—checked in on them, he'd be less likely to be suspicious if he saw mine as the empty room. It wasn't as if I could just black them out. That would be the equivalent of a bright, flashing neon sign saying I was on to them.

Once I was certain I wasn't being filmed, I did a thorough sweep of the room, checking all the likely, and less likely, spots for other surveillance bugs. The walls were rough-hewn wood, and it took ages to check every nook and cranny. The bathroom, with its marble floors and counter tops, reminded me of high-end resorts I'd stayed in while on the job. I ran a finger along the cool stone and slumped onto the toilet lid.

Only then did I pull out the phone.

Again, time was against me, but I had to read as much as I

could. We'd taken a huge risk allowing Aaron to bring us here, one I hoped wouldn't come back to harm us.

The second to last of the entries only bore a few lines of writing. A flash of anger slid under my skin as I stared down at the screen, the words blurring in my too-tired vision.

I've done my part to complete this phase. The subjects have been extricated. Watching them sleep, trusting me, makes me hope it will all be worth it.

Shutting off the screen and gripping the phone so tightly, I worried I might break the thing. After prying it out of my own grasp, I set it on the bathroom counter and tried to wrangle my anger into submission. Everything lately felt ramped up higher than anything I was used to. Everything felt unreal, including my own self. *What was I?*

I had to get downstairs soon or it would become obvious something was going on. But the temptation of continuing to search for answers in Aaron's phone was almost too much to bear. And David. What about him? It didn't seem as though he was part of the nefarious plot with his father, but with the general lack of answers, it was impossible to tell.

I pushed myself to my feet and turned on the sink faucet, letting the water warm a bit before ducking down to rinse the travel grit from my face and smooth back my hair. A shower would be heaven, but that could wait. Right now, I had to eat.

Downstairs, the enticing aroma of something grilled wafted into the foyer, and I followed the scent through the living room—huge, with a fireplace large enough to roast an ox, and leather couches that made me wonder if someone had —and then past double doors that led into a dining room that could have comfortably sat a hundred at the long table. That room was empty so I kept moving, continuing down the hall, again decorated with tasteful and expensive art, toward the sound of voices.

Eleanor met my eyes as soon as I stepped into the kitchen.

She'd strapped Joey, fast asleep, to her back, and was perched on a tall stool at the counter.

The servant was cheerfully chatting away as he worked at an indoor grill that glowed with embers under a huge, hammered copper hood. Lined up in front of Eleanor were at least fifteen wooden bowls filled with all manner of enticing foods, including various salads and potato dishes, though the potato chips called out to me. My mouth watered and I managed a small smile at Eleanor as I settled in next to her.

She nudged my shoulder and I shook my head. No more information quite yet. An unspoken code in our funny DNA. Were all the clone cohorts like this, or was it just a by-product of our odd brains? Things like the ability to catch the way Eleanor's hands shook—just a little—as she filled her plate, or the way her breath caught at the creak of footsteps.

Joey stirred in his sling and I patted his warm, fuzzy head. I was just as genetically related to the boy as his mother.

"Sarah?" I asked, taking a hand-painted plate from the stack and reaching for the smooth wooden bowl before me to ladle out a giant portion of what smelled like garlic mashed potatoes. For one selfish moment, I contemplated just keeping the larger bowl. I could have eaten all of it.

"She's still upstairs, sleeping," Eleanor said before leaning in close. "It's all safe," she breathed to me, pretending to brush my hair back from my face.

I frowned and shook my head at her, but she just smiled and waved off my questions. Later I'd be asking her for more information, most definitely. I trusted that she was right, something I would never do with anyone else. The fact that I even contemplated eating in this stranger's house before being certain I wasn't about to be poisoned frightened me. The stress of the last few days, coupled with so much shock, really did a number on my normally acute self-preserving intuition. Hopefully we had a day or so to recoup, or God only knew what else I'd start to slip on. Like, perhaps, the hot clone whose father was clearly up to something.

I loaded my plate and ate like there was no tomorrow. David soon joined us, exchanging few words as perfectly grilled, juicy ribs were served across the counter. I ate until my fingers stuck together from the grease and my stomach groaned.

"Where's your dad?" I asked nonchalantly as I wiped my hands on the wet towel the servant—Chad—provided.

"He said he misplaced something, so he went to the car to look for it." David frowned and looked around as if he expected his father to suddenly appear at the brief mention.

"Yeah? What was it? Maybe one of us saw it." Eleanor's tone was perfect, curious without being pushy. She played the Game well.

"He didn't say. I'm sure he'll find it. It's not like there are a lot of places where something could be." David shrugged. He was either an extremely good actor, as good as Eleanor or me, or he wasn't worried. It didn't take much introspection to realize I desperately hoped it was the latter.

The edge of the phone dug into my hip, but I didn't say anything. I had to be sure of David's innocence before I brought him in on his father's deceit.

Chad waved off our offers of help in cleaning up, and I couldn't help but be grateful. Exhaustion settled into me like a dark sea, threatening to pull me under. But before I gave in to it, I followed Eleanor up the stairs to her room, bearing a plate of food for Sarah.

Once inside, I motioned for her to go and tend her children while I went to work on her camera systems. After another sweep of the room, I felt reasonably confident we were not being watched, though it would take a great deal of effort for me to feel completely safe in this place.

"What are we doing here?" Eleanor asked, nestling Joey into a cocoon of pillows. Sarah had disappeared into the bathroom and the sound of the shower prevented our voices from carrying.

I rubbed a hand across my face, sinking onto the edge of the bed next to her. "I don't know. Perhaps we should have made our move before we ended up in the middle of nowhere in the woods."

Eleanor shook her head. "I'd rather keep the enemy close. And then we'd never get close to the weird company we have to expose. And plus, David. Do you think he knows anything?"

I swallowed hard. "I have no idea."

Eleanor rubbed a hand on my back and I sighed. "We need some kind of plan."

Eleanor's yawn was impressive, triggering one of my own. We both giggled. "I think the plan for this evening, at least, is to get some rest. Then we've got to find a way to figure out if David's on board with us or his dad. If he's one of us, we could use his help."

Our eyes met and it went unspoken that there was something a little more going on between David and me. Maybe. It was all contingent on what he knew, or didn't know, along with the fact that we were both being hunted.

"He has feelings for you, too." Eleanor flopped back onto her bed, careful to miss Joey's pillow nest.

"Or he's just able to fake it. I could, if I had to." I shrugged, peering at the identical face staring back at me. That would never cease to be weird.

"There are parts of social interactions we can all fake. We've probably been programed to be particularly good at observing others and reading, and therefore faking, social cues. But David's not faking."

I raised an eyebrow in silent challenge and Eleanor laughed. "God, it's weird to see you make my face back at me."

"Tell me about it. I keep seeing you do the same things I

do. I never would have thought they were so highly heritable. Is anything about us due to nurture?"

Eleanor shrugged, but before she could answer, another thought seemed to tug her away and her expression widened into a teasing grin. "David keeps glancing at you, and I can see his pulse jump every time you look at him. I've never been terribly good at seeing the whole pupil-dilation thing, but I'd put money on that going on, too. He's got it bad for you, just as much as you do for him. He couldn't fake all that. Too much of it is a purely biological response. Autonomic."

I paused, contemplating her words. He could probably fake it if he really wanted to, or be so immersed in the Game that he began to believe it himself. There were too many variables to tell. "Maybe," I finally conceded. I wanted to believe her, but I also knew that was the path to getting shot again—and this time without a vest.

Eleanor laughed again and tossed a pillow at me. "You've got your orders. Go find out if David's in on whatever his father's got going."

I stood and fished the phone from my pocket. "You keep this, okay? Read through as much as you can. I can't have it on me..." I couldn't quite finish that thought, and Eleanor waggled her eyebrows.

"Yeah, I gotcha. I'll go through it and report back."

I wanted to hug her, craving on some strange level the affection she could offer as my sister, loving the way she seemed to get me. Instead, I left her room with a wave. I'd only just met the woman, I reminded myself. Even if it certainly didn't feel that way.

Two doors down and on the right, I typed in my code and the door lock clicked.

I cracked the door and heard someone else breathing in the room.

CHAPTER
TWENTY-TWO

"WHO'S HERE?" I demanded, flicking on the rest of the lights. I'd only left the lamp by my bed on, and as I edged down the wall toward where the room opened up, I flipped through ten different scenarios in my mind.

Damn gun was in my bag, stashed in the closet. It was beyond stupid of me not to think I might need it. Seriously, I was getting back on my game and being more careful… just as soon as I figured out who was around the corner.

"Seriously, who the hell is in here?" My heart thundered in my ears but I kept moving. It was only a few paces to reach the edge of the opening, but every inch felt like a mile.

One last, deep breath and I swung around the wall and into the room, careful to keep low and moving, which would make it harder for someone to hit if they had a weapon—or at least, it would be harder for them to hit anything vital.

No shots followed. Instead, a shuddering deep breath came from whomever had settled onto my bed.

I slowly stood and stared down to see David half-lying on my bed, his long legs still bent to the floor, fully clothed, and fast asleep.

Well, at least it wasn't his father.

I approached David's side and spent a quiet moment enjoying his profile. There was no doubt he had been well made. His square jaw carried just enough scruff I wanted to reach out and touch. Instead, I placed a gentle hand against his shoulder and pressed to wake him. A little voice in the back of my mind thought of all the ways I'd like to rattle his teeth to get the truth from him. There were all sorts of ways I could make it fun.

My grin was automatic when David's eyes flashed open. Alert in an instant, he sat up so fast, I toppled backwards in my haste to avoid knocking heads.

"Well, that was graceful," David quipped, rubbing a hand across his face.

I pushed myself up onto my knees, shaking my head ruefully at my own smooth move. "What are you doing in here?"

"Checking on your security. Nice patch, though." He held out a hand and pulled me up from the ground, the two of us awkwardly close. I backed away, not at all sure what to do with the space between us. I didn't trust him, yet my heart desperately wanted to. The way the phone notes were worded suggested that Aaron was fooling his son as much as the rest of us, but that didn't mean much. It could just be all part of the Game, meant to make me doubt myself.

If that was really the case, it was working.

"I was impressed, really. Went back to my room and did the same. It does concern me that whoever owns this place thinks it's appropriate to spy on his guests. Did you find the camera in the shower?"

I wrinkled my nose. "I haven't seen that one. Does your father know about what I did to my system?" The last thing I needed was Aaron knowing I was avoiding being watched. With a sigh, I slumped to sit on the bed.

David shook his head, darkness flashing behind his eyes. "He's in a foul mood. I went to his door, but he just shouted that he was going to sleep. I imagine he knows well enough how to take precautions here."

I nodded, debating about what this meant. Frustratingly, there were too many variables and not enough data. But how to get that information out of him? Torture was too messy, at least emotionally, and I couldn't draw attention. And really, seduction, while effective, was nauseating. David was far too canny for me to try to deploy an indirect approach.

Which left what? The direct approach, I supposed.

"What are you thinking about?" David leaned in, closing far too much of the carefully cultivated space between us.

I looked away, picking at the expensive raw silk comforter. The tiny little nubs in the dark blue of the fabric caught under my nails and I resisted the urge to pull them free. "What else do you know about your dad's involvement with his company? About his intentions for us? *All* of us?"

David fell silent and I peeked over at him, not at all surprised to find a blank mask mirrored back at me from where he stood next to the bed. It wasn't as if I expected any outward sign of emotion, not when it didn't suit his needs.

"What are you implying?" His tone, calm and measured, reminded me of the many times I'd treaded carefully on the job, making sure I didn't betray a source, ensuring that a deal didn't sour.

"I'm not completely certain, just that I'm not sure he's been honest about cutting off all association with Future Solutions, and that maybe he has some kind of motive in gathering us all together. Something else is going on."

David got to his feet and walked away a few steps. I was almost startled by the obvious sign of his discomfiture. Maybe he did have some kind of tell that would clue me in on his knowledge of the situation?

"What leads you to think that?"

The truth, or a lie? With one glance at David's expression, the lie slid easily from my lips. "The security system. Why bring us somewhere that might have someone watching our every move? Don't you think that's odd? Why not get us out of the country, or find some other remote hiding spot?"

"Maybe he's certain this place is as safe as we're going to be. And leaving the country won't keep any of us safe." David's eyes met mine and I caught my lower lip between my teeth, leaning away a few more inches at his expression. "Just ask my brother."

Corbin. I knew far too little about his death.

"What if that's not enough? What if he's acting under duress? I just don't know how we can be certain." I pressed a hand to my cheek, letting just a little of my own anxiety over the situation shine through. It certainly wasn't difficult to conjure.

David traveled to my window and back again. "Which means you're not certain about my own motivation, either."

"Honestly? Not completely." With a sigh, I followed his gaze out the window, a peek of lake in the distance a deep blue in the gathering sunset.

He went quiet, allowing too much time for unease to filter into my blood. I was locked in here with him. He outweighed me by probably fifty pounds, all of that in height and muscle. I might get in a few good hits, but he'd been trained just as I was. That's all I'd manage. It wouldn't be hard to get rid of me. An image of being thrown bodily through the window flashed through my mind.

But would he actually do that? It was one hell of a gamble.

"Why are you questioning this now? What did you find out?"

Again, the logical next question. Sometimes it really was easier to deal with dumb people.

"I've never trusted you entirely. Not after what happened. But," I paused, both for effect and because I couldn't believe I was actually doing this. Keeping him in the dark was the better, safer move, but I also couldn't help hoping that he wasn't in on all of this. "But I found the thing your father has been looking for. It's a phone, with his notes from the last few days. He mentions a few things that are very suspicious."

David cocked his head to the side. "Are you certain it's real? I'd never peg my dad to have notes about something so important that he could accidentally misplace."

The thought did cross my mind. "I know what you mean, but why else would he have it? Why write those things if it was fake? It's obvious he didn't want us to find it. He's upset that it's gone, right?"

David frowned, and I knew, somehow, he was thinking back to the way his father reacted to him knocking on his door. "Still."

"Still, what? He's up to something. We don't know what, but wait until you read the entries. It's..." I closed my eyes, thinking about the words and the way he described us. Like we were things, not people. But maybe that was how he justified his actions, by making us all something not quite human, no matter how we walked and talked. Maybe that was how all the scientists viewed us. But why? They were logical beings. Could they all be so heartless?

Aaron didn't seem that way, but how could I tell for certain? He might not have been as good at the Game as David, but he could still probably fool us all. Obviously he had been for the last two days.

"Do you have it with you?" David suddenly looked far too interested, and I was grateful I thought to leave the phone with Eleanor.

I explained the situation, and David nodded before slumping into the plush chair in the corner. What he actually felt about the situation seemed as elusive as before.

"What do you think?" I looked at him closely and answered as directly as possible.

"He's my father. I want to trust him. But if he's doing something nefarious behind our backs and still working for

FS, I'm going to leave him here in this fancy prison and we're all going to disappear as best we can." The vehemence in his tone and the hardness in his eyes reminded me that he'd had the same day job as me. It left little room for second guessing one's actions, especially in the face of a threat.

"I want to believe you, but really, you two were the ones who found me." I returned his gaze, wanting him to feel the weight of my words.

"All I wanted to do was keep you safe. To give you a chance to learn the truth slowly. And then everything went to hell, and now you're accusing me of actually working with the fucking company that killed my brother?" David huffed a sigh, the tight set of his shoulders and rigid pose of his body fairly radiating anger. "Let me see these entries. I can prove that I have nothing to do with what's going on, if my father is even up to something."

I could do that. I wanted to be convinced of the truth. But... "Not tonight. It'll be suspicious if I go back over there."

David nodded, seeming to accept my explanation. His gaze wandered back to my window and I attempted to take a few breaths to bring my brain back into focus. There had to be a logical way out of this mess, one that kept Eleanor and her kids safe. One that didn't mean I had to hurt someone else.

Peeking at David, I added one more condition: one that didn't mean he was lying.

With no more progress possible for the evening, a yawn built in my chest and the weight of the last few days settled on my shoulders. David, though I knew he heard, made no motion to move.

"So, look, I'm exhausted. Aren't you tired?"

David looked at me like he had startled awake again. "I'm never going to be able to sleep now."

Which meant what? I thought about asking, but really, it didn't matter. All I wanted to do was crawl into my bed and sleep. David was not catching on. "Aren't you going back to your *own* room?"

"Not after what you just told me. I'm staying here and keeping an eye on you."

My laugh was almost a snort. "I'm pretty sure I can take care of myself."

"That's not the issue. I just don't think we should be alone right now."

Frowning, I shook my head. "That's not really comforting, or true. Because if it were, why wouldn't you be over with Eleanor? Children who don't know how to handle a weapon should come first."

David's sigh was long and pained. "A couple of reasons: One, I'm already here, and we don't want to draw suspicion." He ticked his list off on his fingers. "Two, Eleanor's kids mean she's not alone, and I have no doubt she'll be able to protect herself with the gun she lifted out of your bag earlier. And three, I'm not leaving you alone to do anything rash. I would never forgive myself if something happened to you."

I hated to admit it, but the little part of me that was altogether girly had a happy-sigh moment. Keeping that to myself with a shrug, I pulled back the sheets on the bed as I kicked off my shoes. Carefully, I set them in easy reach, in case I needed them in a hurry.

"Well, if you're not going to sleep, I am. If you need to switch off, wake me." Slithering under the covers and tugging them over my head felt so childish, yet at the same time sent little sparks of energy through my blood. Sleeping with him so close was an odd mix of concern and adrenaline. Fun, even. I hoped that he was telling the truth when it came to not being involved with whatever Aaron was up to. For tonight, all I could do was try trusting him, or at least trust my own judgment of him.

CHAPTER
TWENTY-THREE

THE SILVER of a too-bright moon streamed in the window when I woke. I silently cursed myself for leaving the drapes open before the reason why I woke settled through me. The creak of the mattress next to me drew all my attention, like a magnet pulling at my consciousness.

"It's just me. Sorry to wake you." David's voice, thick with sleep, rolled over next to me.

"What the hell? Go sleep in the chair. Or on the floor!" I demanded. Perhaps not my most hospitable comment, but all my filters were down with the combination of middle-of-the-night awakening and the strangeness of waking next to David. Again.

He muttered something incomprehensible and rolled closer. I could feel the heat and weight of him, despite the space between us.

My jaw opened and closed a few times, unable to come up with a good way to tell him off, or push him off, until the warmth of him so close, his breath relaxing into an even rhythm, melted me. It was just… nice.

So, he could kill me in my sleep. Not that he couldn't have before, but being so close made it easier. In the moonlight and my half-asleep awareness, I realized I wanted to believe David. I wanted to trust him. I didn't—not really—but I wished I could.

Wanting and reality might be two vastly different things, but I let the wish ease the tension in my muscles, relaxing into the bed.

I would never have imagined being able to sleep, but it didn't take long for my eyes to flutter closed.

———

In the split second it took for my brain to wake up enough to remember what happened during the night, I nearly launched myself out of bed.

"Do you wake up every morning like that?" David asked with a smile in his voice.

Running my hands through my hair in a futile attempt to smooth it down, I peeked over at him with his eyes still closed, in a fetal position, facing me. His hair was all adorably mussed, his stubble more pronounced.

Of course he looked great. I had a feeling my breath could kill a pig from ten paces.

"Only when strange men decide to become my bedfellow in the middle of the night," I answered.

David cracked one eye and the ghost of a smile quirked his lips. "You didn't seem to mind when we were spooning earlier."

I glared at him. "It's not considered spooning if you're both not under the covers."

"Is that an invitation?"

I threw back the blankets and shoved my feet to the floor. "You're more than welcome to them while *I* go get some breakfast." Last night's massive meal meant I was famished this morning.

While I tugged on my shoes, David pushed himself up to

sit with his back against the headboard. I heard his palms rasp against his cheeks and tried not to think about how I'd like to know how that felt. I didn't remember what I'd dreamt, but my hormones were running high and I got the sense that my subconscious had been having a heyday with the incredibly hot man in bed with me. Even if we had most certainly not been spooning.

"How can I convince you that I have nothing to do with whatever my father is doing, beyond trying to help the rest of the clones?" David's tone was calm, but I could sense the steel in it. He was playing the Game well this morning. Or telling the truth. I hoped for the latter.

I paused, halfway through forcing my feet into my clogs. "I'm not certain. But the person you're cloned from is up to something." I glanced at him, catching his wince at my words.

David sighed. "Why would I want to do anything to harm the clones? I *am* one."

"Because he's your father. Your emotional bond may exempt you, or something else is at play. How am I supposed to know what's really going on?" I stood and turned to look at him, feeling my features settle into hard lines. "And I have no idea how to tell when you're playing the Game or not."

It took him a moment to catch the reference from our emails from what felt like eons ago. His brow furrowed as he considered my words. "Is there any way to prove to you that I'm being honest?"

I sighed, considering. "Nothing other than helping us figure out what's going on with your father."

David's lips pressed together and he nodded. "I really wish you could find some way to trust me."

My laugh was bitter and hurt as it escaped. "Would you trust *me* if our situations were reversed?"

"Of course." Not one hint of doubt colored his words.

Standing and dropping my hands on my hips, I shook my head. "No, you wouldn't. Not a chance. And you know it."

David stood, his movements sure and lithe, and two steps across the room brought him toe to toe with me. I had to crane my head up to look at him. "I would trust you," he repeated.

I scoffed, but it wasn't convincing. I wanted his words to be true far too much.

"I would, if only because I know you. You wouldn't back anything you didn't feel was right. And if what you say is true, then," he closed his eyes for a moment, "then it's not right. And we have to do something."

My mouth was so dry, my tongue made a little sound as I fought to find the right words to respond. Nothing seemed good enough. Finally, I managed a nod and a shrug. "Thanks. I thought I knew you. I thought I could say those things about you. But after all this, after all the subterfuge, I need more proof."

David nodded once, his eyes clouding over. I wanted to comfort him and thank him for his trust, but I couldn't. Because I was right. I didn't know enough about him. Maybe one day, hopefully soon, I could trust him enough to do that. For now, I had to keep my head.

Without another word, I used the bathroom and then went to my door. I pulled it open, my thoughts wandering to the potential breakfast feast that awaited us, when Aaron's face pushed right into mine.

"Did you two have a pleasant night?"

All those years of playing the Game, making sure I portrayed just the right image, almost went out the window as the urge to bring my knee up to Aaron's groin hit me. Instead, I held back, took a breath, and dropped my eyes, for all the world looking embarrassed.

"I think that's absolutely none of your business, Dad," David chided, coming up behind me. His fingers curled around my shoulder, his chest pressed to my back—the perfect image of what we might have looked like if last night had been more about seduction than subterfuge.

Aaron shrugged, nodded, and finally stepped out of our way.

"What's going on?" David asked Aaron as we all started down the hallway.

"I was coming to see if anything was wrong with Diana's security system. Seems to not be working properly, or so the head of security says."

"Oh? I didn't notice anything." I knew my wide-eyed innocent look was pure perfection.

"I can take a peek after breakfast," Aaron offered.

Which meant we had the length of one meal to learn more of the truth about this man. Enough to convince David and see where his loyalties lay.

"Did you find what you were looking for last night?" David asked, changing the topic as we entered the kitchen.

The smell of another amazing meal greeted us, an assortment of hot English fry-up ingredients set out for us to enjoy. Eleanor was already seated at the table, feeding Joey with one hand and helping Sarah cut something with her other. She gave me a relieved grin when I took Joey and settled him into a high chair that Chad appeared with as we entered the room. Joey was instantly fascinated with the bits of eggs his mother placed before him, while Chad disappeared through the back door with a little wave.

"No," Aaron answered shortly.

"So, it wasn't in the car? Do we need to go back to the motel? You and I could do a quick trip today, leave the ladies here," David suggested while piling his plate with eggs.

Keeping my head down, I grabbed a plate and filled it with too much food, keeping quiet so I could discern any underlying inflections in Aaron's words.

"It's fine. No one is going to find that motel. Maybe I'll ask and see if I can get one of the men here to help out." Aaron shrugged. "It'll be fine."

"What was it you forgot?" I asked, all innocence and far too much bacon.

Aaron didn't even hesitate. "My old phone. Disconnected, of course. It had some photos on it I hadn't backed up and was sad to lose." He waved a dismissive hand.

Echoes of what his notes said, of the dirty way they made me feel, washed through me, but I didn't dare show my reaction. Instead, I loaded some sausage on my plate and settled at the table.

Sarah was chattering with her mom about how much she wanted to go outside and explore the woods this morning. Eleanor was nodding and half listening, but her eyes met mine, her expression shrewd, as we joined her at the table.

"Speaking of documents, is there any chance I can see some of this fabled evidence about this clone conundrum?" she asked, eyes alight with interest. "There's the paperwork evidence Diana mentioned yesterday, right?"

"I'd like to know more about this old associate of yours whose house we're staying in," David added, his tone just as light at Eleanor's. But, for just a moment, I caught a hint of malice within David's words. Aaron didn't miss it, either. Father and son looked at each other across the table for a long moment. Even Sarah fell silent.

So much for finding a subtle way to handle this.

After giving Joey a few more pieces of egg, I rose and went to close the door we'd entered through, as well as the one that led into what I assumed was the garage. Aaron didn't have a chance to get to his feet before I turned back to him, arms crossed.

"I think we need to know more about what the meaning of this is." Eleanor held up Sarah's kiddie tablet, packed with her things last night when we left their home. Now it displayed a photo of one of the note pages from Aaron's phone.

Aaron glanced around, his eyes wide and the perfect mask of incredulity settling his features into a facsimile of concern. "I don't understand. What's going on here?"

"Those are your notes, aren't they? From the phone?" I motioned to the screen.

"Do you know what it says about us? About what we are?" Eleanor added

Sarah chose that time to speak up. "I do! Mommy asked me to memorize it last night."

Eleanor pressed her lips together. "She's got a photographic memory. Lucky for us."

Something about Sarah seeing those entries twisted my gut, but I hoped she didn't understand most of it. At some point, it would be important for her to understand what she was. Just not like this.

Aaron's breathing was careful and controlled as his gaze circled the table, meeting each of our eyes. Finally, he spoke up. "Where did you find it?"

"Under your bed, when I was wiping down the motel room yesterday morning."

"And you read my notes?" Aaron's eyes settled onto mine, unwavering, the skin around them taut. "How did you even unlock it?"

I scoffed. "Your password was hardly difficult to guess. And I read parts. Enough." No sense lying.

Eleanor cleared her throat. "Care to let us know what the next phase is now that you've gotten us here?"

Aaron placed both of his hands flat on the table in front of him, like maybe if he stared at them he wouldn't use his fists in some way he shouldn't.

"What are you doing, Dad?" David's pointed tone caught my attention. Darkness seemed to swirl from the words, enveloping them in hate. I almost reached for Sarah and clapped my hands over her ears to keep her safe.

"What else did you learn?" Aaron asked instead.

"That this was all part of your plan," Eleanor began. "That the other clone you raised, Corbin, his death wasn't an accident. And that—"

David's half snarl, half expletive cut Eleanor off. "What did you say about Corbin?" He turned to his dad, and suddenly the room was far too small—particularly in the confines of the table.

While the guys were busy, Eleanor pressed the phone into my hand beneath the table. I tucked it into a pocket without anyone the wiser.

Eleanor waited a beat for Aaron to speak up, but when he didn't, she pitched her voice to convey a semblance of calm and spoke to David. Somehow Sarah knew to be quiet, watching the proceedings with wide eyes. Joey, the smartest of us all, was still merrily eating. "There weren't any details, just that what happened to Corbin wasn't an accident, and the implication Aaron knew it was coming. That your understanding allowed you to handle it so well."

David stood up so fast his chair skittered across the floor several feet before tipping over. "I've taken his death well? How would you know anything about what I've felt since he died?" he fumed, planting his fists on the table and leaning forward to look at his father. "You have no idea what I've been through."

If I was worried about him faking things before, that fear no longer mattered. Not one bit. This was David. His anger and frustration were so real, I felt like I could reach out and pet it. No, he didn't know about Aaron's plans.

Even sitting there, watching the older and younger versions of the same DNA, I could feel the shift between the men. Their bonds seemed to splinter and break, and I half expected to hear them scattering to the ground.

I didn't mean to do this to them. I didn't intend to break their relationship, but it was better for David to know the truth, and for Aaron to know we were on to some facet of his plan. Part of me still felt like I betrayed them both.

"This is not the time, nor the place to discuss this." Aaron somehow managed to keep his face expressionless, his eyes locked unwaveringly on his son's.

"I need to know what *really* happened." David didn't budge, and I started planning ways to get Joey and Sarah out of there if we needed to. The side door was close enough to let us escape. The main door was farther, but if Eleanor gave us cover, we could make it, if we kept to the far side of the room by the giant stove.

"You already know what happened," Aaron pleaded. "Think, David, of the situation. They got to your brother." Aaron's resolve seemed to waver, and I willed David to sit and try and discuss this rationally. Not that my thoughts did anything.

Eleanor spoke up. "That's not what the notes said. You said that Corbin's death *had* to happen."

David's fist connected with Aaron's nose so fast, I actually blinked and missed the impact. Aaron slumped in his seat, hands pressed to his face. Blood gushed between his clasped fingers.

"Corbin didn't have to die! *None* of us had to be put in this kind of danger. All of this…" David sat down, arms crossed, and his expression made me wish he had stayed standing, stayed mad. The hurt was painful to see. "All of this is your fault. All of us running for our damn lives. We're your fault."

Eleanor's eyes caught mine at his words, and I knew without a doubt what she was thinking. The same as me—the gut-twisting truth that we weren't the same as we'd been just days before. That the truth we were *made* set us apart. Changed us.

"Corbin was trying to expose the truth of what you are."

Aaron's soft voice made me lean forward, wary of missing any tiny detail or breath. "He wanted to go to the media."

Expose us? While I didn't have a problem with the idea, I imagined the men who attacked my workplace, shot me, and broke into Eleanor's home would have a serious problem with it. As would Aaron.

"What would happen if everyone knew the truth about us?" Eleanor got there first, her arms going around her daughter and pulling her tight.

"You can imagine what that might do." Aaron met Eleanor's eyes.

My mind raced ahead. No more need for pregnancy. The ability to clone yourself, or even improve yourself. It would bring the fantasy of "perfecting" the human race so much closer to reality. Humanity wasn't remotely ready for such a thing.

Science was more than ready, and had been for some time. The three of us sitting there were proof enough of that.

"So, Corbin was murdered," David breathed.

"To spare you. To give me time to get you away. Before the rest of the program was terminated."

"But why terminate it?" Eleanor asked, though it brought a dark look from David. "Why not just find a better way to hide it?"

Aaron pressed his lips together, making it clear he had more to tell, but couldn't quite weigh out the heaviest consequences of his words.

Just then, the door to the kitchen swung open. It felt like we'd been captured in a bubble that suddenly burst, reminding us that we were indeed in the real world.

"Good morning everyone! I am so glad you've joined me here at my humble abode."

CHAPTER
TWENTY-FOUR

I TRY to avoid instantly not caring for people. It goes against rational thought to judge a person by a first impression. My boss, for example—he was a cheating jerk with horrible dandruff the moment I saw him, but he did run the company well and I could at least appreciate him for that. Until I got him killed, at least.

The middle-aged blond man who waltzed into the kitchen wearing a white track suit and running shoes that had obviously never seen a trail or treadmill made me long to run screaming into the mountains. Add to that a prodigious fake tan and a tiny man bun, and Eleanor and I exchanged an incredulous glance over Sarah's head. We were on the same page.

Aaron jumped to his feet, all smiles and cheer, and went to our apparent host's side for a handshake and hug that looked entirely awkward, especially since Aaron had to wash his own dried blood off his hands before the other man would let him touch him. Aaron brushed aside the injury as an accidental encounter with the hood over the grille, which no one bought or questioned.

David watched like he longed to drag Aaron out back and make use of the gun tucked into his waistband.

"Is everyone doing alright? There seems to be a rather dour mood in the air." The man stepped forward to the table, grinning around at us.

The gap between his two front teeth made me think of the uncomfortable years of orthodonture I'd endured—another mark not in his favor. My parents had insisted on the headgear and other torture, and it certainly left me staring at teeth a lot.

"It's a pleasure to meet you. Thank you so much for providing such a beautiful and comfortable place to stay." Eleanor pulled herself together first, reaching out to shake the man's hand.

He smiled and kissed hers.

"I'm afraid I haven't gotten your name," Eleanor remarked as she wiped her hand on her jeans beneath the table.

"Oh! I'm so sorry not to have done the proper introductions," Aaron cut in. "Everyone, this is Dr. Timothy Mendel."

"No relation," Timothy acknowledged with a little laugh.

I had to fight the urge to roll my eyes.

"Is this your house?" Sarah asked, playing the perfect five-year-old role.

"Yes, yes, it is. Do you like it?"

"I do! I want to go explore in the woods. Can we do that?" Sarah gave her mother a sideways glance but seemed to sense that this man might be able to override her mother's earlier refusals.

"Of course! I'll even get Chad to set up the four-wheelers. Would you like that?"

Sarah clapped her hands together and nodded, all eyes and smile.

Eleanor began to protest, but the man waved her off. "I'll

ensure the perimeter is secure. We have the best security here outside of Columbia."

That didn't make me feel any better, but what choice did we have? Before we could work out our next move, we had to lay low, and that wouldn't be easy with two small kids. Eleanor, biting her lip, sat back and nodded. "Okay. We'll figure something out."

Timothy laughed and went to the wall, using an intercom to call for Chad.

"So, has the food been satisfactory?" he asked good naturedly, returning to the table and staring at us like we all might present him with the best Christmas present ever.

"It's been very nice, thank you," David observed mechanically. I could tell he was still mad from the stiff set of his shoulders, but I doubted Timothy could. David's mask was back in place, and I struggled to get myself into character. I wanted to get back to Aaron's duplicity, and to make sense of the whole situation, but now I just had another person here who I didn't trust but who could probably snap his fingers and have us all our bodies thrown in the lake.

From Aaron's jarring behavioral switch, it was apparent Timothy needed to be wooed to help us. It was almost certainly because he was a class-one narcissist, but I couldn't be completely sure based on five minutes of interaction. I could play the part as long as it meant we got the help we needed.

Because damn, did we need it. From inside and out. I didn't know which was the worse threat at this point: Aaron's revelations in his phone, or the men who were surely still trying to find us. And it was very possible one was helping the other.

And we still had more clones to protect. Faith and the rest of my cohort had to be saved. And the goal of saving her without a safe space to take her was dead in the water—for us all. So, being forced to suck up to man-bun fake-tan… Well, I'd done worse things on the job.

I leaned forward and smiled at Timothy, pushing my arms together to wedge my boobs up and together a tad. "Why don't you join us, Dr. Mendel? I'd love to hear more about your house here."

"Please, call me Timothy." His wide grin made a disgusted shiver go down my spine, but I kept my grin and nodded to the empty chair next to me.

He sat down, all smiles, and Aaron settled back into his seat, watching me like I'd lit the fuse on a bomb he didn't trust I could disarm.

"So, how long have you had Fireside Cottage?" I shifted to face him and crossed my legs to give the good doctor all my attention. I caught a very nasty black look David shot at me when he was certain no one else could see it.

Really? How clear could I make it that I was simply playing the Game? Certainly he realized that, or I'd end up with him somehow marking me as his territory—and I'd prefer not to be peed on.

"I bought it after my company went public, about a decade ago." He smiled, soaking up my attention like a sunbather at the beach.

My brain rattled through what he said: his company was available for stock purchases, but that didn't necessarily mean his investors knew about all that he did. From the way he shifted his shoulders, his eyes locking onto mine, I knew he wasn't above secrets. Lots and lots of secrets.

"I'm afraid Aaron hasn't had a chance to fill us in on all that your company does." I dropped my tone just a touch, putting a little purr into my words. It wouldn't be terribly obvious—unless someone knew what to look for, like Eleanor and David.

They both gave me looks I hoped Timothy would be prudent enough to ignore.

Timothy took the bait, and with a wide flourish, launched into the broader scope of his work (biotech, of course), and some other burgeoning areas of research that he was spinning off out of the country. "Too many restrictive laws stateside."

I nodded along, cataloguing what he claimed, noting he didn't ask who we were, which would have been the polite thing to do even though I knew full well Aaron must have told him.

Aaron was the one who broke in about ten minutes later, motioning toward the anxious expression Sarah wore. "I believe our younger contingent would appreciate a little more action and a little less adult chatter."

"Of course, of course. Come on, let's go!" Timothy raised his hands and ushered us along as if we were all part of a larger pack, perfectly content to follow him.

David hung back with me, resting a light hand on the small of my back.

I gave him a raised-eyebrow look. He shrugged. A part of me wanted to lean into him, but there were too many issues. Timothy might need additional manipulating. And despite all we'd seen, I still didn't fully know which side David would land on. Aaron was his father. His clone. I was only beginning to wrap my head around the implications of that—especially after meeting Eleanor. The line of cascading dominoes was moving forward, but what that meant to me hadn't yet fallen into place.

For a moment, looking at Eleanor strap her son more tightly to her chest, I hoped we'd have time to figure it all out.

As Aaron walked in front of us, I stared at the back of his shirt, wishing I could see into his head. The set of his shoulders told me he was uncomfortable, but then again, who wouldn't be after our confrontation?

A gargantuan garage opened off the left side of the house, rife with the sound of revving engines. Chad had assembled a small fleet of ATVs, and helmets sat at the ready off to one side.

"Who among you has ridden one of these before?" Timothy asked, his gapped smile almost convincing.

The last time I rode, I was being shot at in the jungles of El Salvador. But that was years ago. Sarah looked around at us, her grin and clasped hands all but shouting her excitement.

Dropping a hand on her head, I stepped forward. "Come on, let me give you a ride."

Sarah wrapped me in a quick hug, and Eleanor seemed satisfied. After a quick overview and instructions, along with the clunky helmets, Chad opened the wide doors and we set out into the mid-morning sunshine.

Sarah settled between my knees, her small frame bouncing with excitement.

Aaron elected to join us, and Chad led the way along the driveway until we turned off on a small side trail that led into the trees. When the soft packed earth gave way to a gravel trail, we picked up speed.

Sarah hooted and laughed as we gave chase through the trees, and I used the time to look for ways to escape the compound if needed. The fence that surrounded the place was a good ten feet tall and at least partially electric. The main road could be seen twisting off to my right, but scaling down to it wouldn't be easy with two small children.

And then I saw it. Just for a moment, while twisting us around a hairpin turn that made Sarah grab the handlebars, I spied the cottage and the rock embankment it perched on. Not quite a cliff, an expanse of stone was exposed below the right end of the house. As we went around the turn, I caught the reflection of sunlight against windows much further down the granite wall than the house.

A quick glance up ahead told me that Chad and Aaron were having a little too much fun racing one another (a wager of twenty bucks had been offered up at some point). Aaron certainly had brushed off his anger from earlier easily, which annoyed me more than anything.

"Are you up for a little adventure?" I asked conspiratorially, leaning in close to Sarah.

She must have sensed the change in my tone, and through the glass of her helmet, her eyes widened as she looked up at me and nodded.

It wasn't hard to find a spot to double back. I followed the granite outcropping and edged around the side of the house until I found a way to come down the slope on the other side of the house. I doubted they'd be able to hear us from above, but when a place to wedge the machine away from sight presented itself, I parked it and patted Sarah's shoulder at her anxious glance.

"Can you walk quietly?" I asked. No way could I leave her alone, and this was just a recon trip. She'd be safer with me.

Without a word, she nodded and slid soundlessly to the ground next to me. The walk around the rest of the small bluff was silent. Sarah was lither than me, her footsteps whispers in the padding of the pine needles. The wind kicked up in little gusts, singing through the tree branches, an eerie sound that didn't offer comfort.

Above us, the cottage rose, all glass and stone, impressive and formidable from this angle. It took navigating through the trees and skirting huge boulders until we reached a vantage point where we could see the windows I spotted earlier. Sarah stiffened next to me as they came into view. Smart little girl didn't ask any questions, but I didn't doubt that she knew what they meant.

"We need to get a closer look," I whispered. She nodded and we set off, picking our way along the stones, doing our best to keep low and hidden as we got closer.

The rim of boulders was angled (artificially, I noticed) to guard against anyone seeing in, as well as to keep the outside view unobstructed to ensure no one was watching. Several cameras were tucked into nooks and crannies in the granite to safeguard against anyone stumbling onto this place. Almost straight above us, the rest of Fireside Cottage emerged from the outcrop, while our current position was almost invisible to them.

They must not have thought someone like me would attempt to get a better view. It wasn't hard to calibrate the angle of the cameras and keep out of their radius. Sarah was my shadow, her eyes wide and alert. Somehow, I didn't doubt that she'd only have to see me do this once to be able to do it herself.

Second generation clone. What on earth did that mean for her DNA? There was something different about her, but what was the root of it?

We ended up coming in from above, skirting around the cliff and keeping to a crevice that offered a slim, shadowy recess we could perch in while staying out of the sun.

The windows themselves were the next issue. They were tinted and the bright sunlight reflected off them, turning them into huge mirrors. That had allowed me to see them in the first place, but made it nearly impossible to see inside. And it wasn't as if I could press my face against the glass and cup my hands around my eyes to get a good look.

Sarah seemed to have guessed this, though, and as we got close enough to see down into whatever the glass hid, she touched my hand. I could see the apprehension in her eyes, and I grinned in a way that I hoped helped her feel better.

With that, I snagged my phone, bringing up the camera. After making a couple of adjustments to get the lighting right, I slid the lens down, flush against the glass. I had to be quick, otherwise there was a good chance it would be seen, backlit from inside, but I snapped a couple of quick photos, angling down and into the room hidden behind the glass.

My breath came hard and quick, and I forced myself to

slow it. Panicking right now would only lead to trouble, and I couldn't afford the luxury with Sarah in tow. Cupping the screen against the light, I checked that the photos were visible on the device.

The first one was blurry, but the sight of what the second one held pressed me against the rock behind me so hard, it dug into my spine.

Sarah tried to tug the phone away from me to see for herself, and I was about to dip it down to her eyelevel, my mind a befuddled mess of alarm and calculated plans, before I snapped the device up and away from the child.

No way would I let her see her mother in that position.

CHAPTER
TWENTY-FIVE

GETTING BACK to the ATV seemed to take forever. My mind tallied the seconds and I knew it wasn't more than ten minutes, but more than once I wanted to pick up Sarah, toss her over my shoulder, and race back.

Not that Sarah lagged far behind; she was quick and quiet as ever. The thought of what was in that photo urged me forward faster, faster. It was taking too long.

Of course we shouldn't have left Eleanor behind. Not with the sleazeball Timothy there to do whatever he pleased. And hell, what did this mean about where we'd go to from here? We didn't have anywhere else to go, and we needed a refuge while trying to save what was left of our cohort. Now I had to find a way to retrieve Eleanor, get us out of here, and escape not only the men already after us, but potentially Timothy as well.

Plans and panic, panic and plans. I almost passed by where we stashed the ATV, but Sarah seemed to know exactly where we were headed and tugged me over to it, shoving the helmet onto her head without question. As I slid into position behind her, I found myself begging whomever and whatever might be listening that my ignorance wouldn't leave her motherless.

The knowledge that the ride back to the house might very well lead to an attempt to get away from a masked gunman, I pushed us precariously around corners and slid into the garage with a roar that echoed through the cavernous room.

"What's wrong?" Sarah asked in a small voice as we dismounted. The ATV smelled like burning oil and heat radiated from it in a way that reminded me I needed to keep my cool, especially now.

Sarah's large, questioning eyes looked at me, her hair in a wild halo from removing the helmet she still clutched protectively to her chest. "What did you see inside?"

A quick shake of my head alerted her to be quiet. She must have realized we couldn't speak about that here, now. Cameras were undoubtedly hidden in the space.

"I had to go to the bathroom really bad. I hate peeing in the woods," I explained, patting her head and smoothing down some of the wayward locks. She was so little beneath my hand, so delicate. And while I knew her mind was sharper than anyone her age (or, hell, potentially a lot older), she was still a kid. A kid who needed her mom.

Sarah giggled a little at my comment, but I knew it was fake. She could play the Game, too. We left the helmets on our ride and went inside the house. I hunted down the first bathroom I could find, ducking inside for a moment, but listening with all I was worth to ensure no one snatched Sarah while I was in there.

A brief glance in the mirror confirmed my fears. Lack of sleep left the dark circles below my eyes. No matter how well I played the Game, the image captured on my phone rocked me. As I washed my hands quickly, drying them on the monogrammed towels, I knew I had to get my shit together. I needed to think of this as a rescue mission. Although I'd been on dozens of those... though not for someone who was my clone, for someone who I felt drawn to on a level I couldn't comprehend. Working for strangers was simpler. Everything was simpler before fucking David found his way into my life.

I stepped into the paneled hallway a minute later and found Sarah huddled against the far wall, her head hidden by the arms wrapped around her knees, her ponytail swinging around in front of her head.

For a moment, I hesitated. What was I supposed to do in this kind of situation? Be heartless and let her worry while I tried to get her mom? Or comfort her and potentially lose valuable time? Neither option was great, but when I heard Sarah sniffle from behind her knees, my heart cinched right down in my chest.

Instincts. Such weird, wild things.

Stepping closer to Sarah, I ducked so I'd be as close to eye level as possible and dropped my hands onto her thin shoulders. "We'll figure something out."

She listed tear-filled eyes to mine. "I want to help."

"Help with what?"

Sarah and I both jumped as Eleanor walked down the hallway toward us. Same clothes. Joey strapped to her chest. Same weariness from before etched into her expression.

But I saw her. Below.

I wanted to whip out the photo on my phone and zoom in on the image once again, but didn't dare. Instead, I got to my feet, moving out of the way so Sarah could race for her mother. Eleanor was almost knocked flat by the force of the small girl launching at her but managed to steady herself with a hand on the wall. She laughed and hugged her daughter, looking at me with questions in her eyes.

"She got worried when we left you behind, alone." I could only whisper the words. Something felt terribly *off* about all of this. My mind clicked through thousands of tiny details, searching for anything that would pinpoint the source of my unease, but I couldn't detect the origin. This just felt off; there was something about the situation I didn't trust, nor know how to handle.

"Sorry about that, sweetie. Did you at least have fun on your ride?" Eleanor asked, rubbing a hand comfortingly against her daughter's back.

"Yeah, lots! Until Aunt Diana had to go pee and we had to hurry back. She drove way too fast!" Sarah's expression peeking out from her mother's embrace was open and calm. The lab we saw, the sneaking around, she'd keep that quiet.

God, that kid was going to make one hell of a spy some-day. Assuming we could keep her alive.

"Come on, let's get you cleaned up. I heard there's a pool around here somewhere. Maybe we could go in later today," Eleanor promised, drawing her daughter in close to her side and heading back the way she came.

I watched them go, a knot of unease settling in my gut. If that wasn't Eleanor in the lab we saw, who was it? What was going on?

What was it about all of this that left me doubting abso-lutely everything about myself, even what I saw with my own eyes?

At least now I could find out without having to drag Sarah along with me, and a bit of my tension dissipated knowing that Eleanor was okay. But that space still existed. Something heinous was going on down there, and after all that had happened in the last couple days, I didn't dare trust anything.

I made it back to my room, doing my best to look as if I weren't about to break into a run any second. Because, seri-ously, that was what I wanted to do. Once I locked the door and did a quick check to ensure my alterations to the security system hadn't been distorted or changed, I slumped into the chair David occupied the night before and pulled out the phone.

The image was a bit blurry, the colors distorted due to the deeply tinted glass, but there was no mistaking what was in the lower left side of the image. A chair, restraints keeping the person in place, a silent scream arching her back and revealing her teeth. *Eleanor.* Her clothes were identical to the ones she'd worn during breakfast. Off to one side, Joey was in a small carrier, his eyes scrunched in an inaudible wail.

Eleanor—who retrieved Sarah from the hallway twenty minutes later, with no sign that anything extraordinary had happened. Not one mark from the array of gleaming, menacing tools on the counter near her.

The rest of the space in the photo revealed a lab with equipment that even the technicians at my company—where money was never an issue—would have drooled over. Stainless steel counters were neatly arranged with machines and racks and test tubes, and a whole lot of other things I barely knew the uses of, despite the effort I'd put into understanding the lab wizardry that went on behind closed doors at work. Whatever else Timothy was up to, not all his research was being done overseas.

But that didn't even come close to touching the hundreds of questions that zipped through my mind at lightning speed. My first concern was to make sure Sarah and Joey were okay. I doubted the real Eleanor was the one I met in the hallway, but now I needed be sure.

For once, I was annoyed with myself for disabling the security in Eleanor's room. It might have made this very simple, but now it meant leaving the relative security of my room.

Making sure I was armed, I strolled down the hallway to her larger room. From outside the door, I could hear low voices and laughter, which eased some of the churning in my gut. If anything happened to those kids…

Eleanor opened the door, just an inch, after my knock. Her expression seemed normal, as best I could tell from the slice of eye and nose I could see. Weariness left lines around her eyes. A straggle of dark hair curled down her cheek. She needed a month's worth of sleep.

"I thought I'd see if you all figured out about the pool. I'd like to join you if I can," I pasted on the perfect smile, feeling a bit of chagrin around the edges at inviting myself along.

Sarah bounded up and yanked the door from her mom's hands, "Yeah! You have to come with us!"

"It sounds really nice, doesn't it?" I said.

The girl shrugged. "Yeah, I also want to go explore the rest of the house, but Mom won't let me." She gave me a sharp glance that suggested she wanted to go explore what we'd seen below the house.

Eleanor rolled her eyes. "I know, I know. But we're guests here. I don't think we should just wander the hallways unescorted." She smiled at me as if to say, *Kids!*

But Sarah stayed serious. "But maybe there's other people to talk to here. Maybe there's someone I can play with."

Her words set off my internal alarms. Sarah knew enough about what was going on that she'd never ask that unless she was hinting at something.

"You could come hang out in my room for a bit, if you want?" I offered. "Let your mom and Joey rest?" I shrugged a little, like it wasn't much of anything, doing my best to keep up with whatever Sarah was up to.

"Yeah!"

"No, no, you took up most of her morning already. We're going to go for a swim soon." Eleanor's words ran right over Sarah's, and the small girl's face crumpled in frustration.

A strange, fierce protectiveness washed through me, wanting nothing more than to grab Sarah by the hand and race off with her down the hallway, even if I couldn't understand why. Eleanor hadn't done anything to convince me something was wrong, other than Sarah's peculiar behavior. Maybe the girl truly was just being paranoid.

"Okay, well, I'll see you later." I held up a hand and backed away, watching as Sarah's horrified expression disappeared behind the door.

But, she'd be safe with her mom. She had to be.

David. I had to find him. Now. Even if I wasn't entirely sure about trusting him, he would still want to ensure everyone was okay. And, shit, make sure he was okay, too.

I swung around and kept up the carefully controlled stroll back to my room. No sense in alerting Timothy any more than we already potentially had. My knock on David's door was a little more forceful than was normal, but I didn't care. In some sense, maybe he did deserve some kind of warning of my inner turmoil.

Angling my hip against the doorjamb, I crossed my arms and waited. Thirty seconds later, I knocked again.

Another round. Nothing. Not a sound from inside, and I sincerely doubted he could sleep through the battering force I inflicted on his door.

He wasn't in there. Or he was restrained. Or worse. Which meant what?

Images flashed through my imagination of him being strapped to that chair, just like Eleanor, and my stomach rolled. Which said something about my feelings that I refused to dwell on until I knew he was safe.

"Okay," I breathed out and turned around. He wasn't in his room. That was all. The house was huge, and he could have easily found someplace else to wander to.

I moseyed down the hallway, humming to myself and looking around without seeing the photos on the walls. Letting my mind wander, I took in the layout of the house, the labs below, and how the two had to map together. The entrance to those labs would most likely be on this end of the house, near our rooms. The kitchen, dining room, and garage were all on the south end, so I'd start looking there. If David were elsewhere in the house, that would be the most logical place to explore.

My intuition didn't particularly like that idea—all the clues pointed to something secretive going on. But I didn't quite have enough pieces clicked together yet to head straight for the lab. If I couldn't find David, that would change rapidly.

The first place I checked was the kitchen and dining area we'd eaten in that morning. A coffee carafe was carefully put together with a tray of assorted fixings, including intoxicating-smelling muffins. To keep up appearances, I fixed myself a small mug and snagged a muffin.

My stomach protested, but I meandered through the room and adjoining ones while eating and slowly sipping from my mug.

No David.

From there, I started down the southernmost hallway I could find, systematically searching each room, opening every unlocked door. If Timothy or someone else was watching the cameras, it would be clear at this point that I was up to something. I just hoped it would be obvious I was looking for David and not randomly snooping.

All my senses were fine-tuned to figuring out my surroundings. I explored every nook, every uneven panel on the wall, each small knot that might allow for some kind of camera or knob, and each small noise—anything that might point to how the house could hide something below.

And I planned. I couldn't very well storm into the lab without some idea of what I might do. While the uncertainty of whatever was inside this place roiled my gut, I was more alarmed by the fact that I was almost entirely blind on who was running it and what they were doing.

TWENTY-SIX

FIFTEEN MINUTES later I reached the foyer that linked the two wings of the house. No sign of David on the north. I slunk into the shadows of the wing of the mansion below our rooms, taking note of any cameras and doing my best to keep out of their range.

I was positive more were hidden in places I couldn't find without a thorough sweep. There was no hope of being unseen. Somewhere I'd trip an alarm, no doubt about it. My heart picked up double-time as I made my way down the main hallway.

First door, bedroom, identical to mine. Second door, bathroom, far too luxurious. Third and fourth doors repeated the pattern. The hallway doglegged around a corner. As I edged closer, shoulder to the wall, I finally heard it.

The scream.

My heart caught in my throat.

It was my voice.

My scream.

But not really.

One of my fellow clones.

Biting down on the panic that slid through me—I had no

time for that kind of thing—I peeked around the end of the hallway.

More doors along the southern wall marked the end of this wing. At the end of the hallway sat one last door. The outline of the house, marked clearly in my head, told me there wasn't enough space for another room to open in that direction.

Another cry, muffled and indistinct, but it still resonated within my skull.

I had to get through that door. Use the element of surprise and see if I could rescue whomever was strapped in that chair.

Eleanor. Was it her? Or another one of us?

Was there really any way to know?

My head swam for a moment as I tried to navigate the strange data. None of this should be possible, none of it real. If I weren't the one living it, I would have politely laughed at anyone suggesting the remote possibility of having a clone, let alone multiples, and then being trapped in a house with a torture chamber in its basement lab.

I could wait. Go back to my room. Use that time to form a better plan. Work out some better details. And hope they didn't come for all of us in the interim.

No, I needed to get down there. Now. Escaping and getting the rest of us out of there—that might be the real trick.

One long blink, a deep breath, and I pushed off the wall, walked around the corner and toward the door. Somewhere below, something beeped. Shit. I set off the alarm. So much for making a surprise appearance.

The door, the same as all the other ones down the hall, was locked. Of course. But I'd had experience with that before. As I brought one leg up and carefully aimed my foot for maximum impact, I briefly wondered if they'd ever considered it a good idea to let me go into my profession of choice. Surely they hadn't considered what I'd learn how to do.

Two kicks later, and the doorjamb hung at an angle. *Thank you, spin class with Celine.* I didn't want to think about how my supposed friend had probably just been keeping tabs on me while forcing me out the door on Saturday mornings.

I pushed the door aside and stepped into a small white room. Twisting around, I took in the low ceiling, plain walls, and lack of windows. It wasn't until my stomach dropped that I realized it was an elevator.

Angling against the edge of the door frame to expose as little of myself as possible, I knelt down and waited. It couldn't be more than a couple of floors down, and I took the precious seconds to breathe deeply and get my heart rate back to normal.

An unseen seam opened against the far wall, slitting the space open to reveal a cement antechamber. I rolled across the floor to keep behind the opening door, mindful of being exposed.

For good reason. As soon as the doors were open far enough, three shots pinged and embedded into the wall behind me.

I peeked an eyeball around the door, noting the security guard. Though dressed in plain clothes, his gun and stance screamed military. I made my move.

It took him one second too long to spot me as he moved to enter the elevator with me. I popped up beside him, silent, a hand on his gun. He still got off another round, this one spitting up cement from the floor. But a moment later, I had the weapon in my hand.

"Nothing personal," I explained, meeting his brown eyes. He tensed, his fist rising to strike, but I was faster.

A lunging kick swept his feet out from under him. A painful crunch made me really hope he never wanted to have children, and as he moaned, I used the butt of the gun to knock him out.

Armed, I had a much better chance. Checking the clip and chamber, I inched my way along the wall to the metal door with bullet proof glass that opened into the gleaming lab I'd glimpsed from outside.

Another cry. Pitiful. Painful. In my voice.

A shiver traced down my spine and I had to swallow back the panic that arced through my chest. I didn't know how I recognized it, really. Most cries sounded the same—enough pain can mask any voice. But this one I knew. Somewhere at gut level, it sounded like me in pain.

The commotion drew attention, of course, and as I ducked through the metal door, hurried footsteps caught my awareness.

Three of them. Tennis shoes. The way they moved, noisy and without grace, told me they weren't trained. I took cover in the first place I could find, slinking, bent at the waist, along one of the rows of waist-high counters that ran down the center of the room. Equipment and open shelving in the middle of the countertop obscured my view more than I wanted, but it still allowed me to get out of the way.

"Carl's out cold!" one of the people screeched, panic taking their voice up enough octaves to pierce my ears.

"Shit!" The heavy door slammed shut behind them and their voices became muffled. I waited a moment, barely breathing, hoping they'd make a run for it and leave me to getting Eleanor the hell out of here.

"Move…psycho in there…loose!" An angry tone seemed to urge the others on. I scanned the lab benches, wondering what I could use as a weapon. Would any of the bottles of chemicals in here burn if I threw it on someone?

"Can't leave her…" Another's voice, the one with the whine kicked up again.

I edged farther along the lab bench, one ear on them, the

other listening for Eleanor, who had fallen disconcertingly quiet.

"Fuck's sake…doesn't even have her own soul!" The last phrase came through the door perfectly clear. There was no question about who they were talking about. Me.

The words slammed into my chest as if I'd taken a solid kick. What. The. Hell?

That seemed to be enough to satisfy the worrier as they all raced to the far wall, the whispering suction of a hermetic door sealing shut leaving the room in ringing silence.

Do they not care because she doesn't even have her own soul?

I didn't know why that mattered. Not believing in such a thing as a soul, it still caught me in some strange way, tangling into my thoughts, and I knew I'd be wondering about it for a long time to come. After I finished what I came here to do.

A quick sweep of the cavernous room told me I was alone down here, though I knew it wouldn't be for long. Along the far wall, the huge bank of windows extended from floor to ceiling. The room still gleamed, despite the tinted glass.

There were rows of lab benches. From the look of things, today's crew was skeletal in comparison to how many people normally worked here, each with individual workstations.

Along the southern edge, a series of clear doors stood open. I edged closer, not worried about someone seeing me, and peered closer. Cot. Sink. Toilet. There were five cells, painfully white in the sun. Four of the doors were open.

The last cell in the back corner housed a tall and lanky figure, sitting on the bed with his head in his hands. Something deep unwound an inch inside me at seeing him alive. Some part of me had been certain he was dead, just like his brother. Whether or not I could trust him had no bearing on how much I wanted to hug him now that I knew he wasn't gone.

"David!" I knocked on the glass door and a ripple of electricity shot up my arm, searing through my senses. I swore and rubbed my arm, desperate to get rid of the stinging ache that made it feel as if it had been doused in boiling water.

David looked up at me. I fought to regain a semblance of composure, knowing we had limited time, but David's amused smirk at my shenanigans made me shake my head.

I raised an eyebrow. It wasn't as if I *had* to rescue him.

"We have about two minutes," his voice filtered through the door, muffled but still tinged with laughter.

The control panel was off to one side, coded, of course.

"It's pound-seven-three-five-oh-eight-five," David recited as I went to investigate.

I stared at him through the glass.

"What? I paid attention when they tossed me in here."

Of course he did.

The doors opened with a soft sucking sound, and the brightly lit cell dimmed behind him. He stepped into the lab next to me and my breath caught. I hadn't fully appreciated how concerned I'd been about him until he was standing beside me. For a second, I stared at him, and before I let my brain think better of it, I wrapped my arms around his middle and hugged him close. Breathing in the smell of him, I couldn't fully brush aside the tinge of antiseptic that had seeped into his clothes from our surroundings. Nor the way a completely different ripple of electricity wound through my body.

"How long were you in there?" I asked, stepping away and studiously ignoring the shocked look David wore. Surely a random hug wasn't that terrible.

"Timothy and some other goon snagged me as soon as you pulled out of the garage." I glanced up to see him frown, eyebrows drawn nearly together, clearly wanting to say and do more.

To spare him the awkwardness after my impulsivity, I waved us toward the windows, feeling stupid for not moving instantly toward Eleanor, even if our little interaction couldn't have been more than fifteen seconds. Still, some part of my brain clung to the feel of him, desperate for the hope he was what he said he was.

In synch, we jogged toward where I hoped she still was, following my mental map of the space from the photo.

"They took her, too." David's tone dropped to deadly, already knowing who I was searching for. "She put up one hell of a fight."

"There's someone upstairs who looks like her—has the same clothes and speaks the same," I murmured. "But Sarah knows it's not her."

David frowned as we emerged in the open space near the windows.

The chair with the restraints was occupied. Eleanor's dark hair spilled over her face, her eyes closed and her chest rising and falling.

"Who's upstairs?" I whispered, hurrying to her side. My fingers found the first strap and I hurried to unlace them.

David joined me, the two of us making quick work of the bindings.

"How do I know you're you, if there's another one of us upstairs working for Timothy?" I asked, keeping my voice low so we didn't wake Eleanor quite yet.

"Schrödinger's cat on the train and you've always liked the pink Power Ranger," David answered quickly, his eyes flashing to mine in challenge.

Perhaps our emails weren't a complete waste of time.

"You studied biotech at Oxford, and you don't have any idea where to find a good cup of coffee," I replied.

He looked around to protest, but Eleanor sighed and shifted, snapping our attention back to the much more pressing issue: getting us all out of there.

David finished unbuckling her restraints while I looked

around. Joey had been strapped to whomever was upstairs. Was this really Eleanor?

"What if this isn't her?" I asked in a low voice while David kneeled next to her feet. I brushed the hair back from the woman's face, the now familiar weirdness at seeing myself lying there settling into my gut.

"Then she's another one of us, and maybe it'll buy us some time. We still haven't gotten Faith, and there are a couple more survivors of your cohort after her."

Pressing my lips together, I didn't tell him that I'd already considered that. "What if they side with Timothy and the rest?"

"Stockholm syndrome only goes so far when they try to kill you all the time." David gripped Eleanor's forearm and hip, twisting to angle her over his shoulder. "We'll work that out when she comes around."

EVEN WITH THE LOAD, David's steps toward the exit were as swift as mine. A glance of frightened faces pressed against glass—the scientists—watched us leave.

"They said something." I spoke in a low tone as we ran. Somehow the words had weight and I needed to share them to lessen their load. "They said we don't have souls." I shook my head like the thought was crazy.

David slowed. It took me a moment to glance back, around an assortment of pipettes, to see his expression.

"It's utterly ridiculous, you know," I snapped, waving for him to pick up his feet, waiting for him to agree with me.

But he didn't speak. For a few minutes we focused on working together to angle Eleanor through the metal door and into a stairwell, almost hitting her head several times. David's breathing grew labored as I helped push him up the stairs. Eleanor remained unconscious, her head lolling against his shoulder.

"Let me make sure it's clear." I ducked around him at the top of the stairs, confident this was where they'd trap us. If it were me, that's what I would have done.

I edged the door open, not sure what I'd be happier to see

on the other side: Timothy's gap-toothed grin or a gun barrel. Both seemed equally sinister.

But the hallway remained empty. The alarm continued ringing, faint and indistinct.

"This is too easy," I muttered as we hurried toward the front doors.

David grunted in agreement. "We still have to get the others. The kids. And my dad."

For a fraction of a second, I debated arguing to leave Aaron behind. Surely he was in on this fiasco. David guessed I'd be thinking along such lines and gave me a pointed look. "We still need his help, no matter what."

"His help to end up in some other 'safe house'?" I emphasized the air quotes a little more than necessary.

David narrowed his eyes, urging me forward with his chin. We rounded the last corner in the hallway, my mind half occupied by a slew of colorful potential comebacks I wanted to use. The hallway ended in the foyer, which was definitely not empty.

Chad stood in front of the door, hands on jean-clad hips, a gun conspicuously gripped in his right hand. Three options: take him out, convince him of the error of his ways, or use him as leverage. I chose the last.

"You should stay there," Chad advised, his Southern accent contradicting the annoyance in his words.

"So you can do what?" I kept my tone light. Friendly. The Game was on.

Chad's eyes darted toward the other hallway opening and David walked toward it, scanning the shadows.

"I think you need to reevaluate some of your life choices, Chad," I suggested with a coy laugh, for all the world acting like I was flirting with him.

"I think you both need to stand against that wall and hold very, very still." Seeming to get himself together, Chad raised his weapon and trained it on David's back.

"Don't you think that might be a bit hasty?" I sauntered closer, all smiles and doe eyes.

"I *think* I have my orders. Now get against the wall and keep your damn mouth shut."

Too late. He let me get too close. His fault.

A sweeping kick and a well-aimed fist to his gut and he was down. I checked the gun, a quick laugh bubbling up. "It's not even loaded. Did we catch you by surprise?"

Chad glared up at me, his face twisted into a snarl.

I kept a foot planted firmly on his chest. If he knew what to do, it wouldn't have been much of an obstacle to take me down. He didn't. "We need a car and a code to get out of here."

"I'm not helping you." His pulse ticked under his jaw like he'd run ten miles, and sweat dripped down the side of his face.

"Oh? Well, I think we'll have to see about that." Tucking the unloaded gun into my waistband, I cinched a hand under his arm, locking my fingers around the tendon there in a practiced move that would radiate pain throughout his entire body.

He swore, and it took very little effort to get him to his feet.

"This one *is* loaded," I promised, grinning like I'd just offered him a chocolate treat. I held the security guard's gun with the business end planted against his chest. "And I will use it."

The temptation to make a run for it flashed behind his eyes, clear as the swift glance he gave the front door. I flipped off the safety, tilting my head as I let him decide.

"Fine," he growled.

Before this was over, I'd have to do something to keep him quiet. I wasn't sure what, but I didn't particularly want to kill him. I would if I had to, though. If it meant we got out of here.

Angling Chad in front of me and using the gun as a means to push him forward, we headed down the hallway toward Eleanor's room—and whomever was in there.

Damn it, I just wanted answers.

"How are we going to do this?" David asked in a low voice. We both ignored Chad's smirk.

How did I think this might work? God, I hated hare-brained schemes like this, planning on the fly with no exit strategy. But today we didn't have a choice.

"We knock, and then drag them out kicking and screaming if we have to?"

David nodded, his mouth pinching at the real meaning of my words: I had no idea.

We approached Eleanor's door at a half jog. The fact that we had yet to encounter any additional guards didn't bode well, but I couldn't see a way to deal with that now.

I knocked, trying to keep the pounding urgency from my fists, when what I really wanted to do was knock the door down and pull Sarah and Joey to safety. Who or what was in there as Eleanor's double, or something. Someone. I didn't know, but I wanted those kids safe above all else.

We heard scampering footsteps, and then Sarah threw open the door. She was dressed in a swimsuit, new tags still dangling from one side, and her eyes went overly huge at the sight of us.

"Who's there?" the woman called from the interior.

"It's, it's everyone," Sarah responded.

"Come on! Grab some shoes," I urged. "We're breaking out of here."

A pause from inside, as if I just asked her to wrestle the Loch Ness Monster.

"What in the hell?" Eleanor, or someone in Eleanor's clothes, came around the corner in the room. The shock in her eyes mirrored her daughter's as she caught sight of us. "Who the hell is that?" She raised a finger that trembled as she pointed to the prostrate form over David's shoulder.

They wore the exact same clothing. Their hair was the same. It certainly made the whole clone thing even more dramatic. Even I, who didn't look like I'd been run through a person-sized copy machine, felt an unnerving twist in my gut.

"Good God," Chad muttered from beside me.

I dug the barrel of the gun a little more forcefully into his side, cocking my head as I stared at him. "What do you know about all of this?"

Chad just bared his teeth in a painful facsimile of a grin.

Reaching out, I used my index finger to poke, fast and hard, against the hollow of his throat, just above his sternum. It would leave a bruise.

Chad coughed and twisted, rubbing a hand against the spot. "What the hell?"

"Think about this, Chad: I have a gun. We are going to get out of here. And if you think I'll leave you alive if you don't help, you're mistaken. Getting on my good side is in your best interest." I only bothered to reason with him so I didn't have to fire the gun and draw more attention. Though working him over a bit might get his tongue limbered up.

Chad shook his head, real fear showing in the white all around his irises. "I, I don't know a lot. They don't tell me much," he sputtered.

"What *do* they tell you?" David's low voice rumbled from behind us.

"You all are the third gen-generation." His voice caught, and for a fleeting moment I felt pity for him. It passed. "Your generation shares whatever it is that makes you alive with the person they cloned you from, but they've upgraded the models. Now, they just need to make the bodies. Then they can pop others into them. Like changing the batteries or something."

"What in the hell?" I breathed, rocking back on my heels.

The dominoes were tipping faster now, and I couldn't keep up. "You've got to be kidding."

Chad ducked his head and looked away, shoulders slumped. He wasn't kidding, not at all.

I didn't see her coming. Not until it was too late, and pain erupted in my jaw as my head snapped to the side.

The imposter, Eleanor the Wannabe, panted next to me, her fists up, giving me a second to gather my wits after her first punch. She shouldn't have made that mistake.

No, it wasn't a mistake. The twitch near her eye gave it away.

"How much control do you have?" I hissed, fingers exploring my cheek, my tongue running over my molars to ensure they were all accounted for.

The way she stared at me was chilling—eyes wide with shock over what she'd done, yet body poised to do it again. Somehow, they learned how to control us, or at least her. She certainly wasn't a third-generation model.

"Then I'm very sorry about this." I used the butt of the gun and swung at her, connecting as she moved to hit me again. Her eyes rolled back and she slumped down.

"If we take her with us, will they be able to use her from a distance?" David asked, looking down.

No one had an answer.

"We'll have to keep her tied up and blindfolded, but I don't want to leave her here." No matter what, she was one of us. She didn't deserve what they did to her. Even though bringing her felt a little too much like tying a homing beacon onto ourselves and shouting for our pursuers to find us.

"Can we go now?" Sarah peeked out from around the corner and my heart twisted.

"Grab your brother and anything you're going to need," I instructed. Hauling Chad further into the room, I watched as Sarah efficiently gathered their things into a small pile. She'd had the foresight to put on normal clothes while the rest of us argued at the door. Smart kid.

Joey, who at this point had to be the most well-behaved baby in the world, was sound asleep. I took the bags Sarah handed me and she scooped her brother up.

"We need to hurry," she whispered.

"What do you know?" I asked, ushering her toward the door.

Sarah's lips were white where they pressed together, but she didn't speak, just cradled her brother closer.

"Pick her up," I snapped to Chad, motioning at the prone form of not-really-Eleanor on the ground.

He shook his head, his glare enough to make me appreciate his gumption a touch more.

Another jab to the hollow of his throat convinced him to heft the woman over his shoulder and make for the door. David was already in the hallway, waiting, somehow balancing the real Eleanor over his shoulder while keeping lookout.

"We need a vehicle," David murmured, motioning us toward the far end of the hallway where the stairs led down to the kitchen and garages.

"How are we…" I paused at the curious look Sarah gave me. No, now wasn't the time to muse over our chances. We would make it out of there.

Dropping down the stairs ahead of the others, I peeked around the corner and my heart rose to my throat. Good God. And we thought this might be as simple as stealing a car.

Okay, I wasn't quite that naïve, but it had been a pleasant dream while it lasted.

Around the corner stood Timothy and five other men—the remainder of his security forces. The lack of earlier resistance suddenly made sense. He knew we'd all want to escape together, so why not let us do the hard work? Then he'd have an easier job of scooping us all up.

Too bad he must have been completely unaware of what David and I used to do for a living.

I held up a hand and the others came to a stop behind me. David slammed a palm over Chad's mouth not a moment too soon, stopping the man from revealing our immediate presence. The chances a camera hadn't already alerted the others were slim.

Okay. We had two plausible options. One, go back the way we came and attempt to get out of this place on foot. But we had two unconscious people, a child, and a baby, which also made any potential open firefight an unpleasant option.

Which left the second option: Negotiation.

And there was one more factor at play. Aside from the five men with guns and two extra clips each, Timothy stood triumphantly over a chair holding the slumped form of Aaron.

David wasn't going to go along with letting his father die, and I couldn't quite work out how to get out of this scenario with him alive.

Which left us exactly in the type of escape scenario I always hated—one we couldn't get out of without collateral damage. How many days of my life had I spent coming up with failsafe plans to ensure I didn't end up in a situation like this at work? Yet here I was, walking right into one when it was my own ass on the line.

God damn it, I really did not sign up for this mess.

TWENTY-EIGHT

"YOU KNOW what I need to do." I shifted and spoke to David, keeping my tone barely above a breath.

He met my eyes, staring at me like I might have the answers to a solution he couldn't quite work out himself. A flare of heat, so at odds with the situation around us, rose within me. Double damn it. I needed to make it out of this alive.

"I've got your back," he murmured, subtly shifting Eleanor's weight on his shoulder.

I turned back to the corner, taking a deep breath and setting up what I would say like a branching web of thoughts. I could do this. I had to do this.

The gun went into my pocket—easy access, but not an obvious threat from the start.

Fixing my face took a few extra heartbeats. I had to figure out the best tack to take, and then arrange my features accordingly. The wide-eyed shock seemed to pull at my features, reminding them it wasn't real. But it was necessary.

A deep breath and I slid a hand around the corner of the stairwell and followed it around. A chorus of hammers being cocked greeted me.

"What's going on?" I stepped back, my hand on my heart, hoping I wasn't totally overdoing it. I searched for Timothy's eyes, knowing he pulled all the strings.

"I would ask the same of you," he answered conversationally, his gap-toothed smile grating. Seriously… why didn't he get that fixed?

"I was just coming down for a bite to eat." The cadence of my lie was flawless. Even someone highly trained in detecting untruths would have been fooled.

"Oh? After raiding my lab?" Timothy wasn't having any of it. Not that he was so bad at the Game himself. His smile was fixed and he seemed for all the world to be enjoying himself.

I took a few steps forward, the hallway opening up as it merged with the kitchen. Wary glances and shuffled footsteps from the men greeted me. None of their faces stood out.

"What were you thinking, going down to the labs?" Timothy tutted, angling a hip against the chair where Aaron was restrained.

"I was curious." I shrugged. No sense lying about it. "What else did you expect from us?"

Timothy must not have expected the truth and it showed. Good. That meant I could still trick him. "I expected you to be smart," he retorted. "To keep your nose out of places it didn't belong."

"Oh really? Because I would say that my nose definitely belongs in the lab where you made me. And my clones. And whatever it is you made that looks like Eleanor. I don't know what you thought you were doing, but making someone like me meant that, yeah, I was going to be curious."

The twitch of a grin on Timothy's lips almost made my rant worth it.

"What were you hoping to find?"

"The truth."

Timothy nodded and I stared him down while he rolled

his shoulders, giving me a narrow-eyed glare. "What if I could give you the truth?"

I pressed my lips together. "I'm not sure I want it now. Not after what I've seen."

Timothy's laugh rang out, causing some of his goons to glance at each other and shift their feet uncomfortably. "I don't think you quite know what I'm saying."

"Maybe I don't, but I do know I'm not willing to sit here with guns pointed at me while you try to come up with a way to explain it."

Timothy seemed to consider this, scanning me from toe to head and back. What did he see? Certainly not what I did when I scoured a person. I knew from the long look I'd already given him that his shoes had only been worn once, his tanning bed had a bulb out, and his nerves elevated his pulse well above what his cholesterol level made healthy.

His perusal was much too long, and I resisted the urge to squirm, which was surely his intention. A gamble he lost, at any rate.

"You've pieced together a few things about your status here, correct?"

"A few."

"And you may have some kind of understanding about Aaron's connection to David?"

No emotion crossed my face, but a distinct urge to gulp was hard to suppress. "David's cloned from Aaron." A small bit of information that wasn't very important to help loosen his tongue.

"Should something happen to Aaron, there's a distinct probability something will happen to David. They share their essence. Their soul, you might call it should you be religious. This connection can be quite fickle. Killing off part of Aaron's soul would hurt him immensely. But killing the root of the soul in Aaron might end all of his clones."

Well, fuck. I hadn't had enough time to consider such a

possibility in the five minutes since Chad had clued me in. It must have been why they were slowly picking us off one by one—a mass attack on us all would probably have killed the root clone, and whomever I was cloned from was too valuable, or they'd just have already offed her and I'd be long gone.

Aaron, on the other hand, might not warrant the same protection. Not after running and saving me. Although he did seem to be working with Timothy. What was I missing here?

"If I kill Aaron, your boyfriend doesn't stand a chance." Timothy smiled at me, and with a sweeping motion, indicated that the others drop their weapons.

The fumble and shuffle of feet effectively hid the swirl of thoughts that came from his revelation. How was I supposed to get us all out of this situation? The new information meant we had to get Aaron out too. To be honest, I wouldn't have minded terribly if Aaron didn't survive this mess, not after he got us into this mansion of horrors, but now... I refused to let David die because of Aaron's mistakes.

"Why don't you bring the rest of your party in to join us?" Timothy asked, confident enough to turn his back and pull up another chair to sit next to Aaron.

Of course he knew. Swallowing a sigh, I cleared my throat and called for the others. "Come on in, guys."

I glanced back to catch sight of David, Eleanor still slumped over his broad shoulders, keeping his gun angled under Chad's chin. Chad shuffled in and unceremoniously dropped the imposter Eleanor, still out cold, to the floor.

Sarah scuttled into the corner, wide-eyed and terrified, still clasping sleeping Joey tightly.

Shit. I would do anything to get them out of this mess. But now that we were in it, only some massive on-the-fly planning would get us free. Oh, how I hated not having a concrete plan.

Timothy grinned at us all, patting Aaron's unconscious

head. "Did dear old dad tell you about that contingency?" he asked David.

David shook his head, a blank mask artfully locked in place. Nothing would ruffle him, not this deep into the Game.

"Well, it did make for a rather interesting failsafe. Of course, we had no idea that would be the case when the first batch of you got old enough for dissection. We damn near killed Dr. Reynolds before we realized what we were inadvertently doing to her." His smug grin didn't reveal the gap between his incisors.

"What do you want from us?" One more second of listening to this man and I'd put a bullet through his brain.

Timothy just let off a braying laugh, chilling me. "Isn't it obvious?"

I fought the urge to look at David and roll my eyes. Instead, I stared at the thinning hair Timothy tried to hide with his bun.

"Well, I would have assumed you would've pieced more together. Though you are new to this, aren't you, Diana?"

"Just tell us what you want," David growled, pressing his gun harder into Chad's throat.

"I'm not terribly inclined to fill the lab rats in on the final project, to be honest. You're merely here to ensure you're not in the way." Seeming satisfied that he'd told us enough, Timothy got to his feet and patted Aaron one more time. "I think I'll keep him close at hand so you don't think of something crude to do in the meantime."

With a pointed look at one of his guards, Timothy spun and made his way toward the back entrance of the kitchen. The guards, who seemed to have been waiting for this, snapped into action.

Too slow.

I hit Timothy in his right shoulder. He had a bulletproof vest on, which left this area exposed, and it meant he wouldn't be able to fire back.

The guards froze for a moment, mouths gaping. David and I lost no time waiting for them to collect themselves.

I didn't want to kill any of them. Not with Sarah watching. Thankfully, I had decent aim. Landing shots that took down their ability to shoot back was first priority. When the first one launched himself at me, I ducked out of the way and landed a clean blow at the nape of his neck. He went down.

David shoved Chad to the floor and was handling another on his own, but Eleanor was a handicap. One security guy cradled his arm, huddled against the wall with blood oozing between his fingers. I almost took pity on him and left him conscious, but that wouldn't be fair.

The last two guards ganged up on me, and even with my training, their bigger size left me at a disadvantage. The blur of moves and evades settled into sharp clarity when one ended up with an arm around my neck, the other poised to pummel me in the gut.

"Mister! Help!" Sarah appeared out of nowhere, tugging on the shirt of the guy behind me. I could just make her out, all wide eyes and little Joey attached to her shirt with two fists full of fabric. The man hesitated. *Perfect.* I slid from his grasp and landed him on his ass. David stepped in and together we took out the last guard.

We spared each other a small grin as the man slid bonelessly to the floor between us.

A moan from across the room made me turn to look at Timothy, blood seeping onto the tile floor behind the breakfast bar.

He glared at me, a streak of red running down the side of his face. "We'll find you. No matter where you go."

"Funny. It seems we can take care of ourselves." I motioned toward his fallen men.

"You have no idea, do you?" Timothy winced as he shifted. "No idea what you really are."

I glanced around the room, cataloguing what we'd done,

measuring the breaths of each of the men, calculating the time we had until they woke, noting the angle of the sun through the windows. "No, I have a pretty damn good idea."

With that, I shepherded Sarah with baby Joey toward the garage as David heaved Eleanor back onto his shoulder. At some point Chad had caught a stray blow and wasn't moving. Fine. We could let ourselves out. I struggled but managed to haul the imposter Eleanor out the door. She weighed less than me—another item against her—and thankfully it wasn't too difficult to heft her with my arms under her armpits.

The garage was cavernous, but after a quick look around we found keys in a mounted cupboard. Choosing a vehicle took a few minutes. There were plenty of fast cars, but with a family in tow, we needed something spacious.

Finally, we found a Range Rover in the back corner. I got the unconscious not-Eleanor settled into the luggage compartment, binding her hands, feet, and mouth with duct tape left on a workbench.

"My dad," David blurted after belting in the limp real Eleanor in the back seat as Sarah slid in on the other side.

"Shit." I groaned. We had no choice but to go back in for him.

David grimaced and slammed the door on the Rover. "I don't want that nut job to be able to drop me whenever he gets sick of my dad."

The sheer scale of that knowledge slammed into me as I made sure the kids were as secured as possible. Sarah had gotten Joey nestled onto the seat between her and her unconscious mother where he was watching everything going on with wide little eyes.

Whoever my root was could be killed at any time, but at what cost? Apparently, it was worth ensuring we were killed off one by one instead of just offing her and taking care of the problem at large. Also, fifteen identical women dropping dead around the country at the same time would surely draw some attention.

David didn't look back as he raced toward the door into the house. Go with him? Or stay and protect those we had already gotten out?

Sarah tugged her little brother closer. That was my answer. Not that I wanted to lose David, but I certainly wasn't going to leave these three at the mercy of the crazies in that house.

Behind the wheel, I flashed Sarah a grin through the rear-view mirror and extricated the car from the dozen others in the garage. A flash of rage made me want to smash the Rover into them all, demolition derby style, as retribution for the anger, frustration, and devastation of my former life. But I knew better. Leaving the car without any identifying marks would be best. We could easily switch the plates later.

That did leave the others with all the vehicles at their disposal, though. Many of them were powerful enough to overtake us without breaking the red line.

I threw the Range into park near the door that led into the house. "I'll be right back."

"You've gotta make sure they can't follow us, huh?" Sarah asked.

God, that kid was going to kick some serious ass as an adult. But what about her? Would she die too, if our root was taken out? There was no way I could fully process all of those implications, so yet again I shoved them aside.

I left the engine running and went out to assess the situation. How long it would take for David to extract Aaron had far too many variables, so I needed something quick and easy that would take out the vehicles. There were too many to individually pop their hoods and disconnect the batteries. Same went for puncturing tires. With how I felt, a little mayhem seemed like the best option.

A large red gas can sat off to the side near the workbench

where I'd snagged the duct tape. From the weight of it, it was mostly full—five gallons at least.

A quick glance around pinpointed the best places to spread the gas to ensure any flames caught the tanks on the cars as well.

It took five precious minutes to splash the gas liberally along the side wall, ensuring the building caught fire, and then along the row of cars, the ATVs, and the doorway itself. No way were they getting a vehicle out of this mess. There were probably others around that belonged to the staff, plus the shitty van we came in, but those would take time to get to, and their speed wouldn't match the Rover's.

I couldn't help looking over at the door to the house every few seconds. David wasn't back yet, and every minute that ticked off in my head made my heart rate creep higher. Something was wrong. He'd been shot. Killed. And I was out here, not helping him.

Snagging a few rags and lighter from the workbench, I fashioned a lousy Molotov cocktail and went back to the car.

"Where's David?" Sarah asked as I got behind the wheel. My heart was in my throat when I looked back at her. She nodded in reply to my expression, her small face pinching in concern.

I wanted to comfort her, to climb into the backseat and ensure she was comfortable and wipe away her frown, but somehow I knew she wouldn't appreciate it. And truthfully, my own thoughts were roaring so loud, cataloging every small detail from the dripping of the gas on the vehicles, to the purr of the Rover's engine, to the time we might have until someone called in reinforcements, that I knew comforting another was out of my skill range.

That was even worse.

The ping of a bullet against the far wall of the garage got my attention.

David emerged less than a second later with blood

seeping down the front of his shirt. Aaron was slung over his shoulders, bouncing against David's backside as he came closer. Behind him, one of the guards gave chase. Clearly, he'd regained consciousness faster than anticipated. Blood ran down his arm.

Rolling down the passenger window a few inches, I shouted at Sarah to cover her ears.

David saw what I was doing and ducked at just the right moment for my bullet to reach his tail. The man slammed to a halt and dropped.

"Get in!"

David all but flung his father into the backseat, letting him thud onto the floor in front of the bench seat. Sarah pulled her feet up and all I saw was her wide eyes as David landed in the passenger's seat and I threw the car into gear.

"Throw this at the puddle near the door," I instructed, handing him the bundle of rags and leftover beer bottle as I sped the car toward the garage door.

David held out a corner of the rag without question as I lit the lighter and set the rags blazing. In one swift movement, David dropped the makeshift bomb out of the window, directly into the puddle of gas I'd staged to get the business started.

We spun into the open air, the whoosh of flame behind us flaring in the mirrors.

"Whoa," Sarah whispered from the back seat.

"We're not out of this yet," I advised, pushing the gas pedal all the way down to the floor board and squealing the tires out of the driveway, down the lane to the main road.

"What about the gate?" David asked.

Shit. The gate. Did I ram it with the Rover? Wait for it to open? The heavy metal contraption would be a formidable foe for the SUV.

David met my eyes across the center console as we raced down the hill.

"Could they have locked the place down already?" I asked.

"The guard who chased me was awake when I got there. They definitely had time to do it."

The trees outside my window whipped past. There had to be a way to get out of this place.

At the last bend in the road, I caught sight of what was ahead of us and laughed. A strangled sound, to be sure, but it still felt good.

The little Jetta was crammed full—I counted at least five heads. The one that twisted around to look at us was one of the scientists from the lab. They were making a run for it, and we were going to follow them out of that gate.

"I want to run them over," I muttered to David.

"I wouldn't blame you," David agreed, leaning forward to peer at them out the front window.

"Hmph." I shook my head, weighing the options and realizing all the issues associated with slamming them off the road—or worse. Instead, I rode their bumper as they sped through the opening gate.

The Jetta, once clear, swung to the side, the driver braking hard enough to give his passengers whiplash. He threw his hands up, the occupants of the car watching as we sped past. I really wanted to roll the window down and scream, "See who has a soul now!" but figured that might not have been well taken. For now, I just wanted to get as far away from Fireside Cottage as possible.

"Where are we going?" David asked, bringing up the next question I didn't have an answer for.

I kept my eyes on the road, wishing there was some answer I could come up with that would somehow solve our problem. No matter how I turned it over in my mind, I didn't have any clue what was best.

"Any ideas?" I asked.

David's silence confirmed my fears.

Behind us, a bloom of orange rose above the treetops, followed a moment later by a roar of sound that seemed to rattle the car.

"Well, I imagine the best option for now is to get as far away from *that* as possible," David observed, watching out the rear window as plumes of black smoke rose into the sky. "What in the hell did you use to blow that place up?"

"Just gasoline, and maybe a few cars." I bit my lip as a strangled laugh rose within me. I'd always worried that if I couldn't control my brain, it might someday crack wide open, like an egg left too long in the sun. The last few days had pushed me closer to that point than ever before.

Would that harm my root clone? What could I do to get to her?

All I wanted was a few days of peace so we could plan our next move. This whole mess was far from being over, but I needed a breather. Too bad there was no time for that.

TWENTY-NINE

"WE NEED to go to San Jose." Sarah spoke up about ten minutes later. I had a death grip on the steering wheel and was driving as fast as my training allowed me to, though the thought of letting David behind the wheel was tempting.

Except David was currently sitting in the passenger's seat, sewing up the bullet graze on his left arm. I'd never been so grateful for tinted windows that kept anyone from looking in to see the mess of bloody rags and the amazing torso David revealed when he peeled off his shirt. Not that I should have been looking at his torso. At least not while driving.

Was it a clone thing that made me attracted to him? Was that even possible? Hell, I didn't even know how much I trusted him. But I couldn't help little peeks when I got a chance.

"Why?" I asked Sarah, squealing the tires a bit as we merged onto the main highway around the lake. A steady stream of traffic clogged our progress as the perfect summer day shimmered off the lake to our left.

Sarah poked her head between the seats to inspect what David was doing. He ignored her, his lips pinched together and face looking pale under his olive coloring. He was going to pass out before he managed to tug up the last stich.

How he even managed to come up with supplies to sew himself back together was utterly peculiar. Sarah had crawled into the back area with the still-unconscious clone, and after digging around a while, came up with an elaborate first aid kit. Who the hell kept suturing supplies in a first aid kit?

"Why San Jose?" I asked again. "The other clone?"

Sarah wrinkled her nose at David before she looked at me. I slowed down behind a rusty truck going five miles under the speed limit and glanced at her pensive expression.

She nodded. "Yeah. The notes mentioned something about her. Aaron wrote that he thought she might be the last one alive."

"There should be more. There were fifteen in our batch," I reported, recalling the paperwork I'd read back in the camper. Some of them had apparently been systematically eliminated by their watchers (fucking Celine!), but not all of them.

"Aaron said there were only you three left." Sarah grimaced and gave me a pained look. "He said he wanted you to think there were more so you'd be 'more invested in planning to save them all.'" She tried to mimic the older man's voice.

My stomach soured and I had to swallow back bile. There were only three of us left out of fifteen. That thing was in the back of the Rover was from another generation, and after what I saw, I was less inclined to worry about it. Something was fundamentally different with it since it didn't think like us. *Couldn't* think like us, more likely.

Faith. What did I know about her? Much less than I knew about Eleanor, since Aaron's file on her was sparse. She was a teacher—an art teacher, which boggled my mind. I appreciated art, certainly, but the thought of being creative in that way mystified me.

"So, San Jose. Do we have an address?" I asked aloud, not sure who to address.

"Yes." The croaked response alerted us all that Aaron had woken up.

David had secured his wrists and legs, pretty much attaching him to the side of the vehicle, soon after we blasted away from Fireside Cottage. He reminded me of a fly caught in a silver web. That was where he deserved to be.

David paused in tugging his own flesh together to look back at his father. Pain twisted his features into something of a grimace, and the look he gave Aaron was downright murderous.

"Don't think I saved your ass out of some kindness. I just want to put a bullet in your head myself," David growled.

The words shot goose bumps up my arms.

Aaron sighed and didn't say anything.

"What happens to me if you die?" David asked next.

Aaron opened and closed his mouth a few times before deciding on an answer. I passed the rusty truck, trying hard to keep from speeding, though I wanted to see just how fast I could manage this road. We had to reach Faith before the Future Solutions kill squad did.

Half my brain waited for Aaron's response, and the other half spun its wheels around unanswerable questions. How could they dispose of us that way? In what universe were we less human? Undeserving of the life they gave us?

Did I really not have whatever it was they called a soul? Did it matter? It was bad enough learning I was a clone. That still settled like something sharp in my chest. I'd been made, created, to be the way I was. In some ways that made sense— it explained the years I'd always felt incredibly weird in the world around me, but it did not make me happy about it.

If I hadn't been created, would I have ever existed? Would anyone? I knew some religions preached that every soul had an identity before and after their mortal lives, but I didn't really buy that. Knowing what I did now, what did that mean exactly? Could souls truly be split and given new bodies, become new identities? My very existence seemed to suggest it. If they were telling the truth.

I pushed the thoughts out of my mind. There would be plenty of time for them later. Right now, I just needed to make sure I didn't drive off the road.

Aaron finally seemed to get his brain together enough to reply. "What did Timothy tell you?"

"Answer the question." Aaron couldn't see the white knuckles on David's grip of the armrest. He radiated agony.

"Every time one of you dies, I feel it. It's… painful. When Corbin was killed, it was like being kicked in the head."

"And if you die, what of me?" David showed no emotion at the way Aaron spoke about killing his twin.

"You die." Aaron breathed the words, as if he hated to say them.

"Why?" I cut in.

"We never quite figured it out. It has something to do with the fact that he's tied to my essence; what makes me human. A life force, soul, whatever you want to call it. Part of me had to be split for you to live, but I carry the responsibility of it." The words seemed to drain Aaron and he slumped against the side of the car.

"Fucking hell." David closed his eyes and rocked in his seat.

"How do we know you're telling the truth? You could lie just to make sure we save your pathetic ass." I didn't know which was worse: the possibility he was telling the truth, or that he was lying.

Aaron pondered this a minute. "I guess it's a risk you'll have to take."

David muttered something under his breath I was glad Sarah couldn't hear. Not that we'd been particularly careful about her sensitive young ears, but David's ideas of what to do to his father were downright morbid. He went back to fixing himself up as the car fell into a tense silence.

"What do they want with us? Why didn't they just kill us at the cottage?" I asked, keeping my eyes on the road and willing the cars ahead of me to part like the Red Sea. Too bad that wasn't one of my abilities. That might actually be useful, rather than the collection and organization of a constant barrage of unwanted information.

"Why should I tell you? It's not as if it matters," Aaron grumbled.

"Answer the question," David snapped. "There are a lot worse things than death."

For a moment, Sarah and I stared at one another through the rear-view mirror. I think we both wore the same shocked expression, and the wild urge to laugh bubbled up within me.

Aaron seemed to consider this, like maybe we were bluffing. David snapped off the last knot with his teeth and twisted in his seat, still holding the small curved needle.

I tried to keep my eyes on the road but couldn't stop myself from glancing back as he grabbed one of his father's hands and jammed the needle under Aaron's fingernail. Deep. Blood dripped down Aaron's hand.

We all winced as Aaron's scream hit a soprano note and he fought against the tape that held him. Where did David learn to do such a thing?

Joey's cries filled the car while Sarah tried to shush him, successfully after a few moments. Eleanor stirred, but slumped over further against the window behind me, her breathing turning into a light snore. Shit, she needed to wake soon. I had no idea what to do for her, or what had been done to her, but I desperately needed her awake to confer about everything.

"Ready to talk yet? Because I've got three more needles and we have about six hours until San Jose."

"Fine, fine, I'll talk. Take the needle out!"

David looked over at me, caught my dark expression, then smiled back at his dad. "No."

"Tell us what's going on. Why didn't they kill us back there?" I asked again.

Aaron didn't hesitate this time, though his voice shook when he spoke. "It's the girl. They're interested in her. In her mind. They hoped that by giving you all refuge, they'd get to see what happened if two clones bred."

David looked over at me and the two of us grimaced at the same time. Well, fuck. Don't get me wrong, having little mini Davids *had* crossed my mind back in our emailing days, but no way in hell was I doing that for Future Solutions. I'd sooner rip my own uterus out.

"That's never going to happen," I snapped.

"It may be the only way to make sure you're safe," Aaron threw back.

Of course. Because if we didn't comply, they would kill us. Just wonderful. "We'll figure something else out."

"What might that be? They'll find you anywhere. You can't run."

I had to pry my hands loose from the steering wheel, where the strength of my grip started to make my fingers ache. My head pounded as I tried to estimate how long until Eleanor woke, and what to do about David's arm. And, of course, work out some kind of plan. Anything. There had to be a way out.

And the idea that had been simmering on the back burners started boiling.

"Are you thinking what I'm thinking?" I asked David, a wry grin settling over my features.

His dark eyes flashed, pain almost masking the deep determination that surfaced. Together, we could make them pay. "It's time for a trip to headquarters?"

I nodded, the thought deeply satisfying. Even if it meant the potential of losing myself in the process, Future Solutions needed to learn that messing with our lives wasn't worth it.

"Faith first," Sarah piped up from the backseat.

"Yeah, Faith." I nodded, redoubling my focus on the road. My mental checklist shuffled and filled in the requirements of our new mission. Since we'd lost most everything back at Fireside Cottage, we needed to figure a few things out.

———

"So, where is their headquarters?" I asked, breathing a little easier as we finally emerged onto a larger highway and traffic started moving. We were no longer on such a twisty road, which made my stomach rejoice. The last hour or so was spent in relative silence, each of us needing time to calm down.

David had removed the needle from Aaron's nail. Sarah dozed off after comforting Joey. Eleanor continued to snore. And whatever was in the very back shifted around a few times, but finally quieted down.

I had run mental circles around the truth of my status. A clone. Someone who shared a life essence with another. That made my life a borrowed facsimile. Eleanor and I were just photocopies of the original, whatever that meant. Made, not created. Not truly human.

I was getting desperate for a distraction.

"Aaron took us there many times as kids to be evaluated. It's outside of San Diego."

Well, having it on this coast certainly made things easier. We could drive that far in less than a day.

Another thump from the very back and I cringed. Even if she didn't seem quite human—less than me, at least—whatever was back there still bore my face. "You don't think they can track her, do you? They can control her, so there must be a way to send and receive information."

David shrugged, then winced from the movement. "I would imagine there's a way, but what else can we do with her?"

"Leave her by the side of the road?" It was only half in jest.

"We should at least try speaking with her... it," he offered.

I grimaced. "That would be a good idea. And I want to have a better look at Eleanor. She should have woken up by now."

David shrugged. Neither of us had any clue just what had happened to her. She seemed to be resting peacefully, but I'd feel a whole lot better if she was awake.

Up ahead, the turnoff for Pollock Pines became visible and I merged to get off the freeway.

"Does anyone have any cash?" I asked, pulling into the parking lot of the gas station and staring at the pumps. Everything important was left behind in our rush to escape, which meant no money. The closest safe house for raiding, if Future Solutions hadn't already gotten there, was in San Francisco. The gas needle was already at a quarter tank. No way we'd make it.

No one responded. Grumbling, I turned left out of the lot and wandered down a few streets. Up ahead, a large warehouse stood empty. I did a quick check to ensure no one was around and pulled around the back of the building. The yard was in shadows, which did little to hide the forest of weeds peeking through the cement, or the smattering of glass that coated the asphalt. The back of the warehouse was a mess of rusted metal and broken glass, enough to completely obliterate whatever it had been used for before.

"We aren't dumping a body here, I don't care what kind of spy you might have been," David chided.

The barely perceptible lilt to his words made me laugh. "I was never that kind of spy."

"Uh-huh," Sarah chimed in from the backseat. She must have just woken.

"Stay in the car. This place'll cut your feet to ribbons," I told her.

"We're going to go to a bathroom soon, right?" she asked.

"That's what I'm hoping to do." Sarah wasn't the only one in need of facilities.

Honestly, I could have used a stiff drink.

CHAPTER
THIRTY

OPENING the back of the car, I stared into the shadows at the bound creature wearing my face. She looked back, my dark eyes narrowed in fury. That was just too damn odd.

Ignoring her grumbles, I patted her down. I hadn't had time to search her previously, and now I wondered if there might be anything on her that could be used for ID, money, or tracking. Would I even be able to identify tracking mechanisms? For all I knew, they were built inside of her, allowing Future Solutions to lie in wait for us at a more convenient location.

When I came up with nothing, I grabbed her arms and tugged her into a seated position in the back of the vehicle. The black felt of the car interior made it hard to move her, and it wasn't helped by her futile attempts to kick me in the gut.

"If I take off the tape, you can scream, but no one will hear you. Answering my questions may be the best way to ensure I don't put it back on." I peeled a small bit away from her mouth, picking at the tape slowly as it came away from her skin.

Duct tape should be used for waxing, I learned. How many men had I secured with the stuff over the years? It was never my job to unbind them, and a nagging stone of worry settled with the others in my gut at the thought of what I'd done to them all. We'd have to soak it off her, and Aaron, if it came to that.

As soon as her lips were free, the clone spit and sputtered as if she'd been forced to taste something terrible. I ripped off the rest of the tape and stepped back, waiting for the… thing to make its move. Sarah twisted around in her seat and peeked over to look at us, dark eyes impossibly wide.

"Who are you?" I asked after a heartbeat of silence. My brain may have been cataloguing details, but I certainly felt at a loss as to what to do with them. This clone didn't move like Eleanor any longer. It's arms and legs were clumsy, uncoordinated. Like there wasn't much heart in anything it did.

This… was just too weird. She looked like Eleanor, and yet when I first met Eleanor, there was an immediate connection; some intangible essence that made it clear to me that she was my sister. Instantly, we'd been able to communicate and trust one another.

With this one, it was almost the opposite. I felt revulsion. A need to dump her from the car and speed away, no matter what David claimed about getting rid of bodies.

Scanning her x-ray style from head to toe didn't reveal anything new. She appeared just like Eleanor and me from the outside. Fewer marks, scratches, and scars than we had, but nothing truly noticeable. The only thing that really struck me were her eyes. I stepped closer, staring into her gaze like it held all the impossible answers.

"She doesn't have round pupils," I breathed. Our dark eyes hid this trait rather effectively, but despite the limited light in the lot, I could make out that instead of a round center to her iris, they were more of a slit.

Reptilian.

Oh my gods.

The sound of David dropping from the car and coming

around to stand next to me did little to stir me from my inability to look away.

What did they do to her? Why did her eyes look that way? How could I not have noticed before?

"I never would've seen that in a million years if I hadn't been looking," David whispered, almost in answer to my thoughts.

"Can I see?" Sarah asked.

"Later, I promise. Stay in the car for now. You don't have shoes."

"Can you speak?" David asked the clone, leaning in close. Too close. She rocked forward to smash her forehead into his nose, and would have succeeded if I hadn't snatched David back.

"I can speak." Her words were in my voice.

"What's your name?" I demanded.

"Six."

Good grief. Alphabetical order to numbers? Future Solutions was clearly the worst at naming things.

"What generation are you, Six?" I continued without missing a beat.

"Fifth."

Okay, so two after me. That made sense in some ways, and didn't in others. Wouldn't they want future clones to be more advanced, less automatons?

"What were you made for?" David asked, standing so our shoulders touched.

Six cocked her head at an angle and shrugged. "I am a full body replacement."

"Which means what?"

She wrinkled her nose, like she was about to sneeze. "You don't know? Aren't you the same?"

Crossing my arms to hide the full-body shiver that coursed through me, I shook my head. "I'm a third generation." Shit, when had I managed to incorporate that into my identity?

"Oh." She shrugged then went quiet.

David and I exchanged a glance. "What's a full body replacement?" he pressed.

Another shrug.

Aaron, still secured to the door, cleared his throat. "She probably can't say. They aren't exactly playing with a full deck. Nor are they given much information about… that."

"What's *that*?" I nearly growled the words. If killing Aaron was an option, he'd be the one I left in the empty warehouse to rot.

"She wasn't created with the idea that she'd be a real person. She's meant to allow someone else to inhabit her. That's what Future Solutions was working toward."

"Someone else to inhabit her." I understood what he meant, but my whole being seemed to rebel against the idea.

"Exactly. Once you get done with whatever body you have, and you've replaced the broken bits enough times, you can inhabit a new body. Like this one. Whatever's keeping it alive now is replaced. By you."

David coughed. "That's impossible."

But I knew that was just wishful thinking. It was real. It was possible. It was sitting before us with reptilian eyes.

"No, not really," Aaron responded matter-of-factly. "Diana, you share your essence with your clone, correct? Well, this allows you to shift that same sort of essence into a new body."

"And whatever's in there now?" I asked, peering down at Six's strange eyes.

"Gets absorbed back into the original clone's main body of their essence. Soul. Whatever you want to call it."

"How?" David asked, his features gray around the edges. I probably looked similar.

Aaron shook his head. "Imagine our surprise when we

were working on human cloning and basically discovered that there is verifiable evidence of a human soul. So far as we can tell, it can be split and shared, but also seems to seep—as in pieces will always return to the original, even if they've been cut away for ages. So, if you were to be killed, what makes up your portion of my soul would trickle back to me." Aaron seemed oblivious to the way David and I both gaped at him.

For him, this was clearly just science, with a very odd metaphysical bent. But for the rest of us, this was what gave us life. Whatever the hell that actually meant.

"Ick," Sarah said. She'd scooted onto her mother's lap and tucked up her legs, as far from Aaron in the back seat as she could manage.

"That goes for all of us," I muttered.

"There are a few more generations after her; additional attempts until the bodies were nearly," he paused, "just bodies. Live shells."

His decision to get chatty undoubtedly had to do with wanting to be freed, but from the expression David wore, and the one I shared, there was no way that was happening.

"What do we do with her?" I asked, ignoring Aaron and turning back to the problem at hand: a life-size me that didn't have access to her full brain. The last few days had worn me too thin to reason more, let alone care. I just wanted a bathroom, a bourbon, and a bed for a few days.

"Can she be controlled remotely?" David asked. He reached out a finger and poked Six. She rocked a little and glared at David like she might try to bite him.

"She was housing Eleanor earlier," Aaron answered. "Or at least a portion of Eleanor."

"Is—"

"Eleanor's still in there?"

We spoke at the same time, the same horrible conclusion hitting us both. If that was possible, did I really want to know? I had no idea how such a thing might work or how we could fix it, and from Sarah's wide-eyed expression over the back of the seat, I wasn't alone in the fear that coursed through me.

"I wouldn't know. It does seem odd she's still sleeping," Aaron mused.

"Well, fuck," I breathed.

David went around to the front passenger's seat and slid it forward so he could fit most of his wide frame in and around to face his root inside the vehicle. "Don't make me get out any more tools. Tell us what you know."

Aaron chuckled. "Free me, and I'll do what I can to make sure Eleanor is returned to her proper body."

"Why would I bother? I think I'd rather torture it out of you." David reached across Aaron's body, gripped his father's injured fingers and twisted them.

The clone and the cloned stared one another down, and for a moment I flashed on two massive male elk, sizing one another up before they locked horns.

A drop of blood splashed on the seat. Aaron's and David's breaths were both elevated. I didn't move, the scene frozen in the still air. Not even Eleanor snored now.

"I don't know any more," Aaron fumed through clenched teeth.

David's eyes met mine through the shadows of the car interior, and he released his father's hand. "There has to be someone who would know. Someone you can ask."

"Perhaps."

"Don't make me ask nicely," David snapped. "I'll give you an hour to think about who would be best to contact."

I knew that hour was mostly so we could plan the safest way to manage the contact. I still had the encrypted phone on me, but even that felt dangerous to use with so many people after us.

Which brought me back to the issue at hand: "We need

some cash."

At this, Sarah finally made a move. Before David could stop her, she wiggled across the bench seat and fitted a small hand into Aaron's back pocket. She tugged for a moment, then managed to come up with a wallet.

"Hot damn!" I crowed, giving her a high five after she handed it to David.

"Thank God," David breathed out as he held up a wad of cash from the wallet.

"I think it's time for a bathroom break." I stared at the strange-eyed other me, watching us like she wasn't quite sure what to think. "After we figure out what to do with her."

David grabbed the jacket that he'd shed while stitching up his arm and brought it around to the back of the vehicle. With a deft hand, he snagged Six's feet and hands—keeping her from kicking him—and laid her down in the back again.

From the funky first aid kit he got some earplugs, which I fit as best I could in her ears. She didn't like it much, but other than thrashing her head around, which David promptly stopped, there wasn't much she could do.

Then we draped the jacket over her, including her head.

If she could transmit anything back, it wouldn't be visual or auditory now. We couldn't leave her in the lot behind the crumbling building, not if a bit of Eleanor was stuck within her.

We would figure out how to get her out. I slammed the back hatch, staring down at the prone form mostly hidden in the back. Whatever fragment of soul she might have within her, it made me ill to think we got it front the same source.

WE WENT BACK to the gas station and took precautions while visiting the bathroom. I undid Sarah's ponytail and arranged her hair to cover most of her face. David watched Joey in the car while we made a quick trip inside. We drove off and found another station for David to fill up the car, as well as make a quick trip to the bathroom.

If anyone caught us on tape, it would be relatively simple to work out what we were doing, but I figured—hoped—that gave us at least a head start. Of course, someone could have planted a private camera, or even hacked into the camera feeds, but that may have been giving Future Solutions too much credit.

Granted, they'd figured out how to clone people. Anything was possible.

We stopped a few towns away at an In-and-Out and ordered enough food to fill all our bellies. I couldn't believe I was hungry with all that was going on, and truthfully my stomach wasn't exactly seeking food, but the stress of it all made me want to gnaw on the steering wheel.

"So, San Jose it is?" I asked, watching the sky open up

over the broad central valley ahead of us, tinged with orange and pink in the gathering sunset.

No one responded. Sarah had drifted off. David was holding Joey low in his arms to make it less obvious that we lacked a car seat. Joey had eaten two food pouch things Sarah had found at the gas station and sucked down some milk from a straw cup before passing out with a full belly. I drove with care, keeping with the flow of traffic, making sure no cops saw us or had a reason to pull us over. The last thing we needed was for the police to wonder why we had a man taped to the car, a woman trapped in the luggage area, and another woman comatose in the back seat.

David gave me directions as we drove, risking using the vehicle's GPS. We discussed our options for visiting the safe house in San Francisco and getting more supplies, but Faith drew me away from the idea. We needed to get to her, the sooner the better. And after the last visit to a supposedly safe space, I wasn't eager to meet any more masked men.

"We'll just have to improvise," David said, attempting to make me feel better.

It didn't.

It was well after dark when we exited the freeway and wound our way into a residential area. The neighborhood was nice. Clean. The kind where I half expected to see rows of white picket fences. The kind of neighborhood my mother would have liked me playing in as a kid. Not the kind I expected a clone to live in, nor for men in black to hunt us down in.

"What are the chances she's even alive?" I asked in a low voice. From the sound of their even, measured breathing no one was awake in the backseat, but I didn't want to freak Sarah out any more.

"Low." David gave me a tight-lipped look in the yellow light of a streetlamp.

I swallowed hard. "Next time, lie to me."

"You'd know if I did."

"Maybe I'd just pretend to go along with it."

David chuckled. "Hardly."

I paused, debating what else I should ask, and what I'd rather lie to myself about for a little longer. "What are we going to do?"

"First, we're going to see if she's alive," David murmured, "and then we're going to come up with a plan. It may involve gasoline. I heard that someone in this very vehicle has some experience with such things."

I sniffed my hands. Even though I washed them at least ten times back at the gas station, the cling of chemicals still lingered. "That might work."

"If it doesn't, we get the hell out of here."

"Toward San Diego," I added, prying my death grip from the steering wheel.

David nodded. "To take them down. That's going to require a lot more planning."

His words warmed some part of me. That was exactly the correct answer. I wanted nothing more than to watch Future Solutions burn—from a safe distance while knowing that my plan had worked perfectly.

"How many lives will that cost?" Aaron spoke from the back seat. Okay, so not asleep then—he was quite good at the Game.

"How many lives has it already cost? How many clones have you killed? How many more will die?" I shot back, my mind turning to all my coworkers, to Ron, to everyone who'd been killed in my wake.

Aaron snorted. "And how many humans will live because of what we've done? How many people will survive because they can have a healthy body?"

"Am I not worth the life I've been given? Are you saying I don't deserve to be here, because someone else can live a better life if I'm killed?" My words all but hissed out. If I could have shouted without waking Sarah and Joey, I would have.

"Perhaps you don't fully realize this, but you aren't truly alive. Not in the same sense as me and the children."

Aaron's words cut deep, and I realized in a blazing sense of clarity that what he said was at the heart of what bothered me most about what we were. Maybe he was right. Maybe I wasn't what I seemed, and even more different than I always suspected. Maybe I wasn't human.

"So you're saying I'm nothing more than a shell that accidentally got too much soul?" David asked, voice bitter.

"Yes, a little too much of *my* soul. But not the real deal. Not a real soul."

"How can you even determine such a thing? You can't measure the depths of a soul."

Aaron chuckled. "No, not measure it exactly, but how else can you explain your connection with the root clone?"

"How do you explain children? How can life be passed on from generation to generation if there are no means to divide and pass along this life essence?" I argued.

"Tell me, how would you know your experience was normal? You've never had anything different since you've always lived with half a soul, or whatever you want to call it. But the fact remains that if your root dies, so do you. That should be proof enough that whatever you want to call your essence isn't the same as mine." Aaron had obviously practiced that little speech, and it rattled around in my mind, seeking holes or some other flaw to pick apart.

"You've never been a clone. How could you possibly assume that my experience is any different from yours?"

"Because when my parents died, that didn't mean I died, too."

"That doesn't mean we experience life any differently, though," I contended. "That my time here means I'm any less human. I still experience things in the same way as someone born normally. I'm not so different as to be unworthy of life."

Aaron's bonds crinkled, and I glanced in the rearview mirror to see him shrug.

"We're just as human as any of them," I muttered to myself. Perhaps I was attempting to placate myself, but I didn't care. He couldn't convince me otherwise. If they'd just leave us be, we could live our lives without trouble. Just because the essence that gave me life was different didn't mean I wasn't alive, real, and human.

"It's around the corner on the left," David said. We'd driven further into the neighborhood where the houses were a little closer together, though still nice, with well-kept, tiny front yards and cars carefully parked along the street. A park opened to the right, the lights on and illuminating a group of teens loitering on the swings.

I made the turn and slowed down enough to allow us a good look at the house.

Dark.

The windows were inky pools of black, the front door firmly shut. The houses on either side mirrored this appearance. The streetlight off to the right of the house flickered on and off as we crept past.

"Creepy," Sarah ventured in a small, sleep-filled voice in the back.

"That's for sure," I agreed. I swept the house from roof to yard, taking in any small detail that might help us understand what was going on inside there.

The blinds were neat and orderly. No windows were broken. Nothing appeared out of place. A plain wreath hung on the door, perfectly straight. Someone had trimmed the hedges under the front windows during the past week—the clippings still clung to the grass.

"Could she be out?" I asked no one in particular.

"There's no crime scene tape, at least."

"Or no one's found her body yet," I added to David's words.

We fell silent at that.

I kept moving forward, going barely over five miles an hour. Even so, I almost hit her.

"Stop!" Sarah shrieked, her hand smacking wildly against my shoulder.

I listened without hesitating, pressing down on the brakes so hard we all tumbled forward. It took me a moment to push my hair—in desperate need of a wash—out of my eyes.

"Huh. I always wondered what I'd look like with a pixie cut." The words tumbled out as some strange corner of my brain took stock.

In front of the car, she—another me—stood, one hand held out imploringly to get me to stop. She wore a scarf wrapped around her neck and dark sunglasses, despite the late hour. A long flowing dress, cinched at her tiny waist, gave her a bohemian look I couldn't have pulled off if I starved myself for months.

"Is it really her?" I asked David, debating whether to hit the unlock button or not. "It could be another one like Six."

"Is there a way to be sure?" David raised his brows.

I rolled the window down an inch, beckoning the clone to come over. I flicked on the interior lights and kept the car in drive in case we had to make a quick escape.

She came closer, her mouth pinched in annoyance. "I'm Faith," she began without preamble. "I assume you're another one of me? We've got to get out of here."

"Take your glasses off and let me see your eyes," I instructed. "We have to be sure."

Faith pulled her Ray-Bans down and angled her face to the light, revealing normal, round pupils. Despite this, my gut twisted. Some strange little part of me, picking up on details that I wasn't even entirely conscious of, set off an alarm. I filed the feeling away.

"What generation are you?" I asked, wondering what she knew, what could possibly be enough of a test to prove she was one of us. Not that I could leave a clone in the grip of Future Solutions, but Six already proved they could use one of us against the rest.

"Third," the clone who claimed she was Faith answered. "I think. I didn't get a ton of information out of my parents before they were killed."

Wracking my brain for all I'd read in the sparse file about the woman in front of me, I tried to come up with something to quiz her on. "What kind of art do you make?"

Faith sighed. "I'm a sculptor. How did you know that?"

"They had a file on you. It's one of the few details we have about your adult life."

Even in the strained light from inside the car, I could see Faith pale a little. "I thought I'd dodged them all so well."

I stared out at her, trying to think of some kind of other test that might make this easier, less of a gamble to let her get too close. "If you could be anything, what would you be?" The question was an odd one, and her eyebrows jumped for a moment. But, if she were my clone, and all of this were real, I knew her answer would help determine the truth.

"I'd be happy. Which at this moment means we'd be getting the hell away from here," she said, a hint of a grin tinging her words.

"What?" David asked.

"Get in, and be quick," I instructed, hitting the unlock button.

I knew exactly what Faith meant. Her words echoed the part of me that sometimes longed to find a quiet corner of the world and enjoy some peace and quiet. Which was exactly the opposite of what we were facing now. No matter what, the same connection I shared with Eleanor was there with this woman. She had to be one of us. And while that didn't put her in the clear, it did give me hope that she would hate Future Solutions as much as I did.

David handed me Joey as he reached through and barely caught hold of Eleanor's arm to keep her from tumbling from the vehicle when Faith wrenched open the door. Sarah yelped, helping David haul her mother across the seat so that her feet flopped across Aaron. Sarah's tiny body nestled into her mother's other side, while Faith tossed her bag into the back and tucked into the bench seat.

Six squirmed and Faith peered over the seat, then looked ahead to give me a searching look, which I caught in the rear-view mirror as I made my way as quickly as I dared from the neighborhood.

"Why is there a woman back there and a man tied up here? And why won't this one wake up?"

"That… is a very long story."

WE DROVE at least two hours, over to the I-5 in the valley, then along the freeway, choked with semis and drivers who wove in and out of traffic like madmen.

"So, what's with the unconscious one?" Faith's first question included pointing a thumb at Eleanor, who was still snoring lightly.

Dragging my attention away from the traffic, I tried to put together the best way to explain things. "That's Eleanor. We don't really know what they did to her. We think there's a part of her… essence, or whatever you want to call it, stuck in Six, the sixth-generation clone in the back."

Faith wrinkled her nose. "They can do that?"

I nodded, rubbing my forehead. God, I needed to wash. "It was their end goal, actually." I took a deep breath and thought through all we had learned. "They started out with cloning, but then worked to create replacement bodies, so that the cloned person could merely move into a new shell once they'd exhausted the last one. It will allow those who can afford it to become basically immortal."

"That's disgusting." Faith narrowed her eyes at Eleanor. "It contradicts all that it means to be human."

I raised an eyebrow at her. "Yeah?"

"We aren't just souls stuck into a body, Diana. Surely you know that. We're a *part* of our body. It's the soul and body together that define us."

Part of me wanted to argue. It sounded too new-age hippie, but at the same time maybe she had a point. It would certainly make me feel better to think I was more than just some leftover bit of someone else's soul.

As David explained Aaron's role at Future Solutions, Faith leaned over and gave Aaron a sharp poke. "So this fucker is the one who helped make us?" she fumed. "Why didn't you just kill him?"

David sighed. "Because if the person we're cloned from—our root—dies, we do, too."

Faith groaned. "That does complicate things."

"What happened to your parents?" I was desperate for a topic to keep me awake. The strain of the headlights, idiotic drivers, and keeping a careful watch to ensure we weren't being tailed had drained me to nearly empty.

"They were killed. Car accident, or so I was told. They always claimed that if I knew too much, there was a chance it would end badly for them. They were right." Her tone shifted and I knew she couldn't fake the bone-deep sadness that came from the loss of her parents. "At least they told me what they knew and did their best to keep me safe."

"How long have you known?" David asked.

"Since I was about eight. They figured I was old enough to start understanding."

Made sense. At eight, I was already doing high school level math and reading adult books. She was probably had a similar mental aptitude, no matter what sort of environment she was raised in.

We fell silent again as I continued reading the license plates around us, checking them against those I'd catalogued during our trip, and reasoning whether any of them might be tailing us or were just fellow travelers. Considering I seriously doubted the ancient Winnebago was anything Future Solutions, home of the most cliché killers-for-hire, would use, I decided that for the moment we were safe.

My mind tilted toward my parents and the way they'd used to joke about the giant camper vans on the road. My father had been a huge proponent of tent camping. Which was when Faith's words connected.

"Could my parents…" The words caught in my throat. "Could they have been murdered?"

No one had an answer to that, though Faith stared at me from the back seat like she had a lot she wanted to say.

"Aaron, I know you're not asleep," I snapped.

He pretended to flutter open his eyes, shifting against his bonds. "What?"

"My parents. What *really* happened to them?"

"They died in an accident, didn't they?" he asked. But I knew him now. He might have been able to Game me on being asleep, but his tells were all over the place when he spoke. The slight way his lips smacked on the words, the little shrug of his shoulders I could see through the mirror.

"You lie. They were killed, weren't they?"

Aaron sighed but didn't say anything.

"Oh my God." I pressed a hand to my mouth, the weight of realization crashing down around me and all but drowning out the real world. The instinctual part of my brain was all that kept us on the road. "They died because of me."

The weight of all the events during the insanity of the last couple days didn't begin to compare to knowing that my parents—my biggest supporters and best friends—were murdered by those cloning bastards.

"We don't know that for sure." David touched my shoulder. "It really could have been an accident."

I shook my head. "I always knew it was strange. The road the crash happened on was so out of the way, but I didn't know what to make of that. Or if it even mattered. It didn't change what happened to them." Tears spilled over my lids and I sucked in a shuddering breath.

"I think we need to find a place to stay for the night," Faith suggested in a soft voice.

Wordlessly, I agreed, while fighting to keep my sobs controlled. I fought to push thoughts of my parents behind a steel wall. Their deaths left a gaping hole in my life, one that still felt raw and terrible some days. Learning my role in their death felt like day one all over again, and I couldn't deal with that right now.

We still had to drive, however, and I managed to make it to the central valley, where I-5 careened for endless straight miles through the agricultural fields. David continued to answer Faith's questions while I stewed with silent fury. We stopped at a Motel 6 parking lot—the only hotel for the next fifty miles, according to David and the sign on the freeway. I let him out to negotiate rooms and pay with nearly the last of our cash.

Faith reached around the seat to give me a hug, or as close to one as she could manage, given the confines of the cramped car. "We'll get them back. For all of it," she promised.

I wondered again about what she knew, what happened to her, and how she managed to get out of their grasp, but then, really, I just didn't care. I wanted a bed. A shower. And if any could be found in this place, a stiff drink. Not that I'd allow myself that: I had to keep my wits about me if anyone in a dark suit decided to show up.

"I wish I'd never found out the truth." I spoke to no one in particular, making the announcement in a car filled with identical copies of my DNA. "I wish they'd just killed me and I never had a chance to run."

"You don't mean that," Faith chided with a little pat on my shoulder. "That's not who we are. We always fight back."

I shook my head, determined to stay on my morbid train of thought. "I wish I didn't have to." Wasn't it enough that I'd spent my life fighting for a better world? That I'd worked so hard to try and keep the terrible crazies from destroying the good of humankind?

"You may still get that wish," Aaron said.

"Shut the fuck up," I snapped. My anger surprised me, overtaking over my soul-sucking sadness in an instant. It took all my concentration to keep from launching myself at Aaron.

Aaron obeyed and I stared past him to the little hotel lobby, lit brightly against the dark. A shabby fake tree leaned against the window and David's tall frame dwarfed the plump woman behind the desk. The dirty windows made me wonder if there was any hope of the rooms being free of bed bugs, or something equally gross.

David saved me from having to delve down that rabbit hole by returning. He dangled two room keys when I rolled down the window. "We're down around the end."

I drove us there, carefully taking stock of the layout of the hotel, memorizing any clues about the occupants of the rooms as well as all the other little details my brain collected without me having to think about it. At this point, I was too tired to control the stream of information: several families with small children (those window decals always struck me as ridiculous), a student, a single man traveling for work, a trucker. Most seemed like they'd be quiet neighbors, and the hum from the freeway a half mile away was all we heard when we parked, tucking around the back of the dumpsters to best hide our stolen vehicle.

"Okay, I've got a double room, then another with just a full bed. They're adjoining and the best they could offer. They're full, otherwise."

"So long as there's a place to shower and lie down, I think we'll be fine." I stretched, the muscles across my shoulders sagging as I finally got out from behind the wheel. "The real question is how we're going to get Eleanor up there. And maybe Aaron and Six."

I never thought I'd wish for handcuffs, but right then I would have found them incredibly useful.

David shrugged. "I was wondering the same thing."

Sarah, carrying her brother as if she were a miniature version of her mother, grabbed their bags. "Can't we leave one of them down here?"

"Good point," I conceded. "Aaron or Six?"

We all looked at one another. "Aaron," David and I echoed at the same time.

With that settled, we got moving. The rooms were small, smelled like Lysol and mold, and the carpet was a matted mess that had been blue at one time. But the beds had fresh sheets and the bathroom towels seemed clean enough. The door that adjoined the rooms locked, which might allow for someone to get some sleep. Every little bit of me craved a few moments of peace to myself to try and make sense of everything. The weight of my parents' lives refused to stay sealed away, instead taking front and center in the stage of my thoughts, making every move difficult and cumbersome.

David carried Six into the room, settling her on one side of the second queen bed. She struggled, but not much. We kept her eyes covered while Faith helped me lift her up and give her water from a paper cup. If she needed more, or even a bathroom, she didn't mention it. Surely she had to pee sometimes—her body was alive, even if it seemed to be vacant of an occupant.

Eleanor was brought in next, and Faith moved her around to rest next to Six. This arrangement meant Faith would be stuck sleeping with the kids, but Sarah seemed fine with her, which was both a relief and a testament to the similarity between her mom and her new "aunts."

David and I spent a few minutes shuttling Aaron in to use the bathroom. We kept his hands bound and David locked

Aaron in a firm grip that anyone who happened to be watching would think was just an old man leaning on his son for support. I stood guard, ready to tackle if necessary. Aaron didn't do much other than piss and wash his face, drink a little, and allow us to secure him back in the car with a blanket and the alarm set to alert us if he opened any of the doors. He'd have to get out if he hoped to hot wire it, and I felt reasonably confident he wasn't going anywhere.

I stood in the doorway between the rooms, staring at the assortment of people settling in. The curtains were drawn and the dusty bulbs made both rooms take on a yellow hue. Faith was helping Sarah with Joey, and for some reason that made me feel better. Maybe the motherly instinct was intuitive in all of us, just needing an excuse to come out.

"I'll take first watch," David offered, stepping up behind me so his warm breath tickled the back of my neck.

"Thanks," I sighed. "I'm going to shower."

I wished the hot water spilling over me in the cramped shower stall made me feel better. I closed my eyes and dropped my head into my hands, swaying a little on my feet. What I confessed in the car was the truth: I *did* wish I hadn't learned the truth. It hurt far too much.

Flashes of my parents ran through my mind, a devilish rerun I couldn't pause. I'd spent months dredging through every minute detail I could learn about their accident, the only consolation being that I was told they both died instantly when the semi-truck collided with them head-on. I still hoped that tiny part of it was the truth.

I had nightmares for months about their last moments: coming around the corner of the small two-lane highway in the mountains, the huge truck barreling down on them, the driver having lost control due to a deer jumping in front of his rig. What were their last thoughts?

Now, I couldn't bear to think of how they might have really died. Was it worse than that? Did they suffer? I couldn't stand it. Tears, hotter than the tap water, coursed down my cheeks and I buried my head in the stream.

As my emotions crashed over me, the underlying question of what all of this meant reared up. Being a clone meant what? What Faith had said didn't help much—clearly Future Solution's discoveries showed that while we had to have a body to survive, there was a whole lot more to it. But being made from someone else meant that I hadn't been given all the pieces.

I felt like someone's unwanted toy, reminded that I'd never be real, and apparently I'd never be whole. Even if I survived all of this mess, I'd never be able to be like everyone else. I'd never even be able to be my own person.

THIRTY-THREE

IT FELT like forever before I pulled myself together. Not that the hollow ache left my chest, or the occasional tear stopped leaking down my cheek, but I finally managed to dry off and stare at my pile of dirty clothes.

The thought of putting them back on made me ill. I could smell them, even through the steamy soap scent from the shower. But I had no other choice. My underwear went on inside out and I shimmied, still damp and sticky, into my jeans. Forgoing my bra for the time being, I pulled on my shirt and made a mental note to stop somewhere tomorrow to get us all another set of clothes, if there were some way to steal them.

I cracked the door to the room while wondering if I should put my shoes back on—who knew what lived in that carpet—only to catch sight of David seated on the small bed, doing his best to appear occupied. He'd been listening to me cry, no doubt. The thought should have made me cringe, but all it did was make me feel heavier. I needed to keep it together here, and what was I doing? Sobbing in the shower. I never had this issue while on an assignment—but I'd never had an assignment that ripped my personal life wide open, either.

"How are you doing?" David asked, not daring to look up from the gun he was cleaning.

I shrugged, realized he couldn't see it, and said, "I don't know. The thing about my parents…"

Our eyes met, and what little restraint I'd managed to shore up washed away. I slumped on the bed next to him and fought to catch my breath. He set the gun down on the side table and scooted over, setting a careful hand on my knee. Its warmth seeped into me.

Despite being in close proximity for the last couple of days, we had scarcely touched. Hell, I hadn't known which side he was on for a good portion of that. A shrinking portion of me still wondered. But, no matter what, I knew he wanted to take down Future Solutions.

Staring down at his hand, I wasn't sure if that was enough. Yet, I desperately wanted it to be. A fact I reinforced by taking his hand in my own.

"We don't know for sure. It still might have been an accident." He whispered the words into my wet hair, inching a bit closer.

"I always knew it was a strange situation. I always wondered. This just confirms it." Bitterness, stronger than any lemon, coated my words. "It's the only thing that makes sense."

David, for his part, didn't question me. Instead, with a questioning look in his eyes, he tugged me closer, wrapping his arms around me in a hug.

I melted into his warmth, letting it slide through me and loosen the parts that had wound so terribly tight over the last few days. For now, maybe I could take a few minutes to relax. Before we figured out how to take down Future Solutions, I could try to catch my breath for a few minutes.

When David pulled me closer, I didn't object. It felt so

comfortable. I wanted to be held. I wanted someone to make it all go away. If I were honest with myself, I wanted my mother.

The spinning overload of sensory information threatened for a minute: the smell of David and his unwashed clothes that somehow smelled utterly wonderful. The comforter on the bed beneath us that had never been washed. The low sound of a couple in a heated discussion a couple rooms down. The light snores from the next room over.

I took a deep, shaky breath and tried to push it all away. The process of quieting my mind seemed slippery and extraordinarily difficult. David shifted next to me, and as I cracked my lids to look at him, I caught sight of the fire in his.

My breath caught, and suddenly it didn't matter what my brain was thinking. This time, the sensation of his warm breath, followed by the touch of his lips, effectively cut through all the static.

I've kissed people before. I've had boyfriends. But nothing on the planet could have prepared me for how hungry I realized I was. In that instant, I could have swallowed David whole. As our kiss deepened, everything fell away, and it was just us, and our breath, and the peace that seeped into me.

A soft fussing sound from Joey broke us apart, and for the first time since I'd met the little guy, I grumbled about him. Although, it was probably a good thing—the door was wide open between the rooms and if things had gone much farther, nothing would have kept me from undressing David.

Not wanting to wake anyone—or for anyone to wake me once I actually fell asleep—I slipped over to the door between our rooms and closed it.

I slid back onto the bed, scooting as close as I dared to David. A thrill sparked through my blood with him so close.

"I-I hope that was okay?"

A shocked glance at David revealed a deeply concerned expression drawing his brows together. "Can't you read me by now?" I asked with a whisper of a laugh. Damn it, I really needed him to be able to.

David grinned, hugging me tighter where I'd ended up lying against his chest. "Okay, but I just had to double-check."

I ran my feet against his, tangled together at the end of the bed. "You're not just playing me? Making sure I'm on your side, luring me with a kiss?" I snorted a laugh at how ridiculous I sounded.

David tilted my chin up so our eyes could meet. "I've wanted to do that since meeting you at that coffee shop. Hell, even since the train when I first saw you. All of the rest of this shit has just gotten in the way."

I swallowed. Okay, even if he were playing the Game, that had been an excellent move. One I rewarded him with by pressing my lips to his and allowing the rest of the world to slip away.

Our kiss deepened until the room felt like the heater was on full blast and I desperately needed to divest us of our clothing. David reached for my shirt, tugging it up to reveal my stomach, where his slightly rough palm rubbed circles. His fingers teased the edge of the fabric, inching slowly upward. I wanted to rip it off, finish the job, but the delectable anticipation kept me still, my breathing ragged as I traced his face and lips, running my fingers through his hair.

A full body shiver coursed through me when he grinned at the realization I wasn't wearing a bra. His long fingers traced my breasts and teased my nipples. Pushing my shirt out of the way, his mouth closed over them, racing electricity through my toes. I pressed a hand over my mouth to keep from making too much noise.

My shirt came off, then his pants. His boxers were stretched tight against him, and I rubbed my hand along the length of his erection, loving the way he groaned and pressed his face into my shoulder.

My jeans were trickier—the dampness from my shower

had molded them to me. After tugging at them, David stood, grabbed both the ankles, and pulled them off. He nearly took me with them, and I grabbed the mattress over my head to stay put. We both giggled like little kids, then paused to listen to make sure we didn't wake anyone up.

The chill of the room forced us under the covers after David dimmed the lamp. His bare skin against mine was electric, and I pressed up against him to allow every bare inch of full contact. His fingers tangled with mine, and his lips brushed along my jaw, my ear, and found my lips.

I pressed my hips up toward him, feeling the heat of him between my thighs. He sucked in a deep breath between his teeth. I repeated the movement and delighted at the low growl it elicited.

The last thing between us was my underwear, and David hooked a finger around the waistband and took a deep breath. "This still okay?"

For a sliver of a second, I asked myself the same question. Was I good with this? The response that roared back from my brain and body shocked even me.

I wiggled, helping him remove the flimsy piece of fabric.

He pulsed against me as his lips found mine again and we rocked together, reveling in the myriad of touch and sensation. He broke away and leaned back, the cool air tingling against my nipples. Palming the pulsing need between my thighs made me groan and press into his hand. He grinned, his fingers slipping inside me, making me gasp. He lost no time in producing a condom that I would ask about later... if I remembered.

Lifting his hips just a bit, he angled himself so that his tip replaced his fingers, hot and hard and promising. Before he could fully enter me, I pressed my hips up, gasping as he went deeper, and deeper still.

"Oh, God," David managed, biting his lip as he brought his hips fully against mine.

My fingers strained white against his biceps as I felt him inside me. The deep warmth almost felt like it was behind my bellybutton.

Carefully, as if I might break beneath him, he rocked against me. I joined in, pressing against him, lost in the delicious waves of sensation.

"Harder," I whispered into his ear, clutching him and pushing him inside me with more force. I wanted him to—hell, I wasn't even sure what, but I wanted to feel every last millimeter of him within me, feel the heat of his breath against my neck, make him lose control.

The blur of pleasure lasted for an unknown amount of time. It felt like forever, yet still too short when we finally broke apart, sated and breathing heavily.

"Good God, when can we do *that* again?" I asked, curling into him. Every part of me felt like I'd finally managed to relax, mainlining some powerful drug that erased the stress of the past few days and allowed my brain to finally settle.

"You know, it's kind of funny," I mused, staring at how my fingers fit perfectly between his.

"What is?" David's words were muffled by the way he spoke into my hair.

"I thought there was no possibility of anything good coming out of this situation. That all this mess, the complete upending of my life, was just one big disaster. Maybe I was wrong."

David's laugh was more of a rumble against me than anything that would wake the others. "While I'm probably not going to have many opportunities to say that you're wrong, this is definitely an exception."

I rolled my eyes and grinned at him, halting any more talk with a long, lingering kiss.

CHAPTER
THIRTY-FOUR

WHATEVER WOKE me made me bolt up, pulling the covers with me and tumbling David to one side. I was instantly aware something was wrong. At some point in the night I'd put my clothes back on, paranoia telling me that being naked was not going to help matters if anyone tracked us here.

Allowing my brain full reign to take in all that went on around me, I listened to the rumble of a truck passing on the freeway, a man who snored the deep rumble of drugged sleep a room over, and the snapping of shitty electrical lines in the walls.

And nothing else.

No breathing from the other room.

"Shit, shit, shit." I struggled to get to my feet, throwing the sheet off from where it tangled around my legs.

Empty.

No, not quite. One figure still slept on the bed, and after a closer inspection I realized it was Eleanor. The bright lights made her stir and she sat up slowly, as if she were suffering from a hangover from hell.

"What happened? Where are they?" I stood in the doorway, surveying the room in hopes that something about the place might give me a clue.

The bag of things for Joey was no longer there. The beds had been hastily made, almost as if no one had been present.

"Huh?" Eleanor managed. The dark circles under her eyes and gray tinge to her skin gave me pause. Was she drugged? It made sense, knowing what happened yesterday. And yet, Six was gone as well. "Where are my kids?"

I went to the window that looked over the parking lot and peeled back the curtain.

The Range Rover was gone. A niggle of a memory told me it was the engine starting that woke me.

"Oh, shit. Just shit, shit, shit." I went back to the other room and rocked David once. His eyelids fluttered and he gave me a bleary grin.

"They're gone. Maybe someone took them. I don't know what happened, but they're gone." I was so close to panic mode, I felt my control slip and dissolve. Dropping onto the bed next to him, I forced myself to take several long breaths and clear my head. "The kids and Six and Faith are gone. And Aaron." *Shit.*

"Did they go for food?" David pushed himself up and wrapped an arm around me. His touch managed to calm me, if only a degree or two.

"No, they would have woken us. I don't know what happened."

Swallowing my fear, I forced my brain to come at this from the most logical place. Not that it made much sense to leave the three adult clones behind. Had Faith been in on things with the company? But why hadn't she killed Eleanor, David, and me? I mean, I was grateful she hadn't, but that seemed odd.

"Did you two sleep together?" Eleanor asked curiously. She leaned against the doorframe between our rooms like there was no hope she'd be able to stand on her own.

"Your kids are missing, and *that's* what you're asking?"

"It's better than breaking down," she replied softly, staring down at her hands clasped in front of her.

Swallowing back any other shitty comment I might make, I went to her and pulled her into a hug. "What... what happened to you?"

Eleanor's dark eyes met mine, and I swallowed hard at her expression. Fear made her eyes go wide and her lips puckered into a painful grimace. "I don't really know. Timothy and a couple other big guys I hadn't seen before dragged me down into that lab. A man and a woman in lab coats strapped me down and," she took a shuddering breath, "they injected me with something. It hurt like someone was scouring my body from the inside out. I thought it had killed me, but then I woke in some other body. It felt like my own, but not—I didn't have full control. One of the thugs told me that if I did anything wrong, they'd kill Sarah and Joey. It was all I could do to try and get the point across to Sarah that something was wrong. Someone was still able to control me, the scientists I guess, watch what I said and did, and even made me hit you! I don't know how they did that. How is it even possible?" Her words tumbled out in a pain-filled rant as she slumped to the floor. Her head rested against the wall, and I wasn't sure she could even hold it up herself.

I sat next to her and pulled her head onto my shoulder. "What a horrible thing to experience, Eleanor. While you were unconscious, we got away from the cottage. Aaron told us the cloning process involves sharing elements of the root clone's soul with their clones. The end goal was to create vessels—empty bodies for people to transfer into when they need them. They achieved it in the sixth generation of clones, and part of you seemed to have been inhabiting Six, who we took with us when we left Fireside."

Eleanor blinked slowly, absorbing that information. "That means immortality. They can just switch into a new body whenever they get too old. Limitless, new body parts whenever they need them." While her mind seemed to be working just fine, her body trembled with the remnants of what they'd done to her.

"No one will ever have to get old, or get sick and suffer," I agreed. Many more implications spiraled from there.

We stood on the precipice of a completely different world. One that meant humanity could really and truly overcome its mortality. But, as was abundantly clear to me now, not its morality—this sort of change would not be for everyone, and certainly not everyone deserved it.

"That's not…" Eleanor paused as if she had to piece all the bits together. "That's not sustainable. It's not ethical. It's going to lead to a world filled with only the rich, exploiting those who can't afford to clone themselves. It's bad enough to see the way things are now, but can you even imagine? Oh, God, it's going to be so much worse. My kids will never have a normal world to live in."

This was why I loved having a clone, though I thought of her as my twin now. I knew how her brain worked and I didn't need to ask questions to see how she got to those conclusions. It was as obvious to her as it was to me. And we both knew that what she said was the truth. The potential for this to destroy humanity was so incredibly, frighteningly great.

"We have to stop them. Not just because they've always intended on killing us, but because there's no hope this won't be put to use in all the wrong ways." David's voice, calm and distant, united us all.

"We get my kids back first," Eleanor added, her chin setting as she nodded in fierce determination. No one disagreed.

"Where do we start?" The thought of taking down a corporation with the ability to manage this impressive bit of science made my plan-driven head spin.

"My guess is they're taking Sarah and Joey to the compound, the part of company headquarters where Corbin and I were regularly examined as we grew up. I can tell you all about that place. Then we're going to steal a car and get down there. We'll work the rest out on the way," David said grimly.

The first step lay before us. Where this road led, none of us could fully grasp.

The three of us shared a look. There was no doubt that this course might mean we wouldn't make it back out. But I would do whatever it took to take down Future Solutions.

WE GOT CLEANED UP, removed any trace of our presence in the room, and left by foot as quickly as possible. The guns had been gone when we woke, another annoying reality that made no sense.

Eleanor leaned on me while we walked, murmuring about Sarah and Joey. I tried to determine what would help her the most. She looked like she needed rest, but what she'd been through was impossible and unprecedented. What could I do for someone who'd had most of their soul, along with their consciousness, sucked into another body?

The morning was cold, and I shivered as we crunched along in the gravel on the side of the road. Stealing from the parking lot of the motel would be too obvious, so we traipsed to the gas station in hopes of finding something there.

"The compound is nothing like the building that houses the headquarters," David began. "It's a building that doesn't distinguish itself in many ways from the outside, but inside is where the clones are made and housed. It's in the hills behind San Diego, isolated and guarded more than most government buildings I've been in."

"Good thing we can handle that sort of thing," I

responded, trying to keep positive. I didn't think I quite got my tone right. Too many days playing the Game and I was bound to slip.

"What, two former spies can't break in there?" Eleanor asked. Even though she struggled to get one foot in front of another, she flatly refused to be carried.

"We can, but it's not going to be as easy without supplies, plans, or backup." I sighed. "Plus all the other things we're used to." The typical plan of attack in this situation was pages long, filled with contingencies and fail-safes. This time, none of that would be possible.

David looked between us, his expression so clear, it amazed me I'd ever wondered what went on in his head at any point. He was worried, tired, and extremely wary of what we were about to do.

"What's the layout of the compound?" I asked, dragging his thoughts back to the present.

"It's laid out in a U shape. The central courtyard is used for exercise and any testing that involves being outside. Both sides of the U house labs, or they did the last time Aaron dragged us there five years ago. We were actually due for another checkup soon." He swallowed, and I could tell his unconscious use of the word "us" bothered him. At some point his trauma from Corbin's death would have to be dealt with, but for now we had to survive.

"And the back part?" Eleanor prodded.

"It's housing and offices. I imagine that's where the newest generations are kept." He ran a hand across his face.

We reached the grassy perimeter of the gas station. The place smelled like burning oil, and the early morning fog gave it an ominous look. No one else was around; it was too early for travelers, and the tiny convenience store was closed.

Thus, no parked cars of any sort.

"Now what?" Eleanor asked. She dropped onto the curb

in front of the store and looked like she might lie down if given half a chance.

David and I exchanged wary looks. Waiting meant more time in the open, to be recorded or otherwise discovered. Going back to the motel to steal something would be incredibly obvious, and the gas station seemed to be the only thing for miles in this desolate stretch of valley.

I was mulling over options when the hairs on the back of my neck stood on end about two seconds before the soft pop of a gun went off. Two seconds was long enough. I caught Eleanor and forced her to the ground, and David ducked behind a pump.

Tugging Eleanor, wide eyed and struggling to catch her breath from my forceful push, I crawled towards David as another shot dinged off the edge of the metal rimming where the machine measured how many gallons had been used.

"What the hell are they thinking, shooting near gasoline?" I grumped, settling Eleanor against the pump and taking a moment to peer around to where we'd been cornered.

"They hope the whole place will go up and take us with it," Eleanor muttered darkly.

"Shit," David supplied our mutual response.

The car was by the freeway—easily four hundred yards away. It was actually rather impressive aim, even with the scope I could see mounted to their weapon. It was too far to get a decent look at them, especially with the tinted windows and dark glasses of the shooter.

"God, there has to be some kind of shitty espionage movie they're supplying their cleanup crews with," I scoffed.

"He *does* have a decent car," David pointed out.

"But it's almost a half mile away," I replied.

As if in answer to our comments, the car window with the gun rolled up, and the vehicle spewed gravel and dust to swing around and come closer to us.

"We need cover," Eleanor mused, stating the utterly obvious.

I tugged her to her feet, bracing against her weight, while David returned to the little convenience store. The signs in the window advertised cigarettes and Lotto tickets.

"Bulletproof glass," he noted, pointing to the little white crater where one of the stray bullets had hit.

"Get us inside," I urged, one eye on the approaching sedan. It was all I could do to keep Eleanor and I upright.

David dropped to one knee in front of the door as if he planned on proposing to it in hopes of getting inside. Instead, he stared at the lock for a too-long second and proceeded to pick it.

"There's not enough time!" I hissed. The car was already pulling around the corner, about ten seconds from getting a clear shot to open fire again.

David made a small sound, but less than two heartbeats later, the lock fell apart in his hands. He pushed the door open with his foot while twisting around to grab Eleanor and fairly flinging her inside.

The three of us landed on the floor of the store in a tangled heap. The door shuddered as we pushed it closed with our feet just as a couple more bullets slammed into it from the other side.

"Behind the counter!" David pushed Eleanor toward the clerk's station, and she scrambled on hands and knees behind it. Her breathing sounded like a dying lawnmower, and I feared mine sounded the same.

Swallowing back a flood of saliva, I surveyed the shop, my brain taking in details. Two short rows of candy and other supplies. More brands of cigarettes than I'd ever seen over the clerk's desk. The floor was a spotted mix of old linoleum and dried, blackened gum.

Basically, it was disgusting. Lit refrigerators hummed along the back wall, stocked with every conceivable type of soft drink and beer. Why was a roadside place selling beer? That made no sense.

"There's got to be some kind of weapon in here," David muttered.

"Check behind the cash register drawer." I turned my attention to the back of the store.

"The guy's out of his car and coming closer," Eleanor called out, a hum of panic in her voice from her huddled spot behind the counter.

"Good," David voiced grimly.

I didn't exactly agree, but if he was out of his vehicle, there was a chance we could still find a way out of this.

"Got it," David whooped triumphantly a moment later, holding up a shotgun with the barrel sawed off.

"Good grief," I muttered. Why couldn't it have been a handgun? Why? That piece of shit was great for putting a billion little holes into someone, but the guy approaching outside was a trained professional, and I would have preferred something that would stop him dead. Like a rocket launcher.

"He's going around the side of the store," Eleanor whispered.

I peeked around a display of peanut snack packs and watched the assassin, dark jacket zipped all the way up, with a cap pulled over his ears. Average height and build, fair skin, and otherwise entirely unremarkable. With his glasses mirroring back the storefront, I would have been hard pressed to pick him out of a line-up. Not that he would survive to take part in such a thing.

The man sized up the front of the store, and as Eleanor said, veered left to circle the back.

"There's no back door, is there?" I asked.

A quick scan of the far end of the store revealed the bathrooms and the ATM. A big, flippin' *thank you* to whomever designed this little hellhole.

David, done checking on the shells in the gun, frowned at the door and then me. We had to find a way to get the upper hand. Locked in the store, we were sitting ducks. In the back corner, a pipe rested against the wall, presumably to pull down the faded and cracked blinds that were out of reach at the top of the windows. I picked it up, weighed it in each hand, and took a deep breath, letting it out slowly as I forced my heartbeat to stop galloping.

I heard the footsteps circling, like some large predator, around the back of the building.

With a wave, David motioned me over to his side. "Get down here, at the end of the counter. I'm going to lure him around to the front."

My mouth opened to protest, but David shook his head. No time. I got that. Fine, let him work this out.

I slid down to the ground, giving the faux wood of the counter a long look. No way it would stop bullets. From the craters in the glass, he was packing something high caliber that would pierce just about anything in here.

Eleanor's breath hadn't eased up, and I gave her a long look, hating the wild fear that widened her eyes to giant rings of white. She managed to stem the noise of her breathing, though, and I hoped that meant she wouldn't pass out in the next few minutes.

David went to the door, his footsteps light, and grabbed the grubby handle, pulling it back slowly. It creaked and grumbled the whole way, as if the thing was comprised of a hundred rusty nails being pulled from old, wet wood.

When he smiled, I realized this was part of his plan. The door hung open, despite the weight of it. With a handful of candy from the box beside him, he tossed them one by one, in rapid succession onto the parking lot outside. It didn't really sound like footsteps, but it would sound like something. Indeed, I could hear the man around the back of the building start to run, his feet crunching solidly in the gravel.

He came around the corner, back to the wall behind him, gun in both hands but raised to shoot ahead of him, as if he expected us to be headed toward his vehicle.

Point to David.

The shotgun blast was magnified in the small store and made my ears ring long after David stepped outside to ensure the assassin wasn't going to be coming after us.

"Is he dead?" Eleanor's voice mingled with the buzz in my ears. She didn't look good. Her eyes were swimming in tears, and if she was back to lawnmower breath I couldn't quite tell; maybe it was just me breathing that way.

When I didn't hear anything from David for a minute, I slid from my spot and tiptoed toward the door.

Please, please don't let him be taken out. My silent prayer resonated deep in my chest; the thought of losing David was inconceivable. Not when we had so much more to do.

Relief swept over me as I stole a glance outside. David stood over the fallen man, aiming the dropped gun at the assassin's head. Most of the flesh on the man's arm was gone, and he whimpered as he bled in little rivulets onto the dusty asphalt in front of the store.

"Where are the others?" David's words came through the residual tinnitus.

The assassin shook his head, his teeth biting down on his lip so hard the skin bleached. He must have been in serious pain if he wasn't making any noise at all. A part of me felt a deep sense of satisfaction by the fact, though mostly I just hated seeing him writhe.

If the man's brachial artery had been hit, he'd bleed out in another few minutes. I couldn't tell exactly how much blood he'd already lost, since some of it was pooling beneath him, probably seeping through the cracks and into the dirt. No matter what, we had limited time.

With a deep breath I stepped closer, waving off David's tight-lipped look of disapproval. Kneeling at the man's side, I did a quick check. The artery had been hit—shit—but there weren't any other weapons on him. Satisfied he was in too poor a shape to try anything physical, I started to undo his belt.

"We need a tourniquet," I explained in a soft, calm voice. It was taking all my patience to channel the good cop to David's bad one. "We need to stop the bleeding in your arm."

The man, pale, with dilated pupils, managed a little nod, though the tight bite on his lower lip grew even stronger.

"We need information about who sent you," David, picking up on what I was up to, growled at the fallen man. "Tell us, or she doesn't have to help you."

This caught the man's attention, and he turned a pleading expression toward me. "He's just bluffing," I promised sympathetically. "I'm going to help you. We aren't killers." Well, not all of us—Eleanor wasn't, at least. "He's just scared after how many people have been chasing us."

As deftly as I could, based on a limited CPR class I'd taken for work, I managed to get the belt looped around his arm and started to cinch it down a few inches above the mangled flesh. Hopefully blood loss wouldn't play too much havoc with his lucidity.

"I'm so sorry. I know that's got to hurt. But otherwise you'd bleed out," I murmured, keeping up the calm, soft voice. The trickle of blood slowed as I tightened the belt, though the man's face twisted in pain. His teeth unlocked from his lip and he gasped as I tied off the leather. His arm was probably beyond repair, if he managed to survive this.

I busied myself with trying to make him more comfortable by tucking his cap under his head and zipping up his coat. "I'm sorry I don't have a blanket."

"He doesn't need a blanket. He needs to talk," David said tightly over at the two of us. His gun hadn't wavered.

"I wouldn't test him. He's been through a lot lately," I

whispered to the dying man. "You've got to know something that would help."

The man gasped again, the air that entered his lungs gurgling somewhere deep. "I don't know anything. Just a job."

David's eyes met mine for a moment before he nudged the guy with his foot. "Who gave you the job?"

Another gurgling breath. "Call. Anonymous. No one gives names. Better if you kill me."

Because when they found out he failed, they certainly would.

"We're not going to hurt you," I whispered, patting the man's forehead and pushing his hair back. "You'll be safe."

I stood and grabbed David's arm, tugging him out of earshot. "He doesn't have any info. Let's leave him a phone and get the hell out of here. We've got bigger fish to fry."

David grimaced but nodded his head, dark hair tumbling into his eyes. "Fine. You're right."

We went to the man's sedan next, inspecting it carefully for any tracking devices or explosives. Whomever the man worked for certainly wouldn't be above such things, but the car seemed clean. The leather interior was spotless, and David clucked in approval that it seemed well equipped in the speed department.

The man's phone sat in the center console and David picked it up, turning it slowly in his hands. It was clear he wanted to unlock the thing, search through the entries, and come up with something useful. But there was no time.

Instead, he dropped the phone into the injured man's working hand and walked inside the store. He stepped back out a minute later, Eleanor leaning against him, with a bulging grocery sack in his other hand. I helped get Eleanor into the back seat, where she laid down and smiled weakly at me. I rode shotgun, the actual shotgun tucked by my door with a handful of extra shells stuffed into the cup holder.

David got behind the wheel and with a long screech of the tires, ripped us away from the little hellhole.

"*And* a full tank," David crowed with a pleased grin.

Through the side mirror, I stole one last look at the man on the ground. He hadn't moved. My stomach clamped down and I looked away. After how many times I'd almost been killed in the past few days, he was the least of my problems.

Too bad I didn't believe it.

CHAPTER
THIRTY-SIX

DAVID GOT us back on the freeway, keeping with the flow of traffic. There was a slew of trucks on the road despite the early hour, and I stared out the window, taking measured breaths and calming my mind.

It took a half hour before anyone felt like speaking. Eleanor fell asleep, which made me feel a bit better. She needed it, and honestly, I prayed she'd wake feeling a bit more like herself so we wouldn't have to tote her around any longer.

"Do you think he'll live?" I finally asked, barely above the sound of the engine.

David met my eyes over the center console. "As long as he can outrun whoever hired him."

I nodded, letting myself be comforted, even though the logical part of my brain screamed statistics and data at me. I turned it off. There was only so much I could handle.

"There will be others," I noted.

David nodded but didn't look at me. "It will take a bit of time to get word back that he failed and send another. I can't imagine why there was only one of them back there."

"I hope you're right." I didn't know if I believed him, but

in the end, it didn't matter much. Either there would be others and hopefully we'd be lucky again, or we'd get to Future Solutions without another assassin trying to take us down. Quite frankly, the odds were not in our favor either way.

"So, to the compound? We need to figure out a plan that doesn't involve us getting shot on sight." I stared at the acres of orchards in orderly lines that made patterns as we sped by.

David was quiet a moment. "I have an idea on that front. What if they think we're the originals?"

I paused, thinking it through. "That won't work. I'm sure they have some way to tell us apart."

"I'm open to other ideas, but I don't think Sarah and Joey should be with those people any longer than possible. They've got a couple of hours on us already."

I took a deep breath and leaned back against my seat. What I wouldn't give for my work resources! All that data and access would have done wonders to at least get us a floor plan or aerial view. Hell, I would've been happy with internet access and a smart phone—something else that hadn't been in the room when I awoke. As it stood, David's knowledge of the place was all we had to go on, and that wouldn't make this any easier.

"So, you think you can convince someone there to let us in by saying your Aaron in a younger shell? And if that by some miracle works, what then?" I tried to tone down the extreme sense that this was all ludicrous, but David still shot me an annoyed look.

How he still managed to be attractive after shooting a man and leaving him for dead, and driving the man's car to escape, was pretty much amazing. But not amazing enough that I didn't need an exact plan in place.

"You know I'm not going in there without some kind of plan. There's too much at stake," I noted when he didn't say anything more.

He sighed. "It would go something like this. We park in the lot by the front entrance. A guard is posted there. It looks very bland, in case someone ends up there by mistake. I talk to the guard, convince him to let us in by pretending to be Aaron for a few minutes. It won't be hard, especially since he's apparently still working with them."

"Right," I muttered, distracted by the sudden thought of how somewhere out there was a woman I was cloned from. Someone whose brain was probably just as odd as mine, memorizing cars we passed, and able to tell exactly which ones were likely to have weapons inside. "Do all of us have to pretend to be our clones?"

David frowned, thinking. "I thought maybe we could try that, but it'll be easier if you're my captives. That will make it less likely to get as much scrutiny. Aaron went after you as his younger self to bring you in. So I'll be bringing you in. And once we're past the guard…"

"You'll instantly free us?" I narrowed my eyes. Hot or not, I wasn't entirely liking this scenario. It almost felt like I was getting handed to the company trying to kill me like a trussed-up turkey.

David grinned at me, recognizing my tone. "We'll get zip-ties. I'll secure them in a way that allows you to take them off whenever. So you'll be able to free yourself. Sound okay?"

"Fine. So, Eleanor and I are free, past the guard, and then what?" I wished there were some way to see David's memories, to sketch out the layout.

"Then we find where they're keeping the kids. They always kept Corbin and me in the back left part of the building when we were little. So long as they haven't moved everything around, that's the most logical spot to hold people. We'll get back there and free them."

"What about guards along the way?" I asked.

"It's a science facility. Mostly the guards are outside. The white coats don't really want guns in their labs."

Okay, that was fair. But cameras would alert security personnel that we were out of place. Based on the manpower they were throwing after us, they would certainly be well guarded in their home base. I asked as much and David shrugged.

"Aaron was always able to move around that place as if he owned it. I think the crux of it will be getting in. Convincing them to think that I'm Aaron from the start. And with you and Eleanor in tow, distracting everyone should be rather easy. You'll pick up a couple lab coats and you'll fit right in."

I nodded, already planning the best way to act like a recalcitrant prisoner that Aaron/David was hauling in. It might work. Maybe.

"And how do we get out?" I asked, knowing that I'd be thinking through this far more times than I wanted to before we arrived.

"We take the kids to the center yard. Act like we're taking them out to play a bit. It's good to get them out of their cells and all that. From there, Eleanor and the kids go down along the left wall, hit the fence that has a gate that opens with the same key to enter the area, and they make a run for the parking lot. Then you and I are going to go in and see just what havoc we can create before following."

Sitting back, I tried to run through the mess of this plan in my mind. David answered my questions, and we bounced ideas off each other on what kind of havoc would disrupt Future Solutions. After three hours, we were both exhausted. I hoped what we had laid out would be enough. It had to be. So many lives relied on it.

The miles sped by while I raced through as many permutations as possible, attempting to find some other way to work this out. But there was insufficient data to create an alternate plan. Maybe when we got there a better option would present itself.

Instead, I riffled through the bag of gas station food David had stolen and ate a small container of Pringles. And a bag of peanut M&Ms. They didn't do a whole lot to make me feel better.

Eleanor finally woke on the other side of the Grapevine as we made our way down into L.A. and the instantaneous clog of traffic.

"God, I hate this city," she grumped, leaning forward between the seats to peer ahead at the endless miles of cars.

"You and me both," David muttered.

I kept quiet, staring at the Knotts Berry Farm amusement park we inched past. Unlike the others, I'd never spent time in this city, and longed to exit the freeway and make our way toward the ocean. The odds of our mission weren't exactly in our favor, and the chances of ever getting to explore L.A. were miniscule. Dipping my toes in the ocean one last time would have been wonderful, but time wasn't our friend.

Eleanor noticed my silence and placed a hand on my shoulder. "What's the plan?"

"Are you feeling better?" David asked.

"Much. That was so odd. It honestly felt like I'd been stuffed into my body wrong. Like if you went to put on a pair of gloves and accidentally put your fingers into the wrong slots. It was… horrible." Her voice fell as she finished, and I didn't have to look at her to know the expression she wore.

Her description sent a shiver through me. As much as I hadn't wanted her to go through such a traumatic experience, I was grateful it wasn't me. If that made me a terrible person, then I was okay with that.

"So, the plan?" Eleanor forced her voice to ask calmly, though I knew under the surface, her whole being vibrated with the need to get her kids back.

"We're going to get into the compound by pretending I am a re-bodied original, and you two are going to be my angry prisoners," David explained, glancing at me.

It sounded even more ridiculous than the first time he'd

said it. I pressed my lips together and stared out the window at the car next to us. A black Honda CR-V. The woman driving it was headed to her boyfriend's for lunch and hoped to get lucky.

I kind of wanted to body switch with her and let her deal with this mess.

"Will that work?" Eleanor asked.

"I don't know," David admitted. "But Diana and I couldn't come up with a better plan."

"So there's no other way inside?" Eleanor asked.

I sighed. "David doesn't remember one, and he would have if there had been one in the sections he visited. We don't have a way to look up schematics of the rest of the building, and no real way of even knowing if that's where they are. We'll be walking in blind, but we don't have any other choice." I took a deep breath, trying desperately to reach some sort of inner calm.

Eleanor slid back in her seat, her head disappearing from between the seats. David let out an echo of my sigh, and I could tell from his posture that he didn't think we had any other option.

I really hated that he was right.

The traffic pulsed for the next hour or so until we finally cleared the other end of the city and started down the 5 toward San Diego. I closed my eyes, forcing myself to concentrate on my breaths and keep from thinking too much, or memorize one more license plate number.

David reached over and took my hand. It was too warm against my own, but the contact felt good. A chill seemed to have settled into us all while we waited to see what our next steps would be.

I opened my eyes when we finally left the freeway. David knew exactly where to go, which didn't surprise me, but it didn't make it any easier to traverse as we wound away from the rest of the cars and any sense of escape. If it weren't for the kids, I would be going in the opposite direction. Maybe there was hope for sanctuary on the other side of the globe.

The entry to the headquarters was an ostentatious driveway landscaped to the point of being almost comical. The building itself was nestled back amongst some trees, its walls of windows reflecting the sun and looking like a beacon on a hill. An evil, twisted, insane beacon.

"The building looks like something out of Star Trek," Eleanor said with a little laugh. "It's all glass. Who the hell cleans all of that?"

The only laugh I managed to muster was an especially hard exhale.

David passed the driveway and made a right at the next intersection—which was really nothing more than a four-way stop in the middle of nowhere. We continued down this road until a narrow driveway appeared and I realized this was all we could see of the compound from the road. I'd hoped for a good look to try and organize my plans more.

David didn't slow one bit as he slid into the overgrown drive and down the incline toward the compound. Gravel pinged off the tire wells and back window. "As I told Diana, the headquarters is technically just over that rise, so we're hidden from their view at the moment. Corbin and I once walked between the two," David noted, waving toward his right where I could just see the tops of the trees that must have been the backdrop of the headquarters.

I held my breath as we made it to the parking lot tucked underneath the swell of the road—invisible from any other angle. There were plenty of foreign cars here, as well as a few domestic, all of them new and glistening in the sun.

"Even the janitors are paid well apparently," David noted.

He pulled into a spot that would allow the next driver to pull through and head directly out the exit. As long as it wasn't blocked. My stomach clenched at the realization that the lot was fenced in and offered no other route to escape except by the way we entered.

The building ahead was solid cement, a far cry from the seamless glass and soaring angles of the main building by the road. This one wasn't for show. This was where the messy work happened.

We sat in the car for a long minute, each absorbing details of the place around us. My brain catalogued the other cars, getting a rough estimate of the number of people inside: about twenty, if only two of them carpooled. Six were scientists, five were lab techs, one a manager, another a boss, and the rest security or maintenance.

Who knew how many prisoners/clones there were.

David was the first to speak. He took a deep breath and looked at Eleanor, then me. "Ready?"

I shook my head. "No." But I gripped my door handle all the same.

In unison, the three of us stepped from the car. The pock-marked cement of the lot crunched underfoot, but we tried to appear unconcerned. David pulled out several zip ties he'd found at one of our gas station stops and gave Eleanor and I long looks. "I'm sorry for this."

I closed my eyes and took a deep breath in order to suck down the panic that bubbled up. "Just get it over with." Either this was the quickest way to die, or David was right and it was our only hope of getting out with the kids.

"I'm putting them on wrong. You'll be able to yank hard on them and free yourself when we get past the guards," David added. We'd gone over this in the car, but it didn't make it any easier to have him bind my wrists until the little black plastic band cut into my skin.

Eleanor whimpered a little as he turned to her.

"Let's do this. And remember, I'm Aaron, okay? Just in a younger shell," David said, looking in each of our eyes.

Eleanor and I nodded mutely. David took hold of both our

arms and led us toward the front of the building. The bubbling panic within was nearly at a roiling boil. I was trusting David far more than I had meant to at this stage. My gut felt like I'd tied it into a giant knot.

"The Range Rover's here," Eleanor announced, just loud enough for us to hear.

It sat off to one side of the building, under an awning, looking as if it had been driven through the countryside without benefit of a road. They apparently missed the "Clean Cars Only" memo.

I caught Eleanor's arm and hung on tight, despite my awkwardly tied wrists, as she tried to make a mad dash toward the vehicle. "No! We need to be less conspicuous. They already want to kill us."

Eleanor tugged and pulled against me, her expression bordering on madness.

"But we know they're here now," David added in a kinder tone. "We'll figure this out."

Eleanor gave one last, half-hearted tug and stopped trying to run to her children. Her shoulders slumped and I pulled her close in a hug, her ragged breath against my neck a horrible reminder of how much she'd been through. How much more we still had to face until we got her kids back.

We kept moving, David taking our arms in a faux tight grip as we skirted the edges of the lot until we made it to the other side of the building. A few trees had been planted around a little garden, making a break area with tables for the employees.

I had to press my lips together against the pain of him dragging me toward the garden lunch area, then past it and around the front. David was right; the building was a big U shape. The arm we walked along contained the main entrance at the top, and David's firm grip on both Eleanor's and my upper arms didn't waver as he pushed us into the dark lobby.

No windows here, either. Just the faint smell of chemicals and antiseptic.

"We've been wondering how long it would take for you to show up." The voice rang through the space, but I knew whose it was even before my eyes adjusted.

Aaron stood about twenty feet back from us in front of a wide set of glass doors leading to the rest of the building. The lobby looked normal—modern, sleek, with a plain white desk in front of the Future Solutions logo on the wall. Live potted trees in the corners. Tasteful rugs on the floor and molding around the walls. It was a showplace meant to fool onlookers. Anyone who stumbled onto this building would enter here and go no further.

Aaron. Right. We needed to run through a modified plan to give David the access he needed. I'd already thought of this at least.

I also didn't miss the multiple cameras, the complicated locking system to get through the glass doors into the building beyond, and the sensors around the door behind us. The parking lot had been devoid of cameras—I made sure of that as soon as we entered—but they probably had some other form of surveillance I couldn't detect.

"Hello, Dad." David's voice, for all the world, didn't sound in the slightest bit shocked. I couldn't help myself. I looked over at him, searching his face for any sign that this might be a surprise. That the rules were changing.

But David was good. No sign of the Game showed.

A cold finger of fear traced down my back and I dropped my head forward, my hair curtaining across my face.

This wasn't a game I could fail at. Because, really, this wasn't a game at all.

CHAPTER
THIRTY-SEVEN

"I TOLD you I'd get them all here, didn't I?" David snapped. He stepped forward, pulling Eleanor and me with him. My shoulders already ached from the strange angle of my wrists.

My heart lodged itself somewhere in my throat. He told Aaron he'd bring us here? What the hell? Or was this just part of his scheme to get us in? I couldn't tell. Damn David and his ability to out-Game me.

"You did, and you've done well," Aaron congratulated him. "The kids are in the back already. They're going to be quite an asset, we can already tell."

Eleanor made a sound low in her throat. David dropped my arm as Eleanor lurched away from us, her dark eyes regaining their wild look.

"What are you doing to my kids?" Eleanor lunged toward Aaron, head down, ready to tackle him. I had half a mind to follow her and take them David out while I was at it, but instead I stood by and tried to ease the zip tie off. It was a more effective use of the distraction.

The zip tie wouldn't budge.

As David struggled to get Eleanor settled, Aaron stood by

as if he were having coffee in a café. I subtly shifted my wrists, working at the plastic.

He told us they would come loose if we tried; if we needed to get loose to do something inside the building, they wouldn't hold us back.

He lied.

That realization hit me in the gut so hard my breath left in a whoosh. How had I let myself trust him? Or fall for him?

I'd fucking slept with him last night!

The plastic didn't release my wrists. Eleanor was putting up a helluva struggle—she'd ended up on the floor and got in a few good kicks to David's gut. That was exactly what I felt like had happened to me.

He tricked us. Led us straight into the lion's den. Right into Future Solutions. In zip ties!

What were they going to do with us now? What were they doing with the kids? Why couldn't I have just gotten killed on the way?

The feel of eyes on me drew my attention and I clicked my Game face back into place. No way I was going to slip now. Not after everything I'd been through. Even if the lying sack of shit wrestling with my sister clone on the floor made me want to cry, scream, kick, and run for the hills. Though he deserved a good kick to the balls before I did any of that.

But I wouldn't get far. This place was a fortress. Aaron watched me, leaning against the white counter, a perfectly calm grin splitting his face.

I'd love to take him out while I was at it. Wipe that smug smile from his face with the butt of a gun. If killing him would kill David as well, it would be an excellent two-for-one bonus.

Instead, I kept my face free of any expression. David *humphed* as Eleanor got in one last hit before he snagged her under both arms and hauled her roughly to her feet.

Eleanor's face was mostly obscured by her hair as she

stumbled around. Her eyes met mine, wide and terrified. She must have realized the bindings weren't going anywhere.

"Well, I think that's quite enough of that. Shall we?" Aaron made a sweeping gesture toward the doors that led into the rest of the compound.

A flare of panic swelled through me, making my feet stick to the carpet and my breathing intensify. If we went through those doors, the odds of us ever making it back out were nil. We could be dissected within the hour.

I hoped they killed us before they started.

David prodded me forward without looking at me. A slumped Eleanor didn't protest as Aaron took her arm and guided her to the door. He placed a thumb against the sensor and the glass slid back with barely a whisper.

"Fuck you, you liar." I kept my voice low, pitched just to David. He didn't even look at me.

Damn him.

I really wanted to find some way to crack his Game, to make that façade fall away as he realized what I was going to do to him. How much it would hurt.

Too bad our roles were reversed. It would more likely be me failing to keep my composure with whatever was coming through the doors Aaron held the door open for me and David to pass before herding Eleanor through.

The pleasant decor and atmosphere of the lobby fell away to an industrial laboratory—sharp, white, and sterile. The smell of antiseptic mixed with too much bleach made my nose wrinkle.

"We're just around the back here," Aaron said conversationally. As he walked behind me, I could almost feel his eyes on me and the heat of his breath on the back of my neck. The cringe of disgust I felt didn't reach the surface, but that didn't mean I didn't experience it.

The cement hallways seemed like a long, dull portal to hell. The cement floors shone under the harsh fluorescent lights, and drains were installed every ten yards or so. I didn't want to think about what they were for.

Windows in the lab doors were the only way to see in, and I tried to peek into each of the facilities we passed without making it obvious. Each of the wide rooms were filled with the same biotech equipment: machines with blinking lights, long rows of pipettes, and cages of small animals. It wasn't until we neared the end of the impossibly long hallway that the rooms shifted to treadmills, CT scanners, and other health-related equipment that signaled this was where they studied more human-like things.

Like me. Human-*like*. That was all I was to Aaron and the rest of the researchers here. I wasn't a person. I wasn't someone who remembered learning how to ride a bike. I wasn't a person who got her first kiss during her sophomore year of high school in the back of the movie theater. I wasn't someone who spent years learning how to be the perfect spy. I was a specimen, being led down this hallway toward something I couldn't even begin to imagine.

No. I gave myself a mental shake and forced back the darkness that threatened to close around me. I wouldn't go down without a fight.

My senses had retreated, dampened by the oppressive atmosphere of the place. Now they roared back as if I'd connected my brain to a fiber optic line. Most of the scientists were in the labs up ahead, attracted by the new specimens. There were at least ten lab workers, based on the cars outside. I still didn't know the number of specimens.

David smelled worried, like he wasn't quite sure of his place in all of this. Well, other than being a fucking traitor. Eleanor was a mess. I wouldn't involve her in any plan that had her do anything other than escape with her kids.

There was another exterior door somewhere ahead and to the left. It would lead to the fenced in central courtyard, which wasn't much better than staying inside but might give us an edge.

Doors, lettering, air currents, the worn parts of the shiny cement floor—it all went into my mind, where it was organized into as much useable data as I could obtain. Not that anything spelled out "easy escape route" or any such nonsense. Still, from experience, I knew that sometimes the smallest detail would be the most useful.

I think David could sense the difference. He looked over at me, his dark eyes probing mine. I didn't flinch. Didn't look away. I hoped he sensed the hatred in my gaze. How foolish I'd been to trust him. To think that perhaps something good could emerge from this mess.

Some small piece of me still hoped this hadn't been his plan all along; that betraying Eleanor and me wasn't his intention. Now would be his chance to show some small inkling that this wasn't what he wanted, but no. His expression didn't change in the slightest. The same blank look stared back at me until I turned away.

"You won't escape." David's words were soft, low enough that only I could hear. They brought gooseflesh up on my arms.

"That's what you think," I replied. "And what sort of cookie are they going to give you for being their good little lab rat?"

"Who says I'm a lab rat?" David's tone filled with mirth, even in whispers.

"You are a poor liar," I breathed. Something in the way he said it—something my subconscious caught easily but would take too long to analyze—told me he wasn't being honest. He was a clone, all right. No doubt about it.

The doors to a room at the end of the hallway opened as we approached. A short man with glasses partially obscured by bushy gray eyebrows held it open, his dirty lab coat pushed back from his protruding belly. A tall, elegant, woman who had clearly had a facelift waited for us at his side, a clipboard clutched in her hand as she stared at us. Probably wanted to dissect us right then and there.

"Well, that *does* seem to be the last of them." Her clipped accent spoke of money and summers at Cape Cod.

The last of us? Did that mean all the other clones were killed off? My stomach flipped and I couldn't help the short, quick inhale of pain at the thought. How many deaths were they responsible for? Did it count as murder if the deceased didn't have a complete soul?

Aaron and David propelled us through the doors into the room beyond. It had a good deal in common with the underground lab at Fireside Cottage. Cells lined the far wall, and in one I could see Sarah huddled against the glass, clutching Joey and watching us with wide eyes. At least they were alive.

Eleanor saw them in the same instant and got two running steps in before Aaron caught her. The other male scientist joined in, tackling her to the floor.

"You'll get to see them soon enough," Aaron snapped, grabbing Eleanor's hair to subdue her.

For a brief moment, our eyes met, and it was as if Eleanor's fear and dread washed through me. My knees shuddered and I wanted to collapse. The way she felt was as palpable as a bat behind my knees.

I turned away, unable to handle the pain in my twin's features. It too closely mirrored my own. Instead, I inspected the rest of the room. Chairs, two of them, were bolted to the floor off to my right, restraints lying idle for their next victim.

Surrounding the black leather, sharp tools seemed to multiply on small, shiny trays. I counted thirty on my first glance, and cupboards behind them surely carried more. What they were used for wasn't clear. Except for the drain in the floor. This one dripped water, and I had little doubt it was used to wash away the blood from whatever atrocities were done in those chairs.

According to Eleanor, transferring souls between bodies wasn't exactly a bloody business, so I had to assume there was something else gory going on here. Harvesting organs? It would certainly be useful to take a lung, kidney, or heart from someone with the exact same DNA.

"Well, it's a pleasure to know that it was *my* clones who were some of the last to survive." The voice preceded a woman entering the lab from a door to an office.

The sight of her really did make my knees buckle, accompanied by a hot thread of shame. There she stood—I stood—my root clone.

It was as if someone had taken my face and body and used special effects makeup on it. Some small, silly part of my brain wanted it to be a mask she'd peel off to reveal... What? Me? The absurdity of such a thought only served to remind me of how close I was to my breaking point. What would happen if I lost my mind? Would they just replace it with another clone's?

No. The only way we would make it out of here alive was if I kept it together.

The woman smiled, wrinkles carving into her cheeks and fanning around her eyes. She'd smiled a lot in her life, though her teeth weren't as straight as mine, nor as white. Too much coffee, too many bottles of red wine.

I made a little note to myself to buy Eleanor and myself some really good wrinkle cream once we got the hell out of here. I didn't want those same crow's feet if I could help it. Because we fucking were making it out of here.

"You must be Diana," my root concluded, her grin never wavering as she looked me over from head to toe. "As much as I'd always hoped to meet you under other circumstances, it's nice to finally get the chance. I always wondered if I could have been a spy." She laughed. The portly short man joined in.

She spun on her heel and went to Eleanor, still panting in Aaron's grasp. Stepping closer, our root inspected Eleanor from an inch away, peering into her eyes and touching the dirty t-shirt Eleanor wore. "And you, you are quite interesting. I never knew myself as having a nurturing side, but I imagine there's a great deal of environmental influence on that suite of traits."

"Or maybe you're just evil," Eleanor hissed.

"Well, if you're my clone, what does that make you?" our root asserted, smiling so that it accentuated all her wrinkles.

Eleanor smirked. "The one who found happiness? Because judging from your outfit and this shitty lab, you don't get out a lot."

The woman laughed, peering down at herself. She wore jeans and a plain blue button-up shirt, coupled with white clogs. Nothing about it screamed stylish, though that would have been my outfit of choice if I'd been granted the option of not caring about my clothes—something the rigors of my job never afforded.

"Well, it seems like you're going to be a fun one to analyze further. I want to understand how you ended up having children. I never thought any of you would concede to that form of narcissism." Our root gave us both a huffing sigh and looked about ready to launch into some other critique.

The other two scientists, impatient with our meet-and-greet, stepped forward. "We should get them settled. Plenty of time to discuss things later," the tall woman pointed out, her tone clinically professional.

Funny how it's possible to vehemently hate someone just by looking at them. My attempt to avoid judging people instantly had been entirely blown out of the water the last few days. Maybe for the better.

Portly nodded his agreement and went to help Aaron haul Eleanor into the cell next to her kids.

This, of course, led to Eleanor putting up one hell of a fight, kicking and screaming that she wanted to be with her children. Her screams echoed through the room and down the hallway.

None of the scientists listened. None even showed a smidgen of emotion. Instead, they dropped Eleanor to the floor of her cell—identical to those in Fireside Cottage—and secured it as she rose to her feet, pounding on the glass while her eyes swam with tears.

Sarah watched it all, her baby brother clutched to her as she slowly rocked back and forth. Fat tears dampened Joey's sleeper.

"You are a fucking monster." I twisted around to make sure David knew I spoke to him.

He just shrugged. "At least *I* won't be the one they cut open."

I'VE NEVER BEEN a fly-by-the-seat-of-my-pants kind of woman. Never. I planned, obsessed, and observed. But right then, without a second's thought, I hauled back and landed a solid knee in David's groin.

The satisfying crunch brought David to his knees, head bent forward so his dark hair spilled over his eyes. I slammed my elbow down on the back of his head and he slouched to the ground before he could cry out.

God, that felt good.

The commotion from Eleanor and hushed conversation between the scientists by her cell gave me ten seconds before they fully realized what happened.

Five steps to the first tray of surgical instruments. I grabbed one and angled it against the plastic surrounding my wrists. Three seconds gone. It didn't take much to snap it apart, the instant rush of blood marking my skin with dark red welts and making my fingers tingle. Seven seconds gone.

Without thinking, I shifted my grip and pulled my arm back so that when I turned, I let the small blade fly. Ten seconds.

I'd never been an ace shot—but it was enough. The little

weapon spun across the open space and embedded into the gut of the short scientist, at least three inches deep. A second blade whizzed and caught him deep in his bicep.

Too bad his fat would protect him. But the grunt of pain and instant welling of blood marring his shirt was enough. Dazed, with the instruments still poking out of him, he went down. His hands fluttered around the blades and he groaned. A part of me really hoped I'd hit his abdominal aorta, but I doubted I even nicked his liver.

Another blade-like tool was already in my hand, and this one I had more of a chance to aim.

The tall, snooty woman took it in her upper right shoulder. Another blade near her left hip toppled her next to the fat man.

It only took fifteen seconds, but my root and Aaron were mobile, coming at me from both sides of the room.

Eleanor watched from her cell, her nose pressed to the glass.

Aaron first. He edged along the bench to my left, his eyes flitting to my root and then to the trays of tools. I knew that look. It meant he was gauging his options. Too bad he was too slow.

The long pointy tool looked like something from a dental horror movie. One end was barbed, and I didn't want to know what it was used for. Certainly not for dissecting me.

He didn't see it coming until it was too late, and the nasty little tool embedded itself like a dart in his eye. It even quivered a bit, up until Aaron squealed and doubled forward.

"Don't remove it—it'll just make things worse," I snapped.

And then there was one.

I turned to the woman who wore my face. God, I wanted to slit her throat. I wanted something permanent; a signal to the others not to mess with us.

But if she died… so did Eleanor and I.

"You know, I'm really quite impressed," she mused. She stopped near the door to the office she'd originally emerged from. "I never thought I had it in me to do what you've done." She made a sweeping gesture toward the bleeding bodies and whimpering humans around us.

"You've never had the chance to push yourself like this," I replied. I moved away from the tray of tools, hoping it would calm her a bit if they weren't in arm's reach. Even so, I did make sure I had a simple scalpel tucked up my sleeve.

She shrugged. "Perhaps." Leaning against the doorjamb, she crossed her ankles and arms loosely, as if she already knew the outcome of what we were doing and wasn't worried.

She was wrong. And weak. Too many hours locked away in here with no windows and no training. They picked the wrong clone to screw with. And now they'd pay.

"You know, it doesn't have to end this way," my root hinted, peering down at her nails. She actually picked at a hangnail as I circled her.

I didn't reply. I knew this Game. Two more steps to the left, and I was clear of the lab bench. A clear shot to the doorway and the woman.

She looked up at me, her features a perfect mask. But I knew that, too. Knew it as well as I knew that inside, she was frightened. That her nonchalance was nothing more than a guise. And that if I used her, we had a chance.

The next time she looked down at her nails, I made my move. To her credit, she put up a fight. I dropped low and rounded to her side, using her momentum to drag her arm behind her and spin her so her face was pressed into the cement wall. I heard a crunch and blood dripped from her nose.

She kicked back at me, though I easily stepped out of the way, and shouted for help in blubbery cries that only grew worse as her nose gushed.

The scalpel pressed against her throat quieted her. "You're going to get us out of here," I breathed into her ear, "and then maybe we'll talk about how to lobotomize you. Make you nice and compliant. Keep you in a defective shell for the rest of your life."

Scaring her would make her easy to handle as we escaped. Though just killing her would be by far the easiest method.

A quick look around revealed a bag of plastic zip ties, suspiciously like those David used on Eleanor and me. Keeping the scalpel pressed against her jugular, I pushed her in front of me until I was able to snag one and secure her arms.

Aaron still moaned behind us, voicing a series of unintelligible grunts and groans, and I wanted to take him out. And then this whole place, leaving it no more than a giant, charred pile of rubble. But first, I had to get out with the kids.

"Tell me how to open the doors," I snapped, kneeing the woman toward the glassed-in cells. Eleanor watched me like I'd lost my mind, but crept to the door of her cell expectantly, eager to escape as soon as I pressed the button.

"No." Her voice warbled the word and she spit blood on the floor. "Never."

I dug the blade into her throat, a thin stream of blood trickling down her throat to join that from her nose. "Open the door or I'll slice you. I can take your eyelids first. It won't technically kill you."

My stomach roiled at the thought. Could I really do such a thing? But looking through the glass at Eleanor, noting her bloody lip and a spectacular bruise that was already forming around both eyes and down the side of her face, made up my mind.

To show I was serious, I took the knife from her throat and traced a faint line down the side of her face, just deep enough to draw blood.

My root quivered where I gripped her arm, and her eyes met mine, wide and confused. "You can't kill me."

I barked a laugh. "Who said anything about killing? Hurting you will be enough." My voice was calm. Collected. Like I'd planned this all. Thank God for all those years of practice playing the Game.

I pressed the woman a step closer to the interface with the cell, once again angling the blade against her throat. "Now let them out."

Her shoulders rose with her next shaky breath, and her hand rose to the screen, her bloody fingers hesitating to type.

"Do it!" I jostled her, feeling more than hearing the rise of noise in the furthest reaches of the building. Someone had finally gotten help. We had to move, and now.

"No." Her voice was calm as she spun around to face me. But the look in her eyes—wide, wild, like a feral cat spooked by a sudden flash of light—chilled me. I still held the blade to her throat and she threw her weight against it, angling herself so that it would have sliced right into her jugular.

If I hadn't moved.

"Are you fucking crazy?" I dropped the blade, letting it clatter across the floor. "*Are* you?"

That was what it took to break through my Game. I stood, trembling, my eyes locked with the insanity-filled ones of the woman whose life force I shared. So much adrenaline sang through my veins, I half expected my hair to raise on end.

"I'm not about to be taken hostage by my goddamn clone." Her voice rose and fell in pitch as if she didn't have any control over it. "You're a fucking science experiment. Not a goddamn person. Without me, you'd never exist! No fucking way am I getting you out of this building. You should be locked in a cage!"

Which was apparently exactly what to say to your clone when you wanted to be knocked out cold.

She went down in a disgraceful heap, her head smacking against the glass of the cell door with a hollow *thunk*.

So much for using her to get us out of here. It took every ounce of self-control not to kick her in the gut.

Eleanor pounded a fist against the glass, dragging me back from the trance of staring at the bruised and bloody woman at my feet. The woman who may have given me life in a test tube, but who certainly didn't realize what she was fucking around with by making me a living, breathing human being.

One of these days, I was going to have enough time for a good, long existential crisis. Until then, I turned to the cell's interface.

"It's two-seven-eight-nine-three-eight-eight," Sarah spoke up from inside her cell, her thin voice yelling to be heard through the thick glass.

Without questioning her, I typed in the code, which brought up a menu that allowed me to open both doors. They hissed open and Eleanor scrambled to her children as if they were the air she needed to breathe.

I hated being a total killjoy as the three of them collapsed together in a happy huddle of arms, legs, and hugs, but the sound of too many feet had grown closer. We barely had any time to get out of there, and I still didn't know a great way to do it.

"We've got to move," I instructed, touching Eleanor's shoulder.

She and Sarah looked at me in unison and nodded, and then Eleanor took Joey and snagged Sarah's hand. I looked down at my root's form and wished I could carry her with me. I didn't want to let her out of my sight, especially if that meant she could kill herself to stop us. But committing suicide would leave her work unfinished, and somehow I doubted she'd be so willing if her own life wasn't already on the line.

"There's a window in the office," Sarah piped up again.

"As much as I really hate that you've had to go through all this…" I mused to the little girl as we hurried to the door that led into an office. "You really are a useful one to have along."

Sarah flashed me a quick grin and bounced past me into the adjoining room.

The office was a hopeless mess of stacks of papers and pinned diagrams covering the walls—an unorganized mess of massive proportions.

"Good to know that tidiness is a matter of nurture," Eleanor muttered with a raised eyebrow as we stepped across the threshold. Some of the stacks looked like they were about to cause a paper avalanche, but over the giant desk off to the left was a broad window.

We were going to have to break the glass. No hinges or tracks allowed it to open, and upon closer inspection, the glass itself was a few inches thick.

"Find something to break the glass with," I advised, already searching the surfaces for anything that might give us the leverage we needed.

Sarah and Eleanor broke apart to search through the jungle of papers. It didn't take more than five seconds before the first giant stack of papers went down, almost taking Sarah with it. We all exchanged a worried glance before going back to our hunt.

We had maybe a minute before we would be trapped by the oncoming hoard, and with all four scientists still technically alive out there, there was little hope we'd get another shot at escape.

I jumped as something thumped against the inside of the window and tumbled to my feet—a paperweight. The window, showcasing the bright afternoon sunshine on the rolling hills surrounding the building, wavered, but only a pinpoint divot was evident.

"Keep doing that!" I cried, rushing around the slippery

piles of journal articles and notes, back into the lab. One of the lab stools would be smaller, easier to swing against the glass.

I skidded to a halt at the sight of Aaron, hands still clutched over his eyes, stumbling toward me. "Diana!" His voice rasped. How he knew it was me didn't quite compute, but then again, if he had to have the same skills as David and me, then he could have worked it out any number of ways.

Yet, the sight of him, blood dripping down his wrist, staining his white shirt, twisted my gut and tugged at my conscience.

"Diana," he implored again, bumping into the counter and stopping.

"What?"

"That's not David," he gasped. "He's not the one here in the room."

For a second, it felt like the room had become a vacuum, leaving it in perfect, airless silence. Every tool, surface, and moaning human became caught in the too-bright lights, the shuddering hope that what Aaron contended, and all it implied, could possibly be true.

Then my brain started again. "Nice try. You're just trying to trick me so I get captured." I reached for the nearest stool, metal and heavy and perfect for breaking glass.

"They're going to kill him, Diana. I raised that boy. He's my son. Please, *please*, find him."

I wanted to believe him. I really, really did. But he already made it clear on several occasions that I'd be a fool to do so. That David and I were subjects to him. Even if my heart sped up at the thought that maybe, just maybe, it wasn't David who betrayed us.

"You should have thought about that before selling us out." The words tasted bitter on my tongue, but I turned and ran back into the office.

The others had made a smattering of craters in the windows during the fifteen seconds I'd been gone and moved out of the way as I raced up, using my momentum to crash the stool into the window where they'd weakened it.

It took two more strong hits before a long, snaking crack opened with a shrill creak. Pushing thoughts of David being caught in the building, surely about to be killed, from my mind, I hauled back and slammed the stool, battering ram style, until the glass shattered in a huge, jagged maw of splinters.

"Watch out!" I demanded, grabbing a sheaf of files and using it to protect my hand as I pushed glass away from the counter tops, then extended a hand to Sarah. With her mom helping, I managed to angle her through the window and down the five-foot drop to the ground.

In our haste, we all but dropped Joey down to her; Sarah caught him like a champ, though Eleanor held her breath as she watched from above.

There was movement in the other room when Eleanor dropped down next to her kids. "Keep low, away from where they can see you," I whispered, waving for them to go ahead. No sense in all of us getting caught at once.

"No one's going to get David?" Sarah asked, peering up at me.

"David's the one who got us captured," Eleanor scolded, dropping a hand on Sarah's back and pushing her forward.

"No! That wasn't him! He's back in the other lab," Sarah cried, twisting to look back at me searchingly.

Damn. So Aaron spoke the truth. The sound of a nearby door opening landed me back in reality, and I waved the others away.

Eleanor, clutching her infant protectively to her chest, took Sarah's hand and raced away. I watched for just a moment, knowing my best chance was to immediately follow, escape with the three of them and get far from here, far enough that we could be safe.

But. But, but, but. *David.*

For a fraction of a second, I debated with myself. The smart thing to do would be to go with Eleanor and get her and the kids to safety. But leaving David behind was wrong. Awful and wrong. And I would not leave him here to be dissected by these evil assholes. Not when I needed him with us, with me. He was definitely the only one who might enjoy playing the Game with me, and I'd be damned before I gave that up. And after all this, I just might actually trust him.

Before my brain could catch up with me, I slid off the counter to the glass covered floor of the lab and stepped away from the window. Either I was about to commit unintentional suicide, or I was going to save another one of us, another clone, that I had developed feelings for. The odds were against me.

With a deep breath, I made my way across the paper littered floor, listening, observing, planning. Which other lab? Sarah saw him, had probably traveled here with him, but how was I supposed to find which room it was? Especially without getting caught?

My rational brain told me there had to be a logical plan.

The minute of breathing room had passed and there were others milling in the surrounding rooms, their hushed voices creeping around corners with instructions for those who planned on coming in to capture us. It was impossible to know how long it would take them, but I'd bet on having just a few more seconds.

Which meant... I had no time. How did I keep them from pinning me down?

Aaron moaned on the floor, and I glanced over to see my root. The motion sparked a stupid, but maybe just possible idea.

A little blood marred the collar of the white lab coat, but that was it. I shucked it off her frame with ease, throwing it over myself as I shoved the unconscious woman into the cell and proceeded to lock her in. The glass door was in the process of suctioning closed when at least eight men thundered into the room, surrounding me and the others.

"Hands where I can see them!" one of them shouted, wearing black like the rest, with a plain black pistol clutched in his hands, though a red stripe down his arm identified him as the leader. That, and the bark of his voice that brooked no choice but to agree.

"Oh, thank God," Aaron groaned. His hands were still over his eyes, holding the eyeball-gouging implement stationary.

I put my hands up, doing my best to angle my hair away so that it better hid my face and the clear age difference between me and the woman in the cell.

"They went out the window," Aaron whimpered, and I watched as half of the men broke off and charged into the office, shouting their findings of the broken glass.

Two of the others dropped to their knees to help the other scientists, who seemed too wrapped up in their own agony to be reliable witnesses. From the angle where I'd dropped them behind the lab bench on the far side of the room, they couldn't have seen much.

Aaron had to know the truth, though—that I hadn't gone with the rest.

I stared at him, not daring to drop my arms, wondering how long it would take for him to give me away. He opened his mouth and I cringed: less than three seconds. That was all it took.

I was going to end up locked in the cell I'd just dragged my root into.

CHAPTER
THIRTY-NINE

"FOR THE LOVE OF GOD, isn't anyone going to help me?" Aaron fumed. "They went out the fucking window! Get a damn ambulance here, now! Before I lose my eye!"

I sucked in a long, shuddering breath, forcing my features to remain neutral, as the armed men stowed their weapons and hurried to Aaron's side.

One came to my side and touched my arm. "You can put your arms down. Are you okay?"

I nodded, gulping. "I'm okay. I managed to force one of the clones in the cell. Please leave her there."

The man looked over my shoulder at the slumped figure on the floor. By some stroke of luck, she'd ended up face-down, so it wasn't obvious how much older she was than me.

"Good work."

I managed a weak smile and feigned leaning against the wall for support.

"You should get some water and a blanket. I'm sure you're going into shock."

Mute, I nodded. He left me alone, joining in the flurry of activity in the back office, where I could hear men jumping to the ground outside.

That gave Eleanor and the kids a head start of a couple of precious minutes. It would have to be enough. They could make it out.

For now, I had to focus on getting David and myself out of here.

While the armed men were busy getting the other scientists taken care of, I was waved from the room with curt instructions to go rest and not leave the building.

I merely nodded, hoping that anyone paying attention to me would pass off any strangeness as shock. Ducking my head, I walked down the hallway, trying to figure out which other lab David could be locked in. I headed down the base of the U of the building, walking toward the far arm. The next two openings branched into offices, far neater than my root's, at least from the glimpse from the window in the door.

Two doors down, I peered inside another lab room, staggering a little as I realized what was inside. Six—still wearing the same clothes as Eleanor—was hanging inside a cupboard-like space from padded hooks under each arm. Like she was a piece of clothing, a thing. A single IV drip hooked into her arm.

But what made me choke back vomit was the scarf next to the cabinet on the counter. It was the one Faith had been wearing the day before. I pulled open the door and slipped inside, praying Faith was here, that there was something I could do.

The smell hit me first—blood and viscera, so overpowering I clamped my hand to my face. But it was what was on the steel autopsy table that had me leaning over the sink in the corner.

Faith's flowy scarf was still tied around her neck, but there was no doubt she was long gone from the world. As evidenced by the fact that the top of her skull had been removed, and an assortment of wires and probes emerged from inside her head. These were attached to several large screens and an assortment of machines, none of which I could guess the function of. Through a thick window, an MRI had its lights on, a long streak of blood smeared down the side.

Why they'd taken Faith last night, and not me and Eleanor, was unclear. Maybe Faith had been in on things, to her own demise. Maybe it had been sheer dumb luck. But I whispered a soft "Rest in peace" to the woman, artist, human being that she'd been.

Tears stung my eyes as I left the room, walking away from the commotion still ongoing in the lab I'd left. At the junction of the next hallway, I heard it. The banging of something against glass. Quick and rhythmic—Morse code.

"SOS. David. SOS."

The next room was a lab. The door opened under my shaking hand and I slipped inside without anyone in the hallway noticing.

The setup of the room was identical to that of the other lab: same long benches down the middle, same chairs, same horrible drain in the floor, same feeling of Satan lurking in the shadows. And along the far wall, the white, plain glass cells.

All but one of the cells were empty, the one farthest from the door. Fluorescent lights lit a familiar dark head.

I stared at David for a long moment, drinking him in. He looked okay, other than a fresh bruise that circled his left eye and a swollen and split lower lip.

As soon as he saw me, he pressed his forehead to the glass, both palms flattened against the door.

"We really need to stop meeting this way," I chided.

He cracked a grin that made me want to melt to the floor. This was my David, the man who wouldn't have ever led us into a trap. How could I have ever been misled by the imposter in the other room? I knew this man in some strange bone-deep way that I didn't fully understand but trusted with all my heart. I *trusted* him.

"When?" I asked, knowing he'd understand my question.

"I woke when I heard noises in the other room. I tried to wake you, but you wouldn't budge. When I tried to stop them, Faith stuck me with a hypodermic needle and I woke up here. What happened? Where are the others?"

"They're okay. They've gotten away, hopefully. I'll tell you the rest after we get out of here."

"I don't know the code." David motioned toward the wall where the touchpad glowed.

I went to inspect it, wondering what the odds were of the code being the same as the other room.

"What did I tell you last night?" I spun back to face him, doubt crowding in after so much insanity of late. Heat rushed to my cheeks and I struggled not to feel self-conscious about our time alone in the hotel room. "After…"

David didn't hesitate. "That you never expected anything good to come out of this situation. And I was glad you were wrong. Also, pink Power Rangers."

I nodded, satisfied that he was my David, although I trusted my gut that it had to be him. With that, I punched in the numbers Sarah supplied in the other lab. The cell door whooshed open and David hurried into the lab, eager to be free of the tiny white room.

There was only a moment for him to wrap his arms around me, but the intense rush of relief, of longing, was overwhelming. Even in the midst of everything, of not knowing if Eleanor was okay, of knowing Faith had betrayed us and been betrayed, I couldn't stop the desire to wrap myself around David and kiss him like there was no tomorrow.

I wasn't the only one, apparently, as David wrapped his broad hands around the back of my head, tangled in my hair, and tipped my face to his. His lips tasted of copper and sweat, but I couldn't seem to get enough.

"Ouch," David broke away, a hint of amusement in his voice as he touched his mouth. "I think I might need to see a dentist."

"I'm sorry. That's got to hurt." I peered past his hand as he gingerly touched his jawline. Up close, I saw more blooming bruises under his rough stubble.

"How did I *possibly* sleep through that?" I wondered.

"I think Faith may have drugged you. You were sound asleep. Didn't even twitch when I got out of bed."

Shuddering at the thought, I added that to my growing list of grievances. "We've got to move. I don't know how long we have before they start looking for me. They'll realize I'm not my root soon."

"Any plan for how to get out?" he asked as we moved toward the door to the lab.

"None. We managed to break one of the windows in an office to get Eleanor and the kids out, but if you know of another way that wouldn't draw so much attention, that would be great."

David frowned, his fingers absently pressing against the split in his lip. "There was another exit down here when I was a kid," he mused. "A back door they used to go out and smoke."

"Think it's still there?" I thought about the fortress the building seemed to be and doubted that something as easy as a door could be found, despite the ping of hope that filled my chest.

"Maybe… It was somewhere down here." David looked out of the small window in the door into the hallway, frowning as we heard someone crying out from one of the other rooms.

Their terrified cries raised the hair on my arms, and a moment later David and I watched as someone was hauled down the hallway on a stretcher, screaming in agonizing pain.

Blood dripped from the wheeled cot, splattering against the floor behind the men in black who raced past.

"What did you do in there?" David gasped.

"Nothing like that," I breathed. None of the scientists were in that much pain before. I just incapacitated them. Anything more would put their clones at risk. Could someone else have been doing something to ensure the scientists wouldn't come after us? Did we have an unknown ally, or were they fighting amongst themselves? There were too many parameters to guess accurately, but I couldn't shake the feeling that perhaps we had someone ensuring we had fewer people hunting for us. Aaron's request that I help his son rattled through my mind and if there were anyone causing trouble, my money was on him. Which was great, so long as he didn't go after my root.

"They'll see us on their security cameras," I noted as David reached for the door handle.

"They'll be able to see us in here," he pointed out.

I grimaced, hating that I hadn't thought of that already, but hoping the diversion in the main lab would occupy their attention for a while. Waving him on, we stepped out of the lab and walked, quickly but with purpose, toward the back of the building.

David motioned toward the right as we met the end of the U shape, though it appeared to be a dead end where the labs met in the corner. He opened the door to one of the offices and ushered me inside.

"Don't they lock these rooms?" I murmured.

"They encourage an atmosphere of openness. Or at least, that's what they always said. If there was anyone they were worried about, they'd just dump them in a cell." David quirked a brow and shrugged. "The scientists are supposed to work together, but the clones aren't human, right?"

I didn't have an answer to that, just made a low sound at

the back of my throat. The sooner we managed to get out of there, the better.

David went to the far wall, the one that should have abutted the outside, but all that was visible was a bookcase filled to the brim with books stacked in a haphazard manner.

"Give me a hand with this," David urged, gripping the shelving so he could pull it away from the wall.

For a split second, I almost protested. No way was there a door behind that, let alone one that would still open. But what other choice did we have? It wouldn't take long for the guards to look for us. So I went to the other end of the book-case, found a handhold, and began to angle it in an effort to pull it away from the wall.

David nodded and together we wrenched the rows of books to form a gap. Or tried to. The weight of it made my shoulders ache, and after both of us put all our strength into it, we'd only managed to move it about an inch. Heaving a deep breath, we tried again. And again. But the massive bookcase wasn't going anywhere.

David took a step back and looked at the progress we made. Dropping his hands onto his hips, he turned to me. "Spot me?"

I bit my lip and nodded, eyeing the precarious stacks of volumes.

David inspected the ceiling and then shimmied to the top of the next set of shelves over. He crouched at the top, somehow balancing on the foot-wide space without kicking off any of the volumes stacked nearby, and peered down into the tiny wedge of room we'd made.

The grin he gave when he looked back down at me made me sigh with relief, even as the time ticking by ratcheted up my panic. Surely Eleanor needed our help, and we'd taken too long already.

"I *knew* there was a door! This was my dad's old office. I

remember him going out here sometimes. I'm going to have to make some noise, though. Stand back!"

"Wait! Pushing the bookcase over will draw everyone's attention. What if the door doesn't open?" Panic crawled up the back of my throat. I needed a plan, some contingency option if the door was sealed shut.

David paused, meeting my eyes from his bird-like perch near the ceiling. "If it's sealed shut, we run like hell toward the front of the building. Hopefully they're so busy with whatever you did to all those people, we can sneak out under their noses."

I opened my mouth to protest his plan was nothing more than a means of getting us caught, but David was already angling himself so his feet were jammed between the crack behind the shelves, his back to the wall behind him. Waving me away, he used his angle to topple the giant bookcase to the floor.

The sound was prodigious. The books hit first, flapping to the ground like heavy birds, followed by the shelving. The bookcase was an old giant made from solid wood, and as it crashed onto the hard office floor, it fractured into several pieces that seemed to each take their time falling into silence.

Behind the bookcase, beckoning, was a door inset into the cement wall. Someone had sealed around its edges with tape and nailed it closed in several places, but the hinges and handle were still there.

"Told you," David boasted. He took the handle and popped the lock, shoving against the bent nails that kept it closed.

I joined him, shoving my whole weight against the door. After two failed attempts, it took us getting a running start from across the room and aiming our shoulders against the recalcitrant door before it screeched open. I wriggled through the crack, pushing on my way out to give David enough space, and then we both stumbled into the sunshine.

"Any way to hold them up from following?" I asked, looking back at the door. David was already moving away but I went back, gave the lock a glance, and grabbed a piece of wood from the broken bookcase. I wedged it into the bottom of the closed door, giving it a swift kick to get it nice and tight. They wouldn't get past that easily.

David watched from ten yards away, crouching low and staying against the edge of the building. I bent at the waist and hurried toward him while he peered around the corner.

"We need to get across to the other side," I noted. We were on the edge of the U opposite the parking lot.

"How are we going to get past the window you busted out?" he asked. "They'll be swarming it."

"They *have* to have moved past it by now," I argued.

"We're clear along this side. You know there aren't any windows." Without waiting for any signal of consent, he was gone.

As much as I wanted to go the other direction, mainly because I was scared to death for Eleanor, I didn't want to go it alone. I needed to trust David—at this point, he had entirely earned it.

The grounds were made of large stone gravel that didn't make for moving quickly. I stood up to my full height and stretched my legs with each step, though I struggled to keep up with David's longer stride.

The length of the building seemed oddly shorter than the hallway I'd traversed inside, and all too soon we reached the end, ducking down as we stared out into the manicured front of the building that buzzed with activity as ambulances ushered away the injured and teams organized to hunt us down.

Eleanor and the kids were nowhere to be seen.

"Hopefully they found somewhere to hide, or else they're already be back inside," I breathed.

"If they already captured them, they wouldn't be putting

together search teams," David murmured. "They couldn't have figured out you and I were missing that fast."

It couldn't have been more than three minutes since we escaped the building, so he had a valid point. Of course, the question now was how to get past the end of the building, along the courtyard, and to the parking lot without being seen.

"How far are we from the main building?" I asked, thinking of the shiny glass structure we passed earlier. It couldn't be too much farther to cross the scrubby hills in front of us and reach the parking lot. There had to be a car to steal there, a way to escape, something to get us away.

David pressed his lips together, clearly debating my idea. I scanned the scene in front of us once more, just to be sure I didn't see Eleanor. They had a better chance of getting away if we drew attention away from their trek to the cars. It was my turn to map out a course in the direction of the glass head-quarters and head off without consulting David. He'd follow.

A small gully opened twenty yards from the edge of the lawn, providing shelter from seeking eyes. Hopefully. With so many gathered, it was a long shot.

I doubled back along the side of the building and ran as fast as the loose stones allowed, reaching the grassy hillside and all but sliding on my ass down into the cleft between the hills.

"You okay?" David asked once we reached the bottom and started moving forward again.

I glanced at him over my shoulder and shrugged. At this point, I was so far from whatever *okay* might have been that the fact I was still alive was all that mattered.

David seemed to gather as much and kept quiet. I bent low, my head below the top of the hill, to be less of an easy target for the guns I knew were searching for us.

The ground was coated in prickly bushes and gopher holes, which slowed our progress as we kept heading toward the main building. No matter how fast we ran, it felt as if we were barely moving away from the armed men behind us.

Five minutes later, David spoke up. "I think we're almost—"

A commanding voice interrupted him. "Hey! Get your hands up!"

CHAPTER
FORTY

"NICE JOB," I snapped. I didn't believe in jinxing things, but that didn't mean I'd ever say anything until we were out of danger. Something David didn't seem to agree on.

His expression belied his fear, as clammy as the sweat sticking my shirt to my back. We crouched lower and picked up our pace. I damn near twisted my ankle off when the earth below my foot crumbled into a hole. I ignored the pain. A broken ankle was nothing compared to being dead.

"I said *stop* and get your hands in the air!" the voice barked, closer now, as he wasn't worried about maintaining cover. "Stop, or I will shoot!"

"Move!" David wrapped an arm around my shoulder and tugged me forward.

I stumbled and gritted my teeth. No way was I falling now. From the angle of the slope we were on, we were finally getting closer to the main building. All we needed was to get rid of the guy following us before he radioed in or shot at us —something to draw the attention of the others.

We reached a dry creek bed that had larger stones mixed with the dusty soil. I grabbed one of them, hefting its weight in my hand. "David?"

He paused, his lips pinched, and I half expected him to yell at me to continue. Instead, he looked at the stone and shifted his eyes to mine.

"David *is* your namesake," I added, offering up a biblical reference. We could both hear the rushing footsteps of the approaching guard. He was alone, for now. This was our best shot.

David reached down and scooped up several fist-sized stones. I nabbed a second. He thrusted his hands in the air, where they rose above the swell of ground so the guard could see them. David took the hill in two swift steps, wound up, and propelled one of the larger stones with all the force he could muster as soon as the guard cleared his line of sight.

The guard was a lot closer than we thought, and the hollow thud of impact was almost instantaneous. I crept up behind David as he wound up and let the second stone fly. As the stone found its mark—the man's forehead—he stumbled forward onto his knees, then planted his face in the dirt.

We stood at the top of the hill for a brief moment, looking at the dark puddle of blood that curdled in the dust surrounding the man's head.

"Is he…?" I asked.

David shook his head. "Just going to have a concussion."

I wasn't certain I believed him. Not with that much blood. But I went to the man's side, ripping his weapons from him and tossing the knife and handgun at David. I took the rifle and slung it over my shoulder. A swift heel to the radio strapped to his shoulder ensured that even if he did wake, he wouldn't be calling for backup.

I peered back over my shoulder, noting that we had put distance between us and the lab, which shone in a dusty haze as the afternoon deepened. The swarm of activity was blurred by distance, but I saw an ambulance speed off, lights flashing.

"Come on," David called, already disappearing into the streambed. I bent over the man's shorn head, grateful to hear his ragged breath, and angled his head so that if he vomited he wouldn't asphyxiate.

Then I took off after David once more, running across the dirt and clawing aside snapping branches and bushes, ears and eyes open at all times, aching to hear any sign we were being followed. Our lower position didn't allow us to see far ahead, so we skidded to a stop right before rounding the final corner that led to the border of a perfectly green, grassy lawn, panting for breath.

"No cover." David stated the obvious. The lawn was broad and open, bordered by low shrubs and flowers, looking like something out of Versailles.

How many cameras were watching us right now? How long did we have to get somewhere safe? I tried to run calculations, but there were far too many unknown variables. Scanning the layout of the space, I deduced that the garage had to be below the main building... the building made of glass—which made sneaking up and underneath it improbable, at the very least. Yet, considering the time of day it was, most non-vital personnel would probably be headed home. Until I knew more, our only option was to keep moving.

David grabbed my hand and tugged us through the gardens on carefully trimmed pathways. His other hand had a tight grip on the handgun; the safety was off.

By unspoken agreement, we didn't run. It would draw far too much attention. But we were on high alert. My brain catalogued flower types, when they were last watered, the fact that no one had been out to enjoy the gardens in months— other than the overly meticulous crew of three gardeners— and about a hundred other minutiae. All utterly useless.

The main building came into view as we exited the gardens and rounded a low row of hedges. Looking down into the excavated alcove, only the top three floors poked up above ground level. The glare on the glass made it impossible to see anyone inside, but we would have been clearly visible to anyone who looked this way.

"Around and down?" I motioned to my right. The edge of the hill dipped to the same level as the front of the building and the front driveway.

"Or over the edge?" David leaned forward, peering down the cement block face.

By unspoken agreement, we turned back and ran down the side of the building, keeping behind the hedge.

We emerged at the bottom, off to the side of the main entrance, just as someone exited the parking garage under the building and rounded out toward the exit to the main road.

David stepped out in front of the small SUV—a Jeep, and not a nice one—and aimed the gun at the driver. Which was incredibly stupid and led to David coming within three inches of becoming a hood ornament.

But the driver stopped reflexively and David charged around, yanked the guy out—one of the gardeners, from the look of things—and got behind the wheel. I buckled my seatbelt next to him two seconds later.

"We couldn't steal something nicer?" I grumbled as David whipped the car out on the fancy driveway and out on the road. I angled the rifle below the edge of the window but kept it easy to access.

"This one won't have tracking capabilities," David explained, "and the guy could use an upgrade." His response was all I expected—there was plenty of method to his madness.

I kicked the trash and soda cans out from under my feet and hoped they wouldn't trip me if we had to make a fast getaway.

"Where would Eleanor have gone?" David asked as we sped along the road that would soon have a turnoff toward the lab we just escaped from.

I scanned the countryside for the second time, watching

the gentle swell of the hills. A road diverted to the right up ahead that would return us to where we started, and as we approached, a black Jag fishtailed around the corner, approaching us with every last bit of speed the car was meant for.

"That's her." I couldn't make out the face behind the windshield glare, but I knew it was her based on her driving skills, the car she chose, and the roar of the engine as she drew closer. Why she hadn't taken the car we'd been in earlier was a question for a much later time.

David didn't question the situation. Rather, he slowed and used the shoulder to whip us around just after Eleanor passed.

She had a death-grip on the steering wheel and all but pressed her nose to the windshield. I wished there was some way to tell her it was us who spewed dust and grit to follow her, but hopefully Sarah would have enough sense to let her know.

We raced back toward the main building, the Jeep coughing and not at all pleased to be attempting to keep up with a high performance vehicle. The driveway approached much faster this time, with plenty of trouble in store for us.

"Shit," David groaned. A private security vehicle— outfitted in a way that reflected all too well that it worked for a company with tons of money—waited in the road, lights on, siren blaring, blocking both lanes.

"Can that car take the shoulder?" I asked, studying the back of the Jag and debating the probability of Eleanor being able to handle the complicated swerve necessary to avoid the rent-a-cop and not flip over.

"Probably not."

"Just stop the car, Eleanor. Just stop," I muttered, wishing there were some kind of added perk to this clone business that would allow me to mentally communicate with her.

Eleanor wasn't listening. Instead, she attempted the

maneuver around the vehicle blocking her path. We slowed behind her, but it was clear from the get-go that it wasn't going to end well.

The shoulder was steep, falling away to countryside that wouldn't mix well with the Jag's race performance suspension. There wasn't enough room between the cop's bumper and the shoulder to avoid going off the edge of the road and the drop-off on one side, or completely going off-road on the other.

Eleanor ended up taking the latter.

———

The Jag sprayed dust and weeds for a good fifty feet before it bounced to a shuddering halt. David, using the fake cop's distraction to our advantage, maneuvered the Jeep to the other side of the blocked road—thanks to the Jeep's high clearance—and motioned toward the gun I held, then the officer.

Nodding, I slid from the car, rounded the back, and cocked the rifle.

"I suggest you get back in your vehicle and stop obstructing traffic." I kept my tone level and moved into the guy's view.

The sweat stains and hunched strain in his shoulders made it clear this wasn't part of his ideal afternoon. Still, he pulled his sidearm and aimed it at me.

"Put your weapon down and get back in your vehicle." The guy had a dog, and at least one kid. No way he wanted to get shot for his job, even if they paid him well. "Slowly put the gun on the ground. Now."

The man, his hand visibly trembling, bent at the waist and placed the gun on the ground. Scurrying, he flung himself into the driver's seat of his security vehicle.

Behind me, I heard David returning from the Jag, accompanied by two sets of footsteps.

"God, this car's a piece of shit," Eleanor announced. Cans and empty cups rolled across the pavement when she opened the back door.

I kept the gun trained on the cop until I heard the doors to the Jeep close. With another sweep of the area and the oddly empty road around us, I backed around to the passenger's side and got in. David already had the wheels moving by the time I slammed the door.

"Nice ride you picked there," I said over my shoulder. The Jag sat off the side of the road, doors open, dust still drifting from its back wheels.

Eleanor looked like she'd crawled through two deserts, but her grin was infectious. "I figured speed would make up for practicality. Perhaps I was wrong, but it's not like I've had much experience in these matters."

David even laughed.

"You doing okay, kid?" I asked, craning around further so I could see Sarah.

"We're going to get out of here quick, right?" Her knees were pulled to her chest, and her ponytail had at some point turned into some kind of looping knot of hair that gave her a deranged look.

"We're getting the hell outta Dodge just as fast as we can," I affirmed.

David had the Jeep maxed out, despite the whine and cough of the engine. Before long we started to pass more businesses, along with additional cars every now and again on the streets.

Soon, we had to slow in order to avoid attention. David took us through several careful turns and back roads to lose any potential tail we'd picked up, but as far as we could tell, we weren't being followed.

Sarah, curled up with Joey in her mom's arms, rattled out

a snore that would have been more appropriate for a teenage boy. I grinned at Eleanor, relief swelling in my chest that we'd managed to get them out and survive that insanity.

Not that we were fully in the clear, but I had hope we'd figure something out now—somewhere safe we could go.

We stole a minivan outside of a strip mall with a nail salon, video rental place (Sarah asked what they did), and adult toy store (thankfully she didn't ask about that one). The new vehicle at least smelled better.

With that, we headed to the border. It was closer than I expected—the middle of the city seemed crowded and clustered that close to the freeway. In mere minutes, we passed under the giant "Welcome to Mexico" sign. The immigration officer barely looked at the drivers licenses I kept on me from our cross-country flight and waved us through.

This didn't mean I breathed any easier. The border wasn't about to stop Future Solutions.

"What do we do now?" Eleanor asked from the back seat.

David changed lanes and we sped through Tijuana. I stared out the window, back to memorizing faces and license plates. "I don't know," I admitted. I hated saying it. Hated feeling it. Because it was true. Who knew what we could do now?

"We get somewhere secluded," David said. "Somewhere they won't think to look. And we lie low. We listen for what Future Solutions is going to do. And someday soon, when they reveal what they're doing, we expose them." David's voice took on an edge that raised the hair on my arms. "We tell everyone about the murders they committed. The atrocities they've done." His voice lowered to a mutter. "And for what—so the rich can live forever?"

I looked over at him, at his sharp profile against the glare of the evening light behind him. The ferocity of his grip on the steering wheel bleached his hands white.

"What about our roots? They could kill them to get rid of

us." Eleanor's voice was taut. I turned to her as she stroked Sarah's head soothingly.

"They'll be the first ones to benefit from their own work," he answered shrewdly. "They won't be dying. Not if they can help it."

David was right. They'd be the first ones in line to get their own shell of a body to inhabit. Their deaths weren't imminent. Which meant neither were ours, if we could stay alive.

"So, where do we go?" I asked. It seemed like such a simple question, but it shaped everything about the kind of future we might have.

"And how do I get in touch with my husband?" Eleanor asked in a small voice.

I'd almost forgotten about the man, but I certainly didn't want to see Sarah and Joey raised without their father. "We'll find a way to get word to him. He'll figure out how to join us." I kept my tone firm, even when David looked over at me with an all too clear "Sure about that?" expression.

I *was* sure. If we were going to give everything up, move to another country, and pray we found safety, at the very least we'd have to find a way to give the kids some illusion of normalcy.

"Where will we be safe?" I mused softly after an hour on the road. We'd exited the jumbled buildings and roadside stands of the city to make our way into the desert that surrounded it. David had taken Highway 20, with the goal of getting us to Highway 2 that led into the heart of Mexico, and from there go further south. That was all we knew for now, but sitting in the car with nothing more than dark desert out the window, I needed to ponder something different.

Eleanor was breathing evenly and deeply, and after a quick check, I noted that she'd fallen asleep with Sarah. Joey was wide awake, all bright eyes and gummy grin. I swore that kid deserved a medal, or at least a huge bowl of ice cream, for being the best-behaved infant on the planet. With care, I plucked him from Eleanor, leaving her asleep on the bench seat with Sarah, and bounced the bubbly little guy on my lap.

"Is there anywhere safe for us?" I asked.

David, lit only by the green glow of the dash, shrugged. "I think so. I know some people in Mexico City. They are, for certain, not involved with Future Solutions, since they're from a raid I did a few years ago with work. We'll go there. They owe me. We'll get ourselves settled, for the time being."

His eyes met mine and we both nodded. It was as good a plan as any. For a moment, I thought about that turquois beach in Mexico that my parents had taken me to as a child. While that wasn't near the giant jumble that was Mexico City, perhaps there would be time to get back there sometime.

I trusted David and his judgment, knowing we were in this together. A small rush of relief that I hadn't been out of my mind going along with David and getting into this whole mess. In many ways, it was the only reason I was alive, let alone able to find the silver lining of finding him despite everything.

"From there?" I asked. I couldn't quite keep the wobble from my voice. I didn't have any more Game in me.

David reached over, slid his hand down my arm, and clasped my hand in his. "We'll figure it out. Together. They should have realized when they made us that we'd put up a fight. We're formidable opponents."

I managed a weak grin at his words. "We can handle anything they throw at us."

We held hands as David drove through the night. Behind us, our creators might have cursed our names, but in the end, they could only blame themselves. We would live to play another day.

———

ACKNOWLEDGMENTS

I honestly only ever read the acknowledgements on books that I deeply enjoyed, because they're often at the end of the story and I'm seeking some small final word from the author, from the world they've created, that I want to cling to for just a moment longer. I don't know why you're reading these, but if it is to search for your name and I've forgotten it, I am deeply sorry.

There are many who I ought to thank for bringing this book into the world, especially for this, its second incarnation: Owl Hollow for taking on all of us Bleeding Ink authors and giving us such a good home for starters. Thank you! And for the many editors and extra eyes who have helped me craft this story. The first of these was the excellent writing group at the Missoula County Library, whose sage advice was some of my favorite. I hope I have done Diana justice for your sakes!

This book started as a funny late-night conversation in college with a roommate who had been reading about Dolly the sheep. It's been whittled away by countless hours of frustration at watching smart people be portrayed as socially incompetent and cold.

While I may not have liked all the lessons I've learned as they've spilled between the lines of this work, I hope they bring you something to think about and an escape from this crazy world we live in for a little while.

ABOUT THE AUTHOR

Meradeth lives in Montana where she's also an anthropology professor and scientist. If you let her, she'll tell you more than you ever wanted to know about getting DNA out of dead bodies and old poop. She specializes in degraded DNA (translation: really old DNA that's decayed), and runs two laboratories filled with students, interns, and maybe a few shenanigans. Her goal is to someday clone herself because that's probably the only way she'll ever get through her to-do list. Well, maybe not really—she'd settle for a really big grant.

Other than teaching, research, and writing, Meradeth enjoys the lakes and ski slopes of Western Montana. It's not uncommon to find her haunting the cafes of Missoula where she enjoys working with an extra large tea.

WWW.MERADETHHOUSTON.COM